Praise for the
Siobhan ~~Siobhan~~ .... Novels

Red Delicious

"Wisecracking. . . . Another defiantly over-the-top yarn that breaks every rule in the book, mostly with advance warning, and succeeds by being even more flagrantly disgraceful than its predecessor."
—*Kirkus Reviews*

"Gritty urban fantasy meets old-fashioned noir in this high-octane sequel . . . entirely original." —*Publishers Weekly*

"A fine balance between *parodying* urban fantasy and *being* urban fantasy: a little grim and a lot tongue-in-cheek . . . a rollicking good time . . . witty and snide . . . just enough parody, just enough narrative fiction—keeps the reader amused and engaged alike."—Tor.com

"Quinn is the sort of fly-by-the-seat-of-her-pants, ask-questions-later, non-detective detective that busts the genre wide-open. This ~~Siobhan~~ Quinn book isn't horror or urban fantasy or mystery, but rather [features] a horrifying, fantastical heroine who finds herself embroiled in a mystery." —All Things Urban Fantasy

"Sinfully delicious. . . . If you like your urban fantasy down and dirty, then you can't freaking pass *Blood Oranges* and *Red Delicious* up!"
—My Shelf Confessions

"A well-written, smart, and unapologetically snarky follow-up to *Blood Oranges*." —That's What I'm Talking About

Blood Oranges

"A pedal-to-the-metal, balls-to-the-wall female antihero who doesn't give a damn if you like her or not . . . which totally made me love her." —Amber Benson

"A memorably exhilarating and engaging experience. Sly, sardonically nasty, and amusingly clever." —*Kirkus Reviews*

"[Kiernan] brings an engagingly fresh prespective to well-trod territory. . . . Colorful side characters and a fully realized setting make this a fast-paced series opener well worth checking out." —*Publishers Weekly*

continued . . .

"Kiernan . . . has made it her business to turn the comfortable genres of imaginative fiction inside out. Now writing as Kathleen Tierney, she introduces a heroine as fascinating and compelling as she is foul-mouthed and impatient." —*Library Journal*

"[A] fast-paced, profane, and combustive little thriller."
—The Black Letters

"A strange (and unmistakably fun) project, a parodic urban fantasy that at once vivisects the tropes of the genre as it currently stands and also employs them with vigor and a backhanded, wild immersion."
—Tor.com

"A lot of fun." —*Locus*

"A dark, twisted ride through the seedier side of life, but it's peppered with enough humor to make it enjoyable." —*RT Book Reviews*

"Tierney has created a marvelous character in Quinn. . . . She keeps readers on their toes." —Fantasy Literature

"A mesmerizing exploration of magic without certainty . . . a must read for anyone drawn to the darker edges of urban fantasy."
—All Things Urban Fantasy

"Sometimes subtle, a little crass, and even lovely . . . for those that like Chuck Wendig's Miriam Black series and even Steve Niles's Cal McDonald series." —SF Signal

Praise for the Novels of Caitlín R. Kiernan

The Drowning Girl

"A stunning work of literature." —Peter Straub

"Incisive, beautiful, and as perfectly crafted as a puzzle box."
—Holly Black, *New York Times* bestselling author of *Black Heart*

"A beautifully written, startlingly original novel that rings the changes upon classics by the likes of Shirley Jackson, H. P. Lovecraft, and Peter Straub." —Elizabeth Hand, author of *Available Dark*

The Red Tree

"A strange and vastly compelling take on a New England haunting. . . . Kiernan's still-developing talent makes this gloriously atmospheric tale a fabulous piece of work." —*Booklist*

Daughter of Hounds

"A hell-raising dark fantasy replete with ghouls, changelings, and eerie intimations of a macabre otherworld . . . an effective mix of atmosphere and action." —*Publishers Weekly*

Murder of Angels

"Lyrical and earthy, *Murder of Angels* is that rare book that gets everything right." —Charles de Lint

Low Red Moon

"Eerie and breathtaking . . . [a novel] of sustained dread punctuated by explosions of unmitigated terror." —*Irish Literary Review*

Threshold

"*Threshold* is a bonfire proclaiming Caitlín R. Kiernan's elevated position in the annals of contemporary literature. It is an exceptional novel you mustn't miss. Highly recommended." —*Cemetery Dance*

Silk

"Remarkable." —Neil Gaiman

"A daring vision and an extraordinary achievement." —Clive Barker

BOOKS BY CAITLÍN R. KIERNAN

Novels

Silk
Threshold
Low Red Moon
Murder of Angels
Daughter of Hounds
The Red Tree
The Drowning Girl: A Memoir

Writing as Kathleen Tierney

Blood Oranges
Red Delicious
Cherry Bomb

Caitlín R. Kiernan
Writing as Kathleen Tierney

CHERRY
BOMB

A ROC BOOK

ROC
Published by the Penguin Group
Penguin Group (USA) LLC, 375 Hudson Street,
New York, New York 10014

USA | Canada | UK | Ireland | Australia | New Zealand | India | South Africa | China
penguin.com
A Penguin Random House Company

First published by Roc, an imprint of New American Library,
a division of Penguin Group (USA) LLC

First Printing, February 2015

 REGISTERED TRADEMARK—MARCA REGISTRADA

LIBRARY OF CONGRESS CATALOGING-IN-PUBLICATION DATA:

Kiernan, Caitlín R.
  Cherry bomb / Caitlín R. Kiernan writing as Kathleen Tierney.
    pages cm.—(A Siobhan Quinn novel; 3)
  ISBN 978-0-451-41655-1 (softcover)
  1. Werewolves—Fiction. 2. Vampires—Fiction. I. Title.
  PS3561.I358C48 2015
  813'.54—dc23   2014031584

Printed in the United States of America
10 9 8 7 6 5 4 3 2 1

Set in ITC Galliard
Designed by Sabrina Bowers

PUBLISHER'S NOTE

For Amber Benson (The Voice), Geoffrey H. Goodwin (The Friend), and Vic Ruiz (Compatriot in Ghūl Lore)

As I've said twice before, if your ears, eyes, and sensibilities are easily offended, this book is not for you. If you want a romance novel, this book is not for you. And if it strikes you odd that vampires, werewolves, demons, ghouls, and the people who spend time in their company, would be a foul-mouthed, unpleasant lot, this book is not for you. In fact, if you're the sort who believes books should come with warning labels, this book is not for you. Fair notice.

THE AUTHOR

I wish to do more violence.

—ILLYRIA

I think a plan is just a list of things that don't happen.

—MR. PARKER

It's only after we've lost everything that we're free to do anything.

—TYLER DURDEN

CHERRY
BOMB

CHAPTER ONE

PUSSY TROUBLE

Jump cut.

I met Selwyn Throckmorton five years after I'd left Mean Mr. B and Providence behind me and arrived in Manhattan, three years after that whole mess with the Maidstone sisters and those two demon whoremongers from an alternate reality, all four of whom were scrabbling ass over tit to get their hands on a magical dildo carved out of a unicorn's horn. No, seriously. You may have heard about that kerfuffle. Or not, but it's something else that didn't go so well for much of anyone involved, all those greedy assholes out to screw each other over just to get their hands on this totem of purportedly unimaginable power, blah, blah, blah. And when it was done and the dust had settled, I told B I'd had enough and he could find himself another bulldog to fetch and heel and do his bidding. All I wanted was to disappear.

I went south to Florida, then New Orleans (bad, bad idea), then west all the way to LA. But every city was a new hassle. For example, the crazy albino kid in Jacksonville who went all *Seven Samurai* on my ass. Or the job I took in post-Katrina NOLA, putting down a cult of Cthulhu-worshipping alligator women. Or the swank gig in Hollywood working for a couple of agents at WME who'd made the mistake of accepting shitwit baby vamps as clients.

Fun fucking times.

Finally, I came back east and took up with a mortal thrill seeker in Brooklyn, this lady who was willing to give me a place to hang my hat in exchange for a sip from my wrist every week or two. Her very own pet vampire. She had no idea about me also being a werewolf. I never told her. Didn't really *care* if she found out; the subject just never came up. Actually, I got more than a roof over my head. I also got a decent meal off her once a week, which mostly kept me from having to hunt. So, *my* very own pet *human*. Probably as unhealthy a mutually beneficial, symbiotic psycho fuckfest as you can imagine.

Her name was Barbara O'Bryan, but she called herself Eve when she wasn't at the office counting other people's money or doing whatever it is that accountants do. She was ass deep in the local BDSM scene, and I played the top to her bottom at clubs and whenever the leather-

and-latex crowd threw a soirée. Sometimes we even had sex, but not as often as you might imagine. She really, truly wasn't my type.

Anyway, it was at one of those clubs—a sweaty Chinatown cellar below a shop that seemed to specialize in the unlikely pairing of Hello Kitty tchotchkes and leather daddy porno—that Selwyn spotted me. I was busy with a riding crop, keeping up appearances and keeping Eve happy, and Selwyn had probably been staring at me a long time before I finally noticed. Selwyn Throckmorton knew enough about nasties to know right off that she was looking at a vampire (though, as with my sugar mama, the *loup* part of me was flying somewhere below her radar). She waited until I was done beating Eve, until I'd sent her off to get me a beer, and then Selwyn just walked right up to me and said, "I know what you are."

Normally, someone pulls that sort of stunt, they may as well have just signed their own death certificate. Normally. But, you see, Selwyn Throckmorton was a lucky girl that night. Because she *was* my type.

"Is that a fact?" I asked her, and she just smiled and sat down next to me on the ratty leather sofa where Eve and I had settled after I administered her thirty lashes.

"It is," she said and smiled.

"That's a fairly strange pickup line," I said and lit a Camel.

"It's kinda obvious, what you are, if someone knows what they're seeing. Not like you're trying very hard to hide it."

"And it's kinda goddamn stupid, you mouthing off about it."

She just kept smiling and held out her hand. I shook it. What the hell else was I gonna do? I was already wet. The possibility that she was working some sort of voodoo sex–magick shit on me very briefly crossed my mind.

"I'm Selwyn," she said and sat back, making herself right at home. "You're not the first one I've met. In fact, I've met several. In my line of work, it's not all that uncommon."

"And just exactly what is your line of work?"

"Occult antiquities," she replied. "Acquisition and appraisal." And wet or not, I'd have wrung her pretty neck right then and there if she'd said one word about dildos and/or unicorns.

Her eyes were the deep blue of a star sapphire, and her hair was the black of a lump of coal. Skin like a glass of ice-cold milk. Hey, I can ladle on the purple prose with the best of them if the mood strikes me. And remembering that night, the mood strikes me. She could just about have been something awful herself, a demon or one of the Unseelie gazing out at me from beneath her glamour. Unlike most of the people crammed into the place, she wasn't dressed in some tacky fetish garb. Just a black Hellboy T-shirt, faded jeans, a leather biker jacket a size or two too small, and a ratty pair of checkered Vans. She was both hot *and* goddamn adorable. Which is to say she stuck out in that crowd like the proverbial sore thumb. Shit, even I caved in and wore the silly dom getups Eve the CPA bought for me from a couple of shops down on St. Mark's, just to keep her happy. I also wore the cosmetics, contact lenses, and dental prosthetics that were *supposed* to help keep people from going all looky-loo on me.

"Acquisition *and* appraisal," I said. It sounded a hell of a lot more interesting than accounting.

"Plus," she said, "I'm a bit of an armchair occultist, and a halfway decent thief. But that last part just sort of comes with the territory."

"Occupational hazard."

"It can be. Hazardous. But I'm careful. Cautious."

"Right now, Selwyn, careful and cautious are probably the last two things I'd call you."

She laughed, winked, then fluttered those sapphire eyes. "Oh, come off it," she said. "You're not gonna hurt me."

"And why is that, Selwyn?"

"Because," she began, then paused to point an index finger at Eve, who was still waiting at the crowded bar. "To begin with, your date there bores you to tears. I'm still trying to figure out what you see in her. I know the sort. Something excruciatingly extra dull by the light of day, a wedding photographer or an accountant or an economics professor. Am I right?"

It's not like I could say she wasn't.

"We have an arrangement," I said.

"Oh, I bet you do."

I stared at her, smelling her; she smelled like blood and clean laundry and vanilla. Suddenly, my mouth was as wet as my pussy. Anyone—living or dead—gets bored eating the same meal week in and week out, no matter how convenient that might be.

"Pollyanna Wannabe over there," Selwyn continued, "she comes home from a hard, tedious, unrewarding day at the office, right, and there you are waiting for her, wilder and weirder and more dangerous a creature than she'd ever hoped to meet, much less swap blood with. And every day, every evening, she knows that might *be* the day or night you finally get bored, decide you've had enough, and finish her off. The cherry on top, so to speak. Living dangerously."

"But I suppose you're different."

"I didn't say that."

"It was heavily fucking implied."

She laughed again, stretched her legs out in front of her, and rested her head on the back of the sofa. I glanced from her to the bar. Wouldn't be long now until Eve was on her way back with our beers.

"Just what is it you want, anyway?"

"Didn't say I want anything. What's your name?"

"Quinn," I told her. "You should know up front I'm a piss-poor conversationalist."

"Lady, if I *did* want something from you, it wouldn't be conversation."

"But you *don't* want anything from me."

"Didn't say that, either. Are you always this prone to putting words in people's mouths?"

I looked up at the low concrete ceiling, hoping that if I ignored her, maybe she'd fuck off, and I could get back to my dull but convenient arrangement with the CPA who never asked more from me than her weekly ration of red sauce, nothing more than a monster willing to play arm candy and give her a halfhearted flogging now and then. A sea of chatter pressed in all around me, the casual rise and fall of talk in a place no one came to talk. I could hear Selwyn Throckmorton's beating heart, along with the dozens of others. I could hear her breath, and gazing at the ugly ceiling did nothing whatsoever to calm my appetite or my libido.

"Kid," I said, "you have absolutely no idea what you're fucking around with."

Her heart beat five times before she replied.

"For all you know," she said, "I've had vampire lovers before. For all *you* know, I'm a regular chew toy."

"Bullshit."

"Fine," she sighed. "If you like the cage, if you're content behind bars, it's none of my business." But she didn't get up. She didn't leave.

"Quinn?" That was Eve. I blinked, and there she was, tricked out in her expensive, custom-made corset, hobble skirt, stiletto heels, leather collar, and her lipstick the color of a nosebleed. She held a sweaty bottle of Bass in each hand. "Who's your friend?"

Now, in the land of the whip and the ball gag, there is an age-old etiquette, which I generally tended to ignore. But here was an opportunity to turn it to my advantage.

"Did I say you could speak to me, slave?" I asked her. "Did I give you permission to fucking ask me a question? I sure don't *remember* doing it."

Eve's face managed somehow to simultaneously express embarrassment and delight. After all, wasn't this precisely what she'd been after all along, degradation and humiliation, but I'd been too indifferent to give her?

"Shut up and sit down," I said. She handed me my beer, and when she started to take a place on the sofa next to me, I told her to sit on the floor at my feet. I took her beer and gave it to Selwyn.

"I don't like Bass," she said, clearly amused. "I don't much like beer."

"Then don't drink it. Makes no difference to me, as long as *she* doesn't get it," and I nodded to Eve, obediently sitting on the filthy floor. It made me grin, and I found myself savoring the thought of how uncomfortable she must be, all trussed up in that bondage couture and forced to try and find a not entirely excruciating position down there with the spilled drinks, cum stains, and fuck only knows what else. Her head was down; she wouldn't dare look at me until I told her she could.

"So, occult antiquities," I said. "Acquisition and appraisal. How's that work anyway?" I took a drink of my Bass, a long drag off my cigarette, then turned my head, much more interested in the pushy, reckless girl in her Hellboy T-shirt than Barbara O'Bryan's kinky alter ego. Selwyn sat up and shrugged.

"Depends," she said. "But, usually, a client comes to me with a request. Maybe they've learned the whereabouts of a particular artifact or talisman or grimoire, but they don't have the skills necessary to procure it. Or just don't want to get their hands dirty. Better to have a third party to blame if, somewhere down the road, the shit hits the fan."

"And how often *does* the shit hit the fan?"

She made a zero with her right thumb and forefinger. "I've been fortunate," she said. "But I'm not so stupid that I don't know it's the sort of luck doesn't last forever. You tell me how I'm living on borrowed time, I'm not going to disagree."

Was this the other shoe dropping? Was she more interested in a bodyguard than a vampire fuck buddy? Insurance against that inevitable rainy day? I thought of Mean Mr. B, my long months spent as his muscle, convinced I'd never survive on my own, and the thought alone was enough to leave a bitter taste on my tongue. I'd gotten used to freedom.

Eve, probably in the early stages of asphyxiation, made a small grunting noise, and I nudged her roughly with the toe of my boot. In the immortal words of Johnny Rotten, this is what you wanted, this is what you get.

"Dad was an archaeologist," Selwyn went on. "Specialized in Near Eastern mysticism and religious stuff. When he died a few years back, he left a shitload of unrealized profit just lying around the house. I needed a quick source of income. All I had to do was find the right buyers, match any given piece of ancient junk to an interested customer."

"Pretty resourceful of you."

"Better than waiting around for his savings account to dry up and finding myself on the street."

I took another swallow of beer.

"I'm gonna ask you again," I said, lowering my voice and leaning closer, "what do you want from me?"

"If *that's* what you're thinking, I can take care of myself," she said, sounding slightly offended.

"Kid, you go and piss off the wrong beast, the Pope and Baby Jesus won't be able to protect you."

I only barely resisted adding, *Take it from me. Been there. Done that.*

"You really want me to fuck off, Quinn, fine. Just say so. You can go back to playing footsie with Little Miss Poser. It'll be no skin off my nose."

I leaned still closer and sniffed at the soft, vulnerable spot beneath her chin. The blood pumping through her carotid artery was, to my ears, loud as a jackhammer.

"See," I said, "that's what I wanted about ten minutes ago. Now you've gone and gotten my attention."

To Selwyn Throckmorton's credit, she didn't even wince. So, either she was genuinely too stupid to be scared or she had balls.

"About damn time," she whispered.

I touched the tip of my tongue to her throat and held it there a moment, savoring the calm *thump, thump, thump* of her pulse. Then I told her, "Just so we're completely crystal fucking clear, it turns out you're stupid enough you believe this is some sort of parlor game, it won't make no difference whatsoever. It won't save your ass if I should lose control, as I have been known to do."

"Quinn, are you always this worried about the welfare of your food? You're awfully conscientious for a—"

"Don't you dare taunt me," I growled. Eve whimpered and I kicked her. "Don't you dare."

"Wouldn't dream of it. I'd just hate to find out you're all talk and no bite."

Well, what happened next, I ordered Eve to get up off the floor and the three of us went back to her place. I had Selwyn strip her and fuck her while I watched. Then I cuffed my CPA meal ticket to her bed, stuffed one end of a silk scarf into her mouth, and made Selwyn watch while I did a messy job of draining Barbara O'Bryan. No, not quite true, even if, at the time, I wanted to think it was. I didn't have to *make* her watch. She was as wide-eyed and attentive as a hungry cat waiting to pounce on an unwary mouse.

That night, I didn't let her drink from me. But I offered her a mouthful of Eve. She smiled that smile of hers, all wicked pretend innocence, and accepted every goddamn drop. And right then, I didn't feel lonely anymore. It was the first time in all those years *since* I'd been murdered by a fucked-up china-doll excuse of a vamp who liked to call herself the Bride of Quiet. The first time since I'd been bitten by a Swamp Yankee *loup* named Jack Grumet. I fell asleep with Selwyn in my arms, the two of us naked and gore spattered, and we slept the day away there by the cold body of a dead woman.

All my dreams were crimson.

That night in Brooklyn I broke my cardinal rule, or the nearest I've ever had to a cardinal rule since the night I died. I caved into the loneliness. I was weak and allowed another person to follow me down. Maybe not all the way. It's not like I *turned* Selwyn, but I did everything but. Now, sure, she'd likely had a certain predilection all her life. Maybe she was the sort of person who eventually becomes a serial killer, that supposedly rare female variety. Maybe not. Or maybe some other vamp or *loup* or whatever would have shown up with open, welcoming arms, willing to take her along for the ride—or worse. She was out there cruising, fingers crossed, praying to dark gods that she'd get lucky. She was willing to die, willing to kill. Hell, if I'd put a knife in her hands and told her to cut Barbara O'Bryan's throat ear to ear, give her that gaping Glasgow smile, I have no doubt Selwyn would have done it. I have no doubt whatsoever. It's what she wanted more than love or money, and she was willing to do anything to show me that she wasn't a tourist. That she was, to her way of thinking, deserving of my companionship, even if she knew right from the start—and I'm pretty sure she did—that I'd never share the curse that I have no doubt *she* saw as a blessing.

Some nights, I wish I'd just given it to her. If I had, maybe everything would have gone differently, and she'd be here, and I wouldn't even be writing this, because there'd be no tale to tell. Should'a, could'a, would'a. Regret is a wicked bitter fucking pill to swallow.

Yeah, I suppose I just dropped a spoiler on you. But it's not like I give a shit. I ain't doing this for your amusement and titillation.

Yeah. You.

I'd like to delude myself into believing that I'm doing it for Selwyn, just so there will be a record of her short life left behind—no matter how unflattering—so she will not have been x-ed out without so much as a trace remaining to show she ever was.

So.

The next morning when we awoke, wrapped in those sticky sheets and each other's arms, she put her lips to my ear and whispered, "It's beautiful."

I slapped her.

"Like *fuck* it is," I snarled. "You want to be a killer, be a killer. Just don't ever let me hear you try and romanticize it."

She rubbed her jaw and stared at the stiff, mutilated corpse beside her.

I continued. "It's not a game. It's not a fantasy. There's no dark gift. There's murder and horror, and one day we'll both have hell to pay. Literally. I ever catch you thinking otherwise, I'll break your fucking neck."

There was a good-sized tear in Eve's throat, just below her larynx, and Selwyn slid three fingers inside it, like some grotesque parody of doubting fucking Thomas and Jesus Christ, a story that's plenty grotesque enough to start with. Yeah, I was raised to be a good Irish Catholic girl, force-fed all that nonsense right up until I ran away to live on the dirty streets of Providence.

"You're telling me it isn't a rush?" Selwyn asked. "You really expect me to believe you don't enjoy this? If so, I'm not buying it, Quinn."

I wanted to slap her again. Instead, I got up and went to the table where, the night before, I'd left my phone.

"I'm not telling you that at all," I replied, trying to remember the number I needed. "It's better than sex ever was. It's even better than heroin, and I never thought I'd love anything better than smack."

"You were an addict?" She took her hand out of the wound and sniffed at her fingers.

"Still am. Only now it's blood, not H. But, Selwyn, what you did last night, that's no different from Jeffrey Dahmer wrapping his cock in some poor fuck's intestines and jacking off. If that's your idea of beautiful, keep it to yourself."

She changed the subject. Smart girl.

"How do we get rid of the body?" she asked.

"I'm about to take care of that right now," I told her, and I dialed the number of a janitor over in Red Hook. Back in Rhode Island, I'd had to clean up my own messes. Here in Manhattan, I'd learned there were people who'd pay for the privilege of wiping my ass for me. They were quick, thorough, and they never asked questions. What they did with the refuse, hey, that was their own business, the sick fucks. I called and was told someone would be around in half an hour or less, traffic permitting. There was already a truck in the neighborhood.

"I need a shower," Selwyn said. "Wanna join me?"

I shook my head. There was a chance the cleaners would arrive early, and if I got in the shower with her, well, I knew where that would lead.

"You go on. I'm gonna tidy up."

I didn't bother getting dressed. Eve's eyes were still open, and I sat on the edge of the bed, staring into them. The shower sounded like heaven. I looked into the blind, blank gaze of the woman who'd sheltered me, but all I could think of was the hot water pounding Selwyn's tits and cunt. After five minutes or so, I wrapped the body tightly in the bloody sheets. Usually, I let the cleaners take care of that, but suddenly I needed to be busy. The night before, dumb bitch that I am, I'd gone and changed the whole goddamn tried-and-true ball game of my existence, and it was a lot easier to try and figure out what came next if I kept busy.

"You trust these guys?" Selwyn asked. I looked up, and she was standing in the doorway, wet and naked, drying her black, black hair with a white bath towel.

"Yeah," I replied. "I trust these guys. Put some clothes on."

"What about you?"

"What *about* me?"

She shrugged and disappeared back into the steamy bathroom.

The resurrection men—they never called *themselves*

cleaners or janitors, always resurrection men, when they called themselves anything—came and went. They didn't so much as bat an eyelash at the nude, gore-smeared vampire. I was a familiar enough sight, me and however many other nasties they knew on a first-name basis. These guys, they were hip to what sorta appalling shit goes bump in the night. After all, they might be mortal, but they did a fair share of bumping themselves. They took away the corpse and the mattress and the box springs. They cut away ruined chunks of carpet and sheetrock. They paid me fifteen hundred dollars for their trouble, for their windfall. Selwyn watched on quietly, and I could tell she was amazed, impressed, enthralled. Yeah, I had a budding psychopath on my hands. I was beginning to wonder if the CPA's was the first murder she'd taken part in.

"What next?" she asked eagerly as soon as they'd left.

"What next is I take a shower."

"I mean after that, Quinn."

"I assume you have a place to live. I can't stay here anymore."

She nodded and reached for one of my cigarettes. She lit it and blew smoke rings. "Yeah, I have a place. So we're roomies now?"

"Sure seems that way."

She smiled.

There you go.

How Quinn met Selwyn.

When I left Providence, I did *try* to give up the whole undead avenger shtick. My heart was never in it, anyway. Like I said already, I traveled south, then west, then I came to the Big Apple, and I decided to live and let live.

Or whatever it is the reanimated dead do when they're minding their own affairs and not being goddamn self-righteous hypocrites. In fact, during my time in NYC I'd only taken out a single nasty, a gutter vamp down in the Village who'd made the mistake of getting in my face about my arrangement with Barbara O'Bryan. Maybe I should have let it go, water off a duck's ass and all that, but I hadn't.

Of course, a lot of folks knew who I was. I'd gotten a reputation over the years. Which happens. Frankly, I was surprised no one came gunning for me. I'd been good at slaying my fellow monsters, and that shit's like it used to be for gunslingers in the Old West. You get a rep, and there's always another asshole with a six-shooter looking to put you down and win your infamy for themselves. But no one messed with me. Maybe, like Selwyn that night at the club, I just got lucky.

I bother mentioning all this because Selwyn asked a lot of questions during our taxi ride to her tiny, rent-controlled apartment in Hell's Kitchen; she'd inherited it from her dad. She grilled me, and I wanted to tell her to shut up. The driver kept glancing in her rearview mirror, shooting us the sort of glances you reserve for people who talk that sort of crazy shit in the backseat of your hack. I didn't much care whether or not she took any of it seriously, and besides, odds were she thought we were a couple of loons or larpers or something like that. Whenever I caught her watching us, I'd just smile the most innocent smile I could manage, flashing the fake teeth that hid the truth of my predator's mouth.

"So, this guy in Providence, he was mortal?"

She meant B.

"Yeah, but it didn't stop him from being the king of all cocksuckers," I replied. "At least demons have an excuse."

"Still," she said, "guess you gotta give him *some* credit. Not many people would have the nerve—"

"Fuck that," I interrupted. "He's a low-life grifter who's found a big con, and he's stubborn enough and foolish enough to hang on as long as he can squeeze out a few more pennies."

"Still," she persisted, "he showed up and saved your ass, didn't he? I mean . . . sorta?"

"Is that how you see it? Shit . . ."

She was quiet a moment, then said, "After that ghoul, and the first vampire—"

"*Both* accidents."

"Still . . ."

"Look, B's the reason a big-time beastie ever had cause to come looking for me. If I hadn't been such a goddamn junkie that I was willing to accept a job as a contract killer of killers, I'd have stayed mortal and the worst that ever would have happened is I'd have died."

"But you did die."

"And *stayed* dead."

I still hadn't put her wise to the fact that I was double cursed, double damned, double fucking dipped, that I was a vamp who'd been infected by a werewolf before Mercy had kissed me with those china-doll lips and left me lying in a weedy ditch near the Seekonk River. So, Selwyn, she only knew half the joke.

"Did it hurt?" she wanted to know.

"Fuck you."

She sighed and looked out the passenger-side window, frowning at pedestrians and storefronts.

"I just don't get why you're so bitter, Quinn. I mean, what's done is done. Shouldn't you at least try to make the best of it?"

"Listen, just for starters, how about you get yourself raped to death. Then come to and remember it all in perfect detail. *Then* we'll talk. And stop pouting."

"I don't want to die," she said. "It's hard for me to imagine anything that's worse than death."

"Then you're not trying hard enough. We'll have to work on that."

It went on like that until we finally, mercifully, pulled up to the curb in front of the apartment building on Ninth Avenue. Selwyn paid the driver, who popped the trunk so I could retrieve the gym bag and cardboard box that was all I'd left Brooklyn with. Some clothes, a few books, two pistols, and the mini-crossbow not unlike the one B had given me what seemed like a hundred years before, a bottle of saline and my contact lens case. A makeup bag. The charger and cords for my iPod and phone. My banged-up laptop. Selwyn had said it was a shame leaving all the sex toys behind, and I'd told her to take whatever she wanted, so she had a plastic shopping bag full of dildos and vibrators and lube.

The taxi pulled away, and I wondered briefly if the driver would tell anyone about us. Selwyn pointed up at the redbrick building.

"This is it," she said. "Welcome home."

"I've done worse," I told her, which sure as hell wasn't a lie.

It was a ten-story walk-up, though the stairs didn't seem to bother Selwyn, and they certainly weren't an issue for me. You can't get out of breath when you only bother breathing if you don't want to draw attention to the fact that you're a cadaver. Anyway, the place was still chock-full of the sort of clutter I suppose archaeologists accumulate. Stacks of yellowing books, ceremonial masks from New Guinea and Japan and Thailand, a mummified cat in a miniature cat-shaped sarcophagus. Et cetera. Plus the spoils and tools of Selwyn's own enterprises, sort of Lara Croft meets Madame Blavatsky. Selwyn set the bag of sex toys by the door, then apologized for the mess and excavated half a couch and a love seat. Both had seen better days and had probably been new when Kennedy was president. The place smelled like dust, old paper, and Top Ramen. Well, those are the smells that would have greeted the living. Me, I also caught the stink of rats and roaches, dirty dishes, mildew, a toilet that badly needed scrubbing, unwashed laundry, an expired carton of milk in the fridge, and . . . you get the picture.

"Sorry it's such a wreck," she said.

"Hey, at least it's an interesting wreck."

I picked up a book on Mesoamerican astronomy and flipped through the pages.

"After Pop died, I just—"

"You don't have to explain anything to me. It's your house. I'm just a guest."

"I didn't want to throw out any of his stuff, you know? Plus, I'm sort of a pack rat myself."

I closed the book and returned it to the teetering

stack beside the love seat. "Didn't I just fucking say you don't have to explain anything?"

I picked up another book, this one on Hindu eschatology. Selwyn chewed at her lower lip and worried at a loose thread in the sweater she was wearing.

"How often do you have to eat?" she asked.

I didn't look up from the book. "Thought you were some sort of an expert on us undead folks," I said. "What with your line of work and all. A regular Abraham Van Helsing."

She rolled her eyes.

"Christ, all I *said* was I can tell one when I see one. I never said I was an expert."

"Every two or three nights," I told her, relinquishing the answer to her question. "Four, if I'm willing to deal with hunger pains."

"That's an awful lot of corpses," she said, and then there was the blare of police sirens down on the street, and neither of us said anything while we waited for them to pass.

I said, "Fifteen a month, give or take."

"About a hundred and twenty a year," she said, still messing with her sweater. She wore that sweater a lot. It was a cardigan, and the yarn was a shade of gray that reminded me of a kitten I'd had when I was a kid. Anyway, I nodded. Grisly arithmetic, especially when you pause to consider that a city the size of Manhattan likely has a dozen or so vamps in residence at any given time. All the resurrection men in the Empire State can't make fifteen hundred bodies a year disappear. And not all of us are careful about covering our tracks. There'd surely be a lot more hunters than there are if it weren't for the blood-suckers who hunt the hunters.

"All these books were your dad's?" I asked, using the one I was holding to motion to the rest.

"Yeah, mostly. I suspect he never even read half of them."

"I don't suppose you have any beer?" I asked, and she shook her head and said she'd run down to the corner store and pick some up. At least there were ashtrays, so I didn't have to ask if it was okay to smoke. I put the book down and lit a Camel.

"Selwyn, it's not too late for you to walk away from this shit." Looking back, I have no idea why I said that. No idea what the hell I was thinking. How the fuck was I supposed to let her off the hook? It was not like I had the thing in Brooklyn to go back to.

"You'd let me do that? Walk away?"

I took a drag on my cigarette and watched smoke curl towards the ceiling.

"Even if you would," she said. "And I don't believe you'd take that risk, no way I could go back to the way my life was before."

"Fine. But here's the rub. Don't you ever get it in your head you're indispensable or safe from me. I don't care how good a lay you are, and I don't care how much you get your freak on playing sidekick. That's not the way it works."

"How long has it been?" she asked.

"Since what?"

"Since you died."

I stared at one of the masks hanging on the wall,

something hideous carved from wood and bone that was clearly meant to be a bird. I had the unnerving impression that it was gazing back at me, that it was waiting on my answer same as Selwyn Throckmorton.

"Five years, almost," I told her, then added, "I was sixteen."

"I'm almost twenty," she said. "You seem a whole lot older than me."

Here I am pretending that I remember a conversation verbatim that I hardly even recall the gist of, right? I just stopped and read back over the last few pages. If I sounded a lot older than twenty-one that day, there in her cluttered apartment in Hell's Kitchen, I can only guess how much older I must sound now. How much older than my actual age, I mean. I know I hardly come across as the same person who—while I was traveling—got so bored that I decided it would be a good idea to write out what happened to me with Mercy Brown and the Woonsocket *loups*, then that whole cock-up with the Maidstone sisters, the dread madams Harpootlian and Szabó and their "Maltese unicorn." I'd say, "Hell, I was just a kid," but I'd have to tack on so many qualifiers it's not worth the effort. Reading this, I don't hear the snarky brat who wrote, "First off, taking out monsters absolutely doesn't come with a how-to manual." It's not the days, the months, the years that wear you down. It's the slaughter, the nightmares that I've seen strolling about in broad daylight and every time I look in a mirror, the close calls and deceit and pain I've inflicted and that have been visited upon me. For that matter, it's the years I spent on the street and the toll that took *before* I had any idea monsters were anything but the stuff of fairy tales and spooky stories.

See, this right *here* is why immortal is anything but, why so few vampires stick around more than three or four centuries. Time and the high cost of survival, it fucks you up. No, I don't want sympathy. I've always had a choice. Just like the living, I can put an end to my existence whenever I please. This might have begun with me being a victim, but it never followed I had a right to embark upon my own reign of terror.

I ain't no more than any serial killer ever was. Most times, I figure I'm a good bit worse.

But I digress, as they say.

That autumn day I was twenty-one going on fifty, and here I am twenty-two going on seventy. That day, I didn't tell Selwyn she seemed older than she was; but, obviously, her own life had also been the sort that increases the gulf between actual and apparent age.

"Well, for what it's worth," I said, "I feel a lot older than you, kiddo."

She laughed, and then there was another silence, and this one we couldn't blame on street noise. I smoked, and she picked at her raveling cardigan. After maybe five minutes, the quiet became uncomfortable, and I volunteered to go for the beer myself.

"Okay, but I'll go with you. I don't feel much like being here alone."

There was a knock at the door.

"You expecting company?" I asked her, stubbing out my cigarette.

"Not really," she said.

I didn't much care for the way she was looking at the door.

"Selwyn, I take it you're thinking this isn't a social call," I said. She was buttoning her sweater and combing her hair with her fingers.

"I don't get those," she said. "Leastwise, not very frequently. And never this early."

"So, what, then? A customer?"

"That's not the way it works. I don't tell clients where I live." She stood watching the door, wary as a cat that's just heard a barking dog. Whoa, three cat similes so far. Anyway, whoever our visitor was, they knocked again, harder and more insistently than the first time.

"I hope you aren't so naive you think that means they can't find out. You're not that naive, are you, Ms. Throckmorton?"

"Shit," she said.

"Want me to get it?"

"I told you I can take care of myself," she replied, but it came out even less convincingly than it had the night before.

"Fine. Then how about you answer the door before they huff and puff and blow the damned thing down."

She rubbed at her forehead and glared at me.

"Hey, I was only joking."

"Who *is* it, and what do you *want*?" she shouted at the door, her blue eyes still fixed on me.

"Ms. Smithfield?" a gravelly male voice shouted back.

"Ms. *Smithfield*?" I asked.

"I'll explain later," she muttered. Whoever was at the door knocked a third time. It was starting to sound like they were using a claw hammer on the wood.

"Yeah. Hold your horses. I'm coming."

Selwyn threaded her way through the maze of books and boxes, relics and furniture, and when she reached the door, she peered through the peephole. There were three dead bolts, along with two sliding chains and a steel bar brace for good measure. She didn't touch any of them.

"I told you never to come here," she said.

"You promised a week," the voice on the other side replied. "It's been a week and a half."

She looked over her shoulder at me. I raised an eyebrow and shrugged. She could take care of herself, right, and I wasn't the one making promises I couldn't keep— or couldn't be bothered to keep.

"Don't think he's a happy camper," I said, not the least bit helpfully. And that's when she stooped down and opened an old cigar box only a foot or so from the threshold. What with all the junk, I hadn't noticed it before. Selwyn took out a revolver, a snub-nosed S&W .44 Magnum. She opened the cylinder, checked to see that the gun was loaded, then closed it again. She slowly pulled the hammer back.

The way she held the gun, I could tell she'd never fired it.

"It's been a week and *half*," the man in the hall reminded her. "Mr. Snow is not a man of infinite patience. You assured him that you know the whereabouts of the Madonna."

She had another look through the peephole. "You tell him there's been a complication. You go back and tell him I'll be in touch when I know more."

I lit another cigarette and glanced at my gym bag, lying next to the sofa. But from what I could hear and smell, the man was just a man, and if worst should come to worst, I wouldn't need the guns or the crossbow to stop him.

"That wasn't the deal, Ms. Smithfield."

"Hey, buddy," I shouted at the door, pitching my voice low, filling it with anger and the assurance of violence. "Why don't you listen to the lady and fuck off!"

Silence. Maybe thirty seconds of the stuff.

"You're not alone?" the man asked. "Who is in there with you?"

Selwyn didn't answer but only looked from the door to me and back again. I noticed she was holding it with its barrel aimed down towards the floor.

"You're gonna blow your foot off," I sighed. She licked her lips, then raised the pistol, pressing the barrel against the door.

"I'm not going to *ask* you again," I shouted.

"And I've got a gun," Selwyn said.

I rolled my eyes.

The man in the hallway laughed. It was an ugly laugh, one that made me wonder if I'd misjudged his humanity. I leaned over and unzipped the gym bag. Just in case.

"We'll be in touch, Ms. Smithfield," he said. "We'll be watching." And he laughed that laugh again, and I heard his footsteps retreating to the stairwell.

Selwyn slumped against the door and smacked herself hard in the forehead. I walked over to her, took the revolver from her, and emptied the cylinder. I pocketed the six bullets and put the gun back into the cigar box. She didn't lift a finger to try and stop me.

"But you can take care of yourself," I said. "And last night, this had nothing at all to do with you being up shit creek with this Mr. Snow and needing someone to watch your back, did it?"

"Not entirely," she said. She didn't really seem upset that I was calling her on the ruse. Mostly, she seemed annoyed and maybe just a little embarrassed.

"Did I maybe neglect to mention how I'm no longer in the hired-hand business?"

"Quinn, no way you think last night . . . this morning . . . no way you can possibly believe that was all a put-on because I needed protection."

"I don't know, Ms. Smithfield. I've met some awfully good con artists. You tell me."

"That's not my real name."

I made my way back past the sofa and the love seat to the room's one window, which appeared to have been painted permanently shut quite some time ago. Out on the sidewalk, I watched a tall, thin man climb into the passenger seat of an idling black SUV with Massachusetts plates.

"Is it even Selwyn?" I asked her.

The SUV had already melted into the stream of traffic flowing downtown.

"Yeah," she said. "Selwyn Throckmorton, just like I told you. Want to see my passport and driver's license?"

"Not especially," I replied, still watching the street. "But I am having serious second thoughts about sticking around. Whatever bind you're in, I've got better things to do than get caught up in it myself."

"Do you? Do you really, Quinn? What would that be? Lurking around the city, keeping an eye out for the next miserable man or woman willing to provide safe haven in return for the occasional hit off your carcass?"

I turned towards her. I'd say that I *spun around*, but I've always hated that phrase. Makes me think of whirling dervishes. I turned around very quickly. And very angrily. I felt the Beast rising, the *loup* swelling beneath my skin, ready to set my entire body and mind on fire. The Beast in me has a nasty habit of showing up when I'm really, really pissed, full moon or no, and suddenly I was really, really, *really* pissed.

"Little girl, you do not want to go there," I said, and the words came out in sort of a half whisper and a half snarl. Every syllable was loaded down with threat. "Whatever the next words out of your mouth are going to be, you're gonna want to choose them very goddamn carefully."

So, there I stood with my back to the window, and there she stood with her back to that locked door. Probably there's some sort of symbolism in that, but if so, I have no idea what it might be. Selwyn didn't appear the least bit afraid, only stubbornly defiant, almost daring me, and that made me even more angry. The *loup* writhed and banged at the bars of its cage.

"I'm not sure just when you got the idea that I'm afraid of dying, Quinn."

I took a step towards her, knocking over a stack of books in the process. Maybe she wasn't afraid, but she jumped at the noise of them tumbling to the floor.

Don't do it, you stupid bitch. Get a fucking grip and do not let that dog out to play.

Something like that went through my mind, again and again and again. The Beast strained at its raggedy leash.

I said, "Sorta thought you might be smart enough to possess at least a scrap of self-preservation. But maybe you're only *book* smart."

"And maybe," she said, that sly, wicked smile of hers returning, "you have it all turned around backwards. Maybe, Siobhan Quinn, I just went out last night to find an interesting way to commit suicide. And here you are, unable to control yourself, about to give me exactly what I want."

No one calls me Siobhan. Even Mean Mr. B knew better than to call me Siobhan.

She took a step towards *me*.

"OK," she said. "If you're too weak to control yourself, come on."

I yanked back so hard on that figurative leash it's a wonder the damned thing didn't snap and take whatever was left of my sanity with it. But hell if I was about to give either one of them the satisfaction, my Beast or Selwyn. Maybe she was bluffing, and maybe she wasn't, but on the off chance she was serious, on the off chance she actually was taunting me into killing her . . . fuck that. I took two steps backwards and bumped against the windowsill. Defeated, the wolf withdrew. It knew from experience there'd be lots of other opportunities.

"Liar," I growled. Yeah, *growled* is the most honest and accurate way to describe the way the word came out. "You might be a grifter, but no way you're in this for the short con. You wouldn't have waited this long if that was your angle."

"Yeah," she said. "You're probably right."

How had she even learned my first name? I sure hadn't told her. I never would learn the answer to that one.

"And don't you *ever* fucking again call me Siobhan."

"Okay, Quinn. I'll try to remember that."

Jesus, she looked smug. Right then, I hated her as much as I'd ever hated anyone, which is saying a lot. It passed quickly, but for a moment that hatred was almost enough to call the Beast back again.

"Now," she said. "Are we done playing chicken? Can we put our dicks away and—"

"You gonna tell me what's going on with this Snow guy?"

"You know, you look a little woozy, Quinn. Maybe you ought to sit down." She nodded at the love seat, which was nearer the window than the sofa was. I sat down.

"Who is he?" I asked again.

"Just a disgruntled asshole client. This isn't the first time I've had to deal with his goons. He gets pushy when I'm late with a delivery."

I covered my eyes a moment. The contacts were stinging, and the room seemed a lot brighter than it had only five minutes earlier.

"And you're worried maybe this time he's gonna do more than send the goons around, even though having a goon of your own on your six isn't *entirely* the reason I'm here. Have I got that right, Ms. Smithfield? More or less?"

"More or less," she said.

I squinted at her from between my fingers. Her pale skin almost seemed to glow. She sat down on the sofa and reached for the pack of cigarettes and my Zippo lying on the cushion where I'd left them.

"So what makes this time different?" I asked her.

She exhaled smoke and tossed the lighter at me.

"How about we discuss Isaac Snow later? I'm starving. You might only need to eat every couple of days, but right now I'd kill for pizza or a bowl of noodles. I'm not used to missing breakfast."

So we went to Famous Original Ray's on Ninth, and I watched while Selwyn scarfed down three slices of meatball and sausage. At least she wasn't a vegetarian. Other than my blood, the CPA *had* been, and I never missed an opportunity to point out the irony.

I asked again about the troublesome client, and once again she dodged the questions.

"Later," she said.

She sat there in her fraying gray cardigan and the same Hellboy shirt from the night before. I sat there in my duster and a black tank top. I had gone to the trouble to hide my true face, my true teeth, because, duh, vamps are a lot more noticeable by the light of day. There was a strange familiarity about that morning. Like, you know, we'd known each other for years. There never was a "getting to know you" period for me and Selwyn Throckmorton. Is that what people mean by soul mates? You meet someone, and the way it goes feels like you've known them all your life?

Once upon a time, as they say, I'd thought that was a girl named Lily.

Selwyn stopped gnawing the crunchy rind that was the only thing left of her third slice and dropped the piece of crust onto her grease-stained paper plate.

"Ever think it might not have been an accident?" she asked me.

"Ever think *what* might not have been an accident?"

"The first ghoul, that night in the warehouse." She wiped her hands with a paper napkin.

I wasn't in the mood for stupid questions—but, then, who the hell ever is, right? I sighed and watched the plate-glass windows, all the people walking past. They looked like a buffet.

"I was there," I told her. "I didn't do shit but scream and try to get out of its way. If the stupid, clumsy fucker had looked where it put its feet, we wouldn't be having this conversation."

The first nasty I ever saw, and the first that ever died because of me. Note that I did not say "first I ever killed," because I didn't do jack shit but scream like the teenage girl I was and try to crawl away—*after* it had murdered Lily. Fuck. I never even learned her last name. She was just Lily, and me, I was just Quinn. We met out back of a They Might Be Giants show at Lupo's, and after that night we were lovers, best friends, inseparable partners in heroin. Yeah, I do know just how sappy that sounds, and no, I don't care. You swear to someone you'd die before you let any harm come to them, you swear you'd die to protect them, and then, well, the shit hits the fan and you pussy out. I hadn't told Selwyn about Lily on our cab ride to her place. I'd kept to the bare bones. That first kill, the ghoul with two left feet, it was an accident. Period. That's all she knew, and it's all she ever found out.

"That's not what I mean," Selwyn said, and I nearly told her to drop it right then. I wish I had. Hindsight and all that, you know. "What I mean is, Quinn, what if it was a setup?"

I didn't answer. But I stopped watching the people and watched her, instead.

"Oh, c'mon. Surely you've thought about this before. Surely it's crossed your mind."

"Surely what's crossed my mind?"

She glared at me like I was the kid sitting in the corner, the one wearing the pointy cap.

"This B dude, he needed a slayer, yeah? So . . . what if he arranged the whole thing? What if he *led* the ghoul to the warehouse that night? What if, after that, he made sure that second one, the vamp bitch, *knew* where you'd be, and—"

I interrupted her.

"Did you somehow miss the part where I was just some homeless kid, strung out and willing to do anything for my next fix? Not exactly chosen one material."

"Sure, I know it looks that way. Maybe it's supposed to look that way. But all those demons and things he was associated with, who also stood to benefit, could be one of them figured it out, your potential, and pointed him towards you."

"Are you done? Because I need a cigarette."

"Does it scare you to even entertain the possibility?"

Wanna know the truth? Yeah, it scared me. Scared me shitless. Because all at once I was having what theologians and philosophers and such call an epiphany. A eureka moment. Pieces started falling into place—that ghoul, the first vamp, Alice Cregan that day Bobby Ng screwed up at Swan Point Cemetery, Jack Grumet, the Bride of Quiet—everything, right on down the line. Might be it made *too* much sense, which is how conspiracy theories tend to work. There's this one crazy idea, but suffering Jesus on his cross, why has no one bothered to think of it before? Because they've all been suckered, of course, just like you've been suckered, but then the scales fall from your eyes and WHAM! Why didn't anyone else ever put two and two together? Why?

Well, could be because the ideas are actually *dumb* ideas. And your eureka moment is the product of desperation and/or gullibility and/or plan ol' ignorance.

But there in Famous Original Ray's, drowning in the stink of pepperoni and garlic and burned dough, ain't gonna lie—I was scared by what she was saying to me.

"Wow, you really *haven't* ever thought of it."

"I'm asking you nicely to shut up, Selwyn."

She leaned back and scowled at me. Disappointment was written all over her face.

"Dad taught me the worst fear in the whole wide world is when people are afraid to look at the evidence before them and—"

What I said next, I didn't try not to sound pissed.

"So, you've known me less than twenty-four hours, but here you've sussed out this imaginary grand and secret shadow show of my fate."

"You believe in fate, Quinn?"

"I was speaking fucking euphemistically." I was also

quickly losing my temper, which is never good in a public place. For the second time that day, I felt the Beast lurking far too close to the surface. "Now, I'm gonna go outside and have a smoke. Or two. You can either come with me, or you can sit here and contemplate the possibility that the Illuminati had JFK assassinated in order to hide the truth about Roswell. Frankly, I don't care."

Have I brought up that thing about how all junkies are inveterate liars? No? Well, there. I just did.

I was scared. She'd hit a nerve.

She'd instilled doubt.

She'd shaken my little ring-tailed lemur world.

Selwyn didn't say anything. But she followed me, and we headed back towards her apartment. The day had turned cloudy and windy, and somehow that sudden change in the weather, it felt ominous.

CHAPTER TWO

THE WHORES HUSTLE AND THE HUSTLERS WHORE

The next day passed uneventfully. If Selwyn was still think-ing how maybe B or Drusneth or even, I don't know, the fucking Bride of Quiet herself had gone out looking for a stooge and found me, and I'd been too dumb to ever catch on—if Selwyn still had that going through her head, she wisely kept it to herself. Me, I tried my best not to let it gnaw at me, but gnaw at me it did. Anyway, yeah, more or less uneventful. She was busy with a couple of customers, and I knew one was this Isaac Snow fucker. I read from her dad's books and slept too much.

On that second uneventful night, the third day I

spent in the company of Selwyn—which I remember was a Wednesday—that night was the first time she let me drink from her. We'd been watching television. She had this huge stack of VHS tapes that had also been her father's, and we'd watched a movie. All I can remember is that it was something black-and-white. Might have had Humphrey Bogart in it, but I'm not sure on that point. When the movie was over, I finished my beer, then got up and pulled on my duster.

"Where are you going?" she asked. She was sitting cross-legged on the sofa, sipping at a Rolling Rock.

"I'm hungry," I said.

She tapped at the end of her nose. It was a habit she had, tapping her nose, and I never did ask her why the hell she did it, or even if she realized she did it, or if anyone had ever told her it was sort of annoying.

"I thought we had a deal. Like you and the CPA."

Thing was, I liked Selwyn. Since that night at the club, I'd come to realize just how much I'd loathed Barbara O'Bryan. I was having trouble thinking of Selwyn as my new sippy cup.

"Maybe later on," I said. "I feel like getting some air, anyway."

She looked hurt and tugged at a strand of that very black hair of hers. "Fine," she said, sounding not even the least bit fine. In fact, she was pouting. I don't do well with pouting, especially when I suspect it's a put-on and I'm being played. "If that's what you want."

"You don't have any idea—"

"So, you're having second thoughts."

I stood there, drumming my fingers hard against the

doorframe. "Stop fucking pouting. I can't fucking stand pouting."

"I don't pout," she said, still pouting. "I'm good enough to fuck, and good enough to let you hide out here, but I'm not good enough to drink from."

I was hungry, and I was in no mood for my first lover's quarrel in—shit, maybe forever, since I don't think Lily and I ever *had* quarreled.

"No," I said. "We are *not* going to have this argument. Not tonight and not ever."

"Fine," she said again.

I sighed and sat down on the floor between the cigar box with the pistol and steel bar brace.

"Selwyn, I could fucking hurt you, right. It could happen. Have you thought of that?"

"You never hurt her."

There was a difference—a big damn difference, but I didn't feel like trying to explain it.

"I won't break," she said.

"Everybody breaks," I replied. "Even I break."

She shrugged, took a swallow of beer, and then very deliberately shattered the empty bottle against the edge a table. Before I could stop her, before I could even protest, she sliced her left palm open. She held it up, smiling.

"Oh, you bitch," I said. There was so much saliva in my mouth, all at once, I probably drooled when I said it. The smell of her blood was so strong and my senses had kicked so far into overdrive I was getting dizzy. And no point denying the fact that I was horny as hell.

"Take it or leave it," she said, all self-satisfied and shit. "No one's holding a gun to your head."

Probably, there are vamps out there with the sort of discipline I'd have needed to get to my feet, unlock the door, and leave her bleeding on the sofa. I'm not one of them. I'm not especially ashamed to admit that.

So, like I said, that was the first night I drank from her, the first night I tasted her. I carried her to the bedroom, ordered her to take her clothes off. She did, quick like a bunny, and I started with that gash in her palm, then punched a couple of holes of my own in her throat, near the carotid. It actually *could* have gone bad, that night. The heady mix of anger and sexual tension, there's a recipe for getting lost in the moment and going too far. I thought, another two or three weeks, the ugly beige comforter would be so bloodstained we'd have to get a new one, but that Wednesday night it was still immaculate when I started. I clearly remember, when I was done with her hand and had not yet moved on to her neck, watching crimson drops soaking into the fabric. I was high as a kite on her, tripping balls, and it was like watching stars being born.

Just before I bit her, she had the cojones to whisper, "I'm scared, Quinn." I saw there were tears streaking her cheeks, but she was also smiling. Her sapphire eyes were two balls of blue fire. Way to go, mixed signals. We have already established how I'm not a nice person, so when I say I wanted to hit her, right there, in that moment, you don't have a whole lot of excuse to be shocked.

"I am," she said. "Really. But . . . damn I wish I had teeth like those."

What the fuck was I supposed to say to that? I had no idea. I lay her bleeding left hand between her thighs, slipping the index finger inside her, and suggested an activity that might take her mind off the pain. She was immediately responsive to the suggestion. As I learned that night, Selwyn was as much a pain whore as she was sadistic. And it was a balance I found very attractive, something that had been missing in the CPA. Selwyn never, ever felt like a victim, regardless of her ability to play the role when the mood struck her.

Fade to black.

Next day, she had a package to deliver to a guy down in the Meatpacking District. Not a part of town I was terribly familiar with. She asked me to go along, said I might get a kick outta him—some dude she called Skunk Ape. I asked right off what the fuck kind of nasty winds up with a moniker like that, and she replied no sort she was aware of, that Skunk Ape was just a guy, mortal as anyone.

Oh, and it turns out she had a house safe, which was parked between one edge of the bed and another overflowing bookshelf. I hadn't even noticed it, as it was also buried beneath a stack of books. The morning we went to see Skunk Ape, Thursday morning, she opened it and took out a wooden box. It was obviously old, made of some dark varnished wood with the finish all scuffed up, a latch on the front, hinges on the back. There was a keyhole in the latch. The thing was about big enough to hold a cantaloupe. I inquired what was inside, but she just said, "You'll see."

Fine. I'd see. Be that way.

Later, I learned that Skunk Ape's real, legal name was Rudyard, and I had to admit that Skunk Ape was an improvement. He ran a weird little shop near the corner of Ninth and Washington, place called the Walrus and the Carpenter that specialized in animal skulls and mounted skeletons, "rogue" taxidermy, and fossils. But, truth was, the W&C was actually nothing but a front for an operation that was his actual bread and butter. Guy was a dealer in the remains of cryptozoological and mythical creatures—which, of course, encompassed a range of nasties, vampires and *loups* included—as well as endangered species and specimens stolen from museums. Pretty much whatever the more discerning and unscrupulous collector was after, I was told, Mr. Skunk Ape could lay his mitts on.

Oh, and I learned that day that Skunk Ape is what they call Bigfoot in Florida.

How he'd earned that particular nickname wasn't very hard to figure out. Hair down past his shoulders, beard that hid a good portion of his face. Total neck beard. He was big. Not huge, but big enough to be intimidating. I doubt he worried much about walking the streets alone at night. Finally, it was obvious he bathed less than often. Dude stank, plain and simple, a problem compounded by the closeness of his shop below the W&C. He was wearing a paisley waistcoat with a sweat-stained gingham shirt underneath. Weird, how I remember crap like what Skunk Ape was wearing that afternoon, but can't remember stuff that actually mattered.

As they say, anyway.

Back to the delivery. There was a very cute girl behind the counter, sort I always think of as Betties, because they're working that Bettie Page look, only with enough tattoos and piercings to find work in any halfway decent sideshow. She told us Skunk Ape would be right with us, and then we waited upstairs for maybe ten minutes. Never did learn the chick's name, but she gave me the hairy eyeball while I perused the wares. Dinosaur and mastodon bones, a ruby-throated hummingbird mounted inside a bell jar, jackalopes and Jenny Hanivers and two-headed cobras in jars of formalin. Et cetera and et cetera. Pretty cool shit, really. Anyway, finally Skunk Ape appeared, introduced himself, stared at me a moment, then ushered us behind the counter and down an exceedingly narrow flight of stairs. He parked himself behind a desk littered with an assortment of taxidermy tools, several magnifying glasses of various shapes and sizes, slips of paper impaled on receipt spikes, bits of hide and bone, and a dinged-up beige PC.

He stared at me.

The *way* he'd stared at me, I knew *he* knew exactly what he was seeing. That he'd seen it before, up close and personal. There was a mix of fascination, revulsion, and lust in his murky eyes. Made me want to snap his neck. Might be, if I had, everything would have gone another way. Might be Selwyn would still be alive and here with me. But, you know, probably not.

"What are you looking at?" I asked him.

He sucked at his teeth. He didn't look away.

"She's with me," said Selwyn, taking my hand, the wooden box cradled in her left arm.

"Always playing with fire, ain't you, Annie?" he smirked. "You've outdone yourself this time."

I didn't bother asking why he'd called her Annie.

"Can we get this over with?" I asked her, instead.

Skunk Ape frowned and sighed. He pointed at me. "Is that really the best disguise you could manage, Lady Nosferatu? Annie, is she at least housebroken?"

There was a stuffed black bear to my left, wearing a red fez and frozen forever rearing up on its hind legs. I reached out with my free right hand and knocked it over. When the fez bear hit the floor, its head came off in an impressive puff of sawdust.

What do you say when someone breaks your bear? You'd think the occasion would call for something imaginative and extra-pissy special, right? Well, the best Skunk Ape managed was a couple of vamp specific slurs and flipping me the Massachusetts state bird.

I kicked the fallen bear, raising another cloud of sawdust. "Think I *won't* kill you, Sumo Boy?"

"Play nice, you two," Selwyn said, then coughed and let go of my hand. She swatted the sawdust away from her face while Skunk Ape muttered and rearranged the junk on his desk until there was room for her to set the box down. He finally stopped staring at me and was watching her expectantly, one bushy eyebrow arched like a dying caterpillar.

"At least tell me that's what I think it is," he said to Selwyn.

"Sorry I'm late," she said and coughed again. "There was some last-minute bullshit. That greedy bastard in Cambridge decided to jack the price on me, right at the last minute. You know how it is."

"Don't think that means I'm paying extra," he replied. "Open the box. Let me see it."

Fairly sure he was salivating.

Selwyn produced a rusty barrel key from a front pocket of her jeans and unlocked the box, lifted the lid, then stepped back from the desk. From Skunk Ape's expression, you'd think he'd just found the world's best girl-on-girl, faux lesbo porn. His mouth was a perfect O, framed by the wild tangle of his beard and mustache.

"You'll pay me extra if you still want it," Selwyn said firmly. "I have a buyer in Thailand who'll gladly fucking take it off my hands."

I'm not sure he even heard her.

"Skunk," she said, "we're friends and all. But I'm sick of greedy assholes trying to rip me off."

The box was lined with dark blue velvet, and he reached inside and lifted out a very, very old skull, its lower jaw wired in place. It looked almost as old as some of the petrified bones I'd seen for sale upstairs. Right off, I knew what it was. Like the love child of a human being, a baboon, and a hyena. The bone had an orange-brown patina, and the teeth were the color of nicotine stains. There was a pentagram etched into the top of the skull, a different alchemical symbol placed at each of the five points.

"Oh, baby," Skunk Ape cooed. "Look at you."

"The fifteen we agreed on, plus my expenses, plus—"

"Yeah, yeah, yeah," he said, interrupting Selwyn and waving a hand dismissively towards her as he gingerly set the Ghūl skull down beside the wooden box.

I wasn't shocked or surprised by any of this. I'd met collectors before. Whatever gets your rocks off, so long as it's not *my* head in a box.

"Oh, Annie, you surely have outdone yourself this time. You, my friend, are the ghostess with the mostest."

She smiled, obviously proud of whatever mad skills and machinations had been required to get Skunk Ape his prize and land her payday.

"Before Rupert Talbye got his hands on it," she said, "it was one of Dick Pickman's. You can see his mark burned into the zygomatic arch, just behind the sutura lacrimomaxillaris."

Skunk Ape glanced skeptically at Selwyn; up went that caterpillar eyebrow again.

"You've got the documentation."

"I do," she said, and produced an envelope from the biker jacket. She handed it over to him. "Before Pickman, it was the property of a necromancer in Marblehead, woman named Cherish Doliber. And she's almost certainly the one who got it from the ghouls. I'm not even gonna guess how that transaction came about, the way the hounds are about their dead."

"Might'a stolen it," said Skunk Ape.

"Or had a ghoul in her debt. Rumor has it she was a fairly formidable witch. So, there you go. The skull and proof of its pedigree, just like I promised."

Skunk Ape was still busy examining the contents of the envelope. "You're totally the cat's bollocks, no doubt about it. But . . ."

Dramatic pause.

"But?" asked Selwyn.

". . . I should at least be able to deduct the cost of the bear your leech friend there destroyed."

I looked around for something else to break and settled on a winged rabbit with baby alligator feet. I held it out over the decapitated black bear.

"Quinn, please don't," Selwyn said to me, and then to Skunk Ape, "Fair enough. What I'm owed, minus the cost of the bear."

I set the rabbit back down on the shelf where I'd found it, and Skunk Ape breathed an audible sigh of relief. I'd seen the price tags upstairs, so I was well aware his man-made freaks didn't come cheap, and I felt a tiny bit of guilt that Selwyn had to pay for the busted bear.

Selwyn shut her eyes and did that tapping at the end of her nose thing. When she opened them again, she told Skunk Ape he owed her seventeen thousand and twelve dollars and seventy-four cents. "But you can knock off the spare change," she said. "I'm feeling generous." She took another envelope from her pocket and handed it to him. "You'll find my receipts and an itemized list of all my expenses right here."

"Like I don't trust her," he mumbled, then opened a desk drawer, took out a metal cash box, unlocked it, and pulled out a sizable wad of cash. Of course he'd be paying in cash. Who writes a check for a Ghūl skull?

Skunk Ape counted out the bills, licking his thumb and slapping them down, nothing larger than a hundred.

"You're actually gonna walk around carrying that sort of cash?" I asked her. She shrugged and said we'd catch a taxi to the bank where she had a safe-deposit box.

"By the way, Annie," said Skunk Ape, passing the stack of bills to Selwyn, who proceeded to count them for herself. "One of Snow's creeps came by a couple of days back, sniffing around. You *know* how I don't like getting involved in your other transactions, especially not with characters like Isaac fucking Snow."

"Sorry about that," she said, still counting. "I'm taking care of it. He won't bother you again."

Skunk Ape put the money box away and leaned back in his chair; it creaked loudly.

"Don't know why you do business with that guy," he said and shook his head.

"Maybe cause he's rich as Croesus? One day, Skunk, I'm gonna retire—for good and forever—and you'll have to find someone else to root about for your goodies."

"When I see it, I'll believe it," he scoffed. "You've got the golden touch. You're a goddamn bloodhound, and—"

"Annie," I said, glancing over my shoulder at the stairs. "Are we just about done here?"

"Just about," she replied, pocketing her payday.

Skunk Ape chuckled, and, because some motherfuckers are too stupid for their own good, he asked, "You got someplace to be, Vampirella?"

She'd been paid. I could kill him now.

But Selwyn put a hand on my chest and said, calmly, "Shitbird's not worth the trouble. Besides, he's a valuable shitbird."

Skunk Ape smirked.

But we left. He didn't escort us to the door. Out of the sidewalk, Selwyn hailed a cab that ferried us to 42nd Street and the great silver spire of the Bank of America building. The second-tallest building in the Big Rotten Apple. I waited outside and smoked while she was inside. Didn't ask what else she kept squirreled away inside that tower of glass and steel, or if she had other safe-deposit boxes, maybe scattered all around the five boroughs. Wasn't none of my beeswax, right? Right. She did say boxes were getting scarcer, what with fewer people using them and the feds having gotten more inquisitive about suspicious financial activity since 9/11. "One day," she said, "I'll have to start stuffing the mattress."

Afterwards, she dragged me to Shake Shack, because she said she was starving.

"It's something about being around Skunk," she said. "I always leave that place hungry enough to eat a billy goat if you slapped some mustard and pickles on it."

From time to time, Selwyn said inexplicable shit like that. Eventually, I got used to it. Frankly, just the smell of the man was almost enough to put me off my feed for a month or so. But go figure. She ate two cheeseburgers with ranch dressing and bacon and whatever else, plus fries, and I had a grape Fanta. I will admit, no matter how delightful the red delicious is, I do miss the taste of a good burger.

"You ever gonna spill the beans about Isaac Snow?"

She looked up from her fries, which she'd doused in ketchup, and she said, "After you left Providence, did you come straight to New York? I mean, if you did, I'm sort of amazed I haven't seen you before now."

"I asked you first . . . for the third time."

"You show me yours, I'll show you mine."

"Annie, after last night, I suspect you haven't got much left to show me I ain't already seen."

"Haven't," she said.

"Haven't what?"

"*Haven't* already seen. And don't call me Annie."

She chewed a French fry, and I marveled at her chutzpah, which was something about her I *never* got used to.

"By the way, is that Annie Smithfield? Or is it Annie Somethingoranotherelse?" I asked.

She swallowed and said, "Smithfield. Annie Smithfield was my paternal grandmother's maiden name. I'm just wondering, if you didn't come to New York right off, and if you made a habit of hanging out in—"

"I didn't come to New York first," I said.

"Aha!" She jabbed a greasy finger at me and winked. "I didn't think so. Then where *did* you go first, after you told Mr. B to go fuck himself?"

I actually hadn't told him to go fuck himself. Not in so many words. Our parting was slightly more civil than that, a fact I've sometimes regretted.

"I went to Florida," I told her.

"Florida? Jesus, Quinn. Why the fuck did you go to Florida?"

"For my health. Listen, you know, if I stick around, sooner or later either you're going tell me who he is or I'm gonna find out all on my own."

Selwyn sighed and stared at what was left of her second cheeseburger.

"He's just this dude from Boston, okay? Old money. Brahmin accent. The whole nine yards. A few years back, his mother died—or disappeared—I'm unclear on that. But he and his twin sister, they inherited everything. Those two, like a bag full of spiders. Total New England Gothic cliché. The whole family—the Snows, the Endicotts, and the Cabots, this little clan all tied up by marriage going back all the way to the Massachusetts Bay colonies and Plymouth. After Isaac Snow's mother died, or whatever she did, and he came into the family fortune, he started buying up a whole bunch of artifacts, and sometimes he comes to me."

I finished my Fanta and set the cup aside.

"Frankly," she continued, "if he wasn't willing to pay twice what I can get from just about anywhere and anyone else, I wouldn't have anything to do with him. They give me the willies, him and his sister."

"Wait. You're having lunch with the vampire you fucked last night, but this guy gives you the willies? He must have some serious hoodoo going for him."

"Look, Quinn. I don't like talking about Isaac Snow, and I especially don't like talking about him in public." She picked up her burger and took a big bite. Nice defense mechanism; hard to answer questions with your mouth full of lightly charred Angus beef and crispy strips of this little piggy.

"Fine," I said, "then once we're not in public we're going to continue this conversation. No more changing the subject or evading the question."

She shrugged.

I was pretty sure whoever this "dude from Boston" was, he wasn't anyone I couldn't handle, if push ever came to shove. Which I had a feeling it probably would. Because no way I was buying that at least half of Selwyn Throckmorton's motive for cozying up to me hadn't been the need for a bodyguard. Still, I'd been through enough shit to know it's good to be clear exactly what you're up against, even if you only *might* be up against it.

When she'd finished lunch, turns out we had another stop to make. Which meant another taxi ride. I don't like taxis—an aversion to wasting money harking back to my spare-changing, life-on-the-streets days. I had legs. And the subway was a hell of a lot cheaper. Then again, I rarely needed to be anywhere in a hurry. On the way to wherever we were going (she didn't bother to tell me, I didn't ask), Selwyn produced a necklace from the jacket pocket that had Skunk Ape's documents of authenticity. All, like, "Hey, Rocky. Watch me pull a rabbit out of this hat." Fuck me, but back in the day that thing would have kept me and every other homeless junkie around Providence in heroin and donuts for years, probably. Dozens of tiny diamonds, with a ruby pendant dangling like a big, bloody teardrop. She held it low so the driver couldn't see, like, what? He was gonna pull over and rob us at gunpoint? Okay, maybe that's not so unlikely a scenario.

"Fuck me senseless," I whispered. "Did you rob Tiffany's or something?"

"Or something," she replied, then put the necklace back in her pocket. "This one, wasn't about to keep it in the apartment."

"The safe-deposit box."

"Bingo."

"*That's* your next drop?"

She nodded. "It's not all dry and dusty bones."

Not that the ghoul skull in its velvet cradle had been dusty, not as far as I could tell.

The taxi took us to the East Village, a tall, narrow four-story Victorian pile of bricks, looked almost like it would topple over in a strong wind. Looked malnourished and sort of stranded there on East 4th Street. The front had been painted the red of a cardinal's cassock. Selwyn paid the driver, then asked him to stick around. When he told her he couldn't do that, she slipped him a couple hundred dollars and he changed his mind. All that money, gotta tell you, it was seriously starting to freak me out.

"Here we are," she said, turning to face the tall red building. "This is the place." She smiled and leaned against me. I already mentioned how her place smelled of vanilla; well, so did she. The vanilla oil she dabbed on didn't quite hide the *actual* smell of her, but it was probably enough to confuse the nostrils of nasties with noses not so keen as mine. I'm not saying that's why she wore it. I'm just saying, that's all.

The ground floor was a dive with a green neon sign that read simply IRISH BAR. There was a GUINNESS IS GOOD FOR YOU sign in the window, along with a framed and faded photograph of James Joyce. Inside, past the entrance to the bar, there were stairs, and Selwyn took them two at a time, all the way to the third floor. I trailed behind, wondering if this customer would be more or less annoying than Skunk Ape. Or just about the same. There was a short hallway with a tiny landing and a door painted exactly the same shade of red as the front of the building.

She knocked on the door.

"Selwyn, what's waiting for us in there?"

"And spoil the surprise?"

"Yeah, and spoil the motherfucking surprise."

Before she could say anything else, the door opened. No *one* opened it. It just opened. Immediately, the odor of honey was so strong I thought for a moment I was actually gonna gag. I covered the lower half of my face, but it really didn't help all that much.

"You'll get used to it," she whispered.

"I seriously doubt that," I muttered from behind my fingers. "What the shit?"

"You don't even breathe, Quinn."

"Yeah, but I can fucking *smell*, okay? A whole bunch better than you."

"Well, I'm not gonna stand out here listening to you complain. We're running late as it is." And with that she stepped inside. I hesitated a few seconds. I didn't *have* to follow her. I could always go back and wait in the taxi. Sure I could. But I didn't.

I crossed the threshold, and the door swung shut behind me. I heard it latch. Click. Which is how long it took me to regret not having headed back down the stairs to the street, the space of a lock clicking. It wouldn't stop me from leaving, unless there was some sort of ward or whatever, but I doubted it had been installed to stop vamps who were also *loups* (and vice versa).

The place was filled with bees.

I shit you not.

I resisted the urge to swat at them.

There was a brightly lit foyer, which led into a parlor that was just as bright. I squinted and dug a pair of sunglasses from my duster. I glanced about me, looking for Selwyn, but half blinded by all that light and seeing nothing much at all. The cloying sweet honey stink was even stronger now.

"Hey!" I shouted.

"In here," Selwyn shouted back from somewhere, and it's a wonder I could hear her over all that goddamn buzzing. Bees had begun lighting on my arms, in my hair, crawling over my face. And the bastards were *loud*.

Like a hurricane wind made out of bees. *A person could go insane in here,* I thought. *A person could go absolutely corn-fucking, ass-banging, cock-monkey out of her mind.*

I did not swat the bees. I endured the noise and the sensation of their prickly legs on my skin, several stings, and the honey stench. I walked in the direction Selwyn's voice had come from, and between the bees and the bright light, I didn't notice much about my surroundings. The parlor led into a much larger room.

And . . .

At least the lights were dimmer.

"Thought you'd gotten lost," Selwyn said. There wasn't a bee anywhere on her. And I realized the buzzing had had faded to a dull roar.

It had to be a goddamn Faerie.

I hate Fae. Maybe even worse than I still hate Mean Mr. B. Which is saying a lot. Only Faerie I've ever been able to stand was a troll named Aloysius lived under a highway overpass back in Providence. I knew right off the pretty creature in front of me, stretched out on the cranberry recamier, was worse than any troll who ever squatted below any bridge. The recamier was upholstered, by the way, in some threadbare fabric about the same color as the red door and the front of the building.

"Quinn, meet Aster. Aster, meet Quinn."

The only thing I hate more than Faeries are Faeries named after flowers. It's just so . . . twee.

"Quinn's sort of along for the ride today," said Selwyn.

The Faerie made an expression that wasn't quite a grin.

"Why, Annie," she said in that annoying, lilting Un-seelie accent. "You have a new lover. I'm so glad. Quinn, it is my pleasure, certainly, I am sure."

The Faerie lifted one long, slender arm. I wasn't sure whether I was meant to kiss her hand or shake it. I didn't do either.

"Charmed," I said, trying to keep a bee from crawling up my left nostril. Selwyn frowned.

The Faerie waved the hand I had neither kissed nor shaken, and all the bees on me flew away. I probably literally sighed a sigh of relief.

I haven't described her. Aster, I mean. I suppose I should. Well, I can't say what she *really* looked like, because I've never been any good at seeing through glamours and shit like that. To my eyes, she could have been some runway model bitch, bulimic and thin as a rail. But still hot, right. Aster's ash-blond hair was cut in a bob, and she had eyes almost the same shade of gray as B's. The dress she was wearing was so sheer I'm not sure why she bothered wearing anything at all. By the way, I'm not sure the Faerie was actually female; these are pronouns of convenience. Beneath that glamour, Aster could have been anything at all. Besides, with Faeries, gender and sex and whatnot tends to be a pretty slippery affair.

The Faerie named Aster studied me, and then she said to Selwyn, "I would caution you against taking one such as this into your bed, child, but you know your own affairs better than I."

"We have an arrangement. I trust her," Selwyn said, and she winked at me. "Mostly."

"We must always be careful with whom we bargain and where we've placed our trust," the Faerie said, "and especially when matters of the heart are concerned."

I ran my fingers through my hair, making sure all the bees were gone, still imagining I could feel them on me.

"Lady, I don't currently plan on eating her," I told the Faerie, not much bothering to hide the indignation at having been dragged across town to be attacked by a swarm of bees and have my character called into question by this Tinkerbelle slut. "Which is not to say that might not change, of course. Being one such as this and all."

Selwyn pulled the shiny, shiny necklace from her jacket right about the same time I noticed the hives.

"Oh," crooned the Faerie. "Oh, it's even more beautiful than the ballads would have us believe, isn't it?"

Hive is the only word I can think of that even comes close to describing the misshapen things lining the walls of the room. Clearly, they'd once been human beings, and probably, in some sense, they still were. Some of them were still alive. I know this because a couple of them were breathing, and one even turned its head. I'd say it was watching me, only it didn't have any eyes. Try to imagine if someone had attempted to mold statues from honeycombs and done a fucking sloppy job. Bingo. It was hard to tell where one began and another ended, and their waxy yellow flesh was pockmarked with thousands of hexagonal pits. And the bees were all over them. The hives had holes where mouths had been, and holes in other places, and the bees crawled in and out, out and in. The honey I was smelling dripped from those horrid fucking things and pooled on the floor around them. Takes a whole damn lot to make me want to puke. Those things did the trick.

"I knew you wouldn't be disappointed," said Selwyn, pleased with herself and seemingly oblivious to the hives. I figured she'd likely seen them at least once before. Maybe shit like that didn't bother her anymore. Maybe it never had.

The Faerie said, "My dear Ms. Smithfield, a treasure is lost—so lost to have been all but forgotten even to the memory of Daoine Sídhe—it is foolish to believe it will ever again be seen. A treasure lost as long as was the Tear of Dis, then I do not hesitate to name its reappearance miraculous."

Me, I was trying to concentrate on anything at all but the hive people. So I stared at the string of diamonds and that huge ruby cupped in Selwyn's right hand. In the taxi, I hadn't realized the way the ruby seemed to shine . . . no, wrong word. How the ruby seemed to *ooze* a soft reddish glow. The stone wasn't reflecting light; it was making it. Wasn't the first time I'd seen that sort of magic, and I still don't know why it took me that long to catch on. Maybe the ruby waited until it was there with the Faerie to show its true colors—ha-ha.

"That's infernal," I said, and Selwyn nodded.

"Taken from the mines beneath the City of Iron," she replied. "Supposedly it belonged to some archduke or another for, I don't know, thousands of years. Took me—"

"Correction, love," the Faerie interrupted. "Your kind would count it in millions of years."

Now that I knew what it was, the ruby seemed a fuckton worse than the hive people.

"So, wait. You traffic in hellgoods?" I asked Selwyn.

I felt her eyes on me, but I didn't look away from the necklace.

"Only when they come my way," she answered, "which isn't very often"

Right then's when it occurred to me the ruby was staring into me, same as I was staring into it. You know, Nietzsche and gazing into the abyss and all. Well, the ruby wasn't some philosophical, metaphysical abyss. It was the real fucking deal. Might sound trite, but it felt as if I actually had to pry my eyes away from the ruby. My head had begun to throb, and I could taste iron.

"A damned shame, too," Selwyn said. "It's a profitable market. Demand always exceeds supply."

"You have such a keen head for business," the Faerie told her. "Quite the acumen, for only a mortal girl."

I think the appropriate phrase is, *I was aghast.*

"Selwyn, do you even *know* how fucking stupid that is?"

The Faerie raised an eyebrow and leaned towards us. The honey smell was coming from her, too.

"Selwyn? Annie Smithfield, why did that dead one name you *Selwyn?*"

Selwyn turned sort of green. She looked like she wanted to punch me in the head.

"It's my *middle* name," she replied, doing her best not to sound as pissed off as she was at having her *nom de guerre* blown like that. "Annie Selwyn Smithfield. Anna-belle, to be precise."

I thought it was a decent enough save, though it was unclear whether the Faerie was buying it. Aster's left eyebrow was still cocked in a very skeptical fashion.

"I shouldn't like to ever learn that you've been less than truthful with me, Ms. Smithfield," Aster said, her voice just as skeptical as her eyebrow.

"I'm not lying." Selwyn turned away from me, back towards the Faerie camped there on her tattered red recamier. "You want to see my driver's license? My passport? My—"

"That won't be necessary," Aster said, leaning back again. "You've brought me such a precious thing, so I shall take your word."

"Thank you," said Selwyn, all obsequious and shit. I wondered if the Faerie could hear as much relief in her voice as I did.

"It is understandable, dear, that such a formality as trusting me with your middle name might slip your merely human mind."

Jesus God, have I said how much I fucking *hate* fucking Faeries. Yeah, well. I haven't said it enough.

I hate Faeries.

Except for Aloysius.

He's my one and only exception.

"May I please hold it now, my sweet dear?" asked Aster the fucking pompous, condescending Fae bitch.

Selwyn started to hand over the necklace, but I grabbed her arm.

"Payment up front," I said.

Selwyn? Mortified.

The Faerie? If, as they say, looks could kill. A bee appeared from her right nostril, buzzed loudly, then flew away towards a clump of the hive people.

Selwyn forced half a strained smile, and she said, "She loves to joke. You know vampires."

The Faerie shut her gray eyes a moment. When she opened them, the irises were an oily black. I guessed that meant she was seriously bent out of shape, that I'd just gone and dumped sand in her vagina.

"I have made a habit of not making the acquaintance of corpses," Aster sneered.

"Your loss," I said. Often, thoughtlessly shooting off my piehole is how I deal with my fight-or-flight response when doing either isn't an option.

Selwyn quickly intervened by placing the necklace in bee lady's hand and then closing the hand around it. Which instantly seemed to placate the Faerie. Her eyes faded to gray again. Just give us monsters our play pretties, yeah, and all is forgiven. No, that's obviously not exactly true, not across the board, I mean, but it certainly seemed the case with Aster the fucking Faerie.

"At first I was afraid it was still in the vaults at Thok," Selwyn said, talking a little too fast, "and no one was ever gonna see it again, like you said. But—"

The Faerie whispered, "The Ghūl have always been careless with the fruits of their thievery. And the Tear of Dis burns. The flame held within its facets betrays its origins, if only one has the sight to know hellfire."

Blah, blah, fuckity blah.

I was beginning to think maybe Selwyn wasn't getting paid for this transaction, that she might be somehow in debt to Aster—happens all the time with humans—and this was a way of buying her freedom. Also, surely

Selwyn had to know about Faerie gold. They pass you a bag full of Spanish doubloons, only later you discover that bag's full of acorns or pebbles or rabbit droppings. Selling shit to Faeries is, in short, almost as stupid as selling hellgoods. And here was Selwyn Throckmorton doing both at the same time.

"It *is* beautiful," she said, "though I know I can't appreciate it as you do."

The Faerie nodded, and the necklace vanished from her hand, only to reappear around her throat.

"You're honorable, Annie Smithfield. You will find that the Host never again troubles you."

So, okay, this wasn't about money, but some sort of exchange of services. Not that the Fae are known for keeping promises. I almost asked what Selwyn had done to get the Unseelie Host on her—that vicious assortment of bogles, goblins, hobs, and flying fucking monkeys.

Selwyn thanked Aster again, bowed, and the Faerie dismissed us with a wave of the hand. Well, dismissed Selwyn. I suspect the Faerie considered reanimated corpses and cadavers and whatnot so disgraceful that we're not worth the trouble.

I hate Faeries.

Once we were out of there and down on the sidewalk again, I tried to conceal how glad I was to not be in the presence of Aster and her hive people. I'll take a hundred Skunk Apes and their BO any day of the week.

The taxi hadn't waited. This came as no surprise, though it did piss off Selwyn. Well, pissed her off even more. She was already so angry at me, she was seething.

"Two hundred damn dollars," she said and kicked a

trash can lying in the gutter. It ripped wide-open, spilling soda cans, Chinese leftovers, and a couple of used pro-phylactics.

"Whatever," I said. "I need a drink anyway."

She pushed me hard enough that I almost lost my balance and ended up in the gutter with all that liberated garbage.

"Are you a total fucking *idiot*? Do you even *know* what could have happened back there?" She was shouting loud enough that several people were staring.

"You're making a scene," I said.

She shoved me again, but this time I was ready for it.

Seemed like a good time for an understatement. I said, "I didn't like her." I said it as matter-of-factly as I could, given I was still seriously creeped out over the hive peo-ple. "Besides, no one who deals hellgoods to the Unseelie has any business calling *anyone* an idiot."

"Quinn, if she'd wanted, she could have—"

"Also, you push me again and I push back. Three strikes you're out. Now, I'm going to get a beer. You're welcome to join me, unless, I don't know, you're late for a meeting with a succubus or something."

"You ass," she hissed.

"I have my moments," I said, and then I crossed the street. No way I was going into that Irish place below the Faerie's human apiary. Fortunately, there was another bar hardly a stone's throw away.

"You think I'm just gonna put up with this sort of crap?" she shouted.

"Your call," I shouted back. "You're a big girl."

"Oh my god," I heard her mutter just before I walked

through the door to the bar. By the way, that door was also painted red, and if I hadn't still been so shaky I might have taken that for an ill enough omen I'd have gone in search of another watering hole. But fuck it.

I went inside and ordered a Pabst and a shot of Jack.

Sure, it sounds arrogant as shit, but I was not the least itty-bit surprised, ten or fifteen minutes later, when Selwyn showed up. I had something she wanted as bad as I'd wanted heroin, back when I was still a breather, as much as I need blood now. And she knew the odds were against her finding another willing donor anytime soon. Or ever.

Could say I held all the cards.

She sat down on the stool next to me and ordered an old-fashioned. I watched while the bartender mixed whiskey and bitters and added a lump of sugar and a maraschino cherry. To each her own poison, but that shit's way too sweet for my liking. I drink bourbon, I want to taste bourbon.

"You told her my real name," she said.

I glanced at her, then back to my beer. "Doesn't work that way. You ought to know that. Faeries and demons, *they're* the ones have to worry about their names. You really ought to know that, Selwyn."

"There wasn't any point to you getting her so torqued."

"Her? You really think—"

"Don't change the subject. You didn't have to do that, Quinn." She sounded tired.

"I hate Faeries," I told her, though she'd possibly already deduced that much.

Her drink came. She pulled out the toothpick with the cherry on it and lay it on the paper napkin.

"I don't have to be told how risky this line of work is," she said very softly.

"I have some serious doubts on that score."

She sighed and sipped her drink and stared at the picture of Karl Marx hanging behind the bar, above all the bottles of liquor. Oh, yeah. The place was decorated in all sorts of Soviet memorabilia—flags, photographs of the late, great politburo and other assorted heroes of the USSR, propaganda posters, et cetera. Turns out, it actually had once been a secret gathering spot for socialists trying to stay under the radar of the McCarthyism and Cold War hysteria. Back then, it was called the Ukrainian Labor Home, and there were dances and potluck dinners. Sitting there, you can almost smell the *kapusniak* and hear the accordions. Sorry. Infodump. But that bar— named after the former Soviet security agency—is one of the few places in Manhattan I ever genuinely fell in love with.

Selwyn stirred at her old-fashioned with a swizzle stick, and I drank my Pabst.

"How'd you get the Host on you, anyway?"

She shook her head and went back to stirring her drink.

"I'd rather not get into that."

"Okay, then, how about we return to the subject of Isaac Snow, or, better yet, why you seem to specialize in ghoul artifacts."

She chewed at her lower lip a moment, then said, "One skull and one necklace hardly constitute specializing."

"So, that was just a coincidence?"

"Is this really your business?"

I finished my beer and ordered a second and another shot of Jack. If the bartender had overheard us, he was either used to hearing that sort of talk because the place was a secret watering hole for nasties and their fellow travelers or he had the good sense to mind his own business.

"Hey, Selwyn, you go and spring shit like Aster and her chamber of horrors on me, then it starts being my business real fast. Never mind getting me involved in your flea market of the damned. Do you even begin to understand what happens when the bad folks from the Nine Hells discover someone's playing Walmart with stuff they consider rightfully theirs? Because I do."

"I take precautions," she said.

I was only almost speechless.

"Congratulations, baby girl. I think you just graduated from 'reckless' to 'too dumb to fuck.'"

She stopped stirring her drink. She tapped at the end of her nose instead.

"He's my cousin," she said, and she took a tarnished silver pocket watch from her jacket and opened it. She checked the time against the clock behind the bar, then closed the watch and put it away again. "Isaac Snow. He's my cousin."

I tossed back my Jack Daniel's and ordered a third shot. I figured, whatever was coming next, whatever she was about to say, I'd need it. See, it tends to work like this with monsters. Not always, but usually. We aren't so big on the "enemy of my enemy is my friend" adage. More like "the enemy of my friend is always my enemy." You hang with troublemakers, or even just someone unlucky enough to be in the wrong place at the wrong time, tends to rub off. There are exceptions, sure. For example, when Evangelista Penderghast helped me put an end to Mercy Brown—see the first thrilling installment of the misadventures and dumb luck of me. But, truth be told, the Bride of Quiet and Penderghast, they were actually playing a very long game of chess, and I'd just been the pawn in the match. Okay, bad metaphor. But you get the gist. I knew sitting there at the bar that afternoon that the longer I stuck around Selwyn Throckmorton, the more of her messes were gonna become messes I could call my own. Hell, the spooky grapevine was probably already humming with the news that she'd found a vamp guardian angel.

"So," I said, watching the bartender as he poured the shot of bourbon, "when you were telling me about Boston's answer to the Addams Family, you just conveniently neglected to mention it also includes the Throckmortons. You know, if I murder you, this very minute, I'll totally get away with it."

She glanced at me, and then she tapped her nose a few more times.

"It's *not* the Throckmortons," she said. "The Throckmortons are all working-class, God-fearing Baptists. Dad's from Pittsburgh. But my mother was an Endicott. Suzanne Endicott. He didn't know about any of it until after they were married. She'd come to New York to try to get away from that bunch."

My shot arrived. I found myself wishing it were something redder and richer than whiskey. I let her talk. I didn't have to. I could have gotten up and walked out, bought a bus or train ticket, put Manhattan behind me, and hoped none of the grief Selwyn had earned would follow me.

I sat on my stool and listened.

"Mom had some money she'd inherited from a dead aunt or uncle, and she enrolled at NYU. She wanted to study art history. Anyway, that's where she met my father. He was doing his postdoc work. They got married, she dropped out, got a job at the Strand, and Dad didn't find out anything about her family until after I was born. She'd told him she was from Alaska."

"Alaska," I said.

"Yeah. Anchorage. He believed her, which is sort of crazy because she had such a strong Boston accent and all. Maybe he just didn't care what the truth was, decided it didn't really matter, whatever. It was three years before he found out, not until after I was born. He wouldn't have found out then if I hadn't been born with a tail."

In one of those old screwball comedies Selwyn liked so much, here's where I'd have done a spit take. But dead girls, we don't do spit takes when we hear our new fuck buddy was born with a tail. Par for the course, water off a duck's back, cliché, cliché, cliché. We're a jaded lot.

"I didn't notice a tail last night," I told her.

"That's because my mother told them to amputate it. When she saw it, she got hysterical. She wouldn't even hold me until the doctors cut it off. Dad used to apologize, like it was all *his* fault I didn't still have a tail."

I imagined that dusty old portrait of Karl Marx was staring sympathetically down at me as if he understood precisely how impatient I was getting, exactly how much I was wishing Selwyn would hurry up and get to the goddamn point already. I lit a cigarette. I didn't offer her one.

"That was very sweet of him," I said. "But how the fuck did your tail lead to his finding out about the skeletons in your mom's closet?"

"She told him. She got it in her head somehow that he'd connect the dots—which was perfectly ludicrous, because it's not like he'd ever even heard of the Endicotts or the Snows or—"

"Promise me this starts making sense eventually," I interrupted, and she took a swallow of her old-fashioned. Most of the ice had melted.

"She freaked out. Got paranoid. I honestly have no idea. But a few days after they came home from the hospital, she started talking and didn't *stop* talking until Daddy knew why I'd been born with a tail and a whole shitload more about her family and their past than, you know, than they wanted anyone who wasn't one of them knowing. I was also born with a caul," she added, like an afterthought.

"Which means . . . what?" I asked. "Come *on*. I'm a blood-sucking freak and a werewolf. It's not like you're gonna *shock* me."

That was the thud of the other shoe dropping.

Her sapphire-blue eyes got very, very wide, and I half expected they were gonna pop out of her skull and go rolling away across the floor.

"Fuck," she whispered. "You're a werewolf? And you were gonna tell me this when?"

"Jesus." I sighed, a great big exasperated sigh and rubbed at my eyes. My stomach grumbled, and I wondered how long it would be before anyone noticed if I ate the bartender. "How about right after you got around to explaining how you got your hands on that necklace, or ever got involved with goddamn Faeries, or—"

"Yeah, but . . . Jesus. I didn't even know werewolves were real. Not for sure. How did—"

"Shut up," I said. "Just shut up. Later. I'll tell you all about it later. *If* I feel like it. Meanwhile, you were saying, your mom blew a fuse over your tail and your caul and ratted out her creepy relatives. Your creepy *relatives*."

"Yeah," Selwyn said, still watching me like I was about to get all hairy right then and there. "I was."

My stomach grumbled again. The bartender seemed like a nice enough guy, but I'd eaten a lot of nice guys over the years, and what was one more?

"You were going to tell me what babies with tails have to do with the Snows and the Endicotts."

"And the Cabots."

"Them, too."

She finally took her eyes off me.

Warning: infodump inbound.

"The families came mostly from north of England, Yorkshire mostly. And they didn't leave England by choice. Frankly, I don't know a lot of the details, but it seems their reputation finally got the best of them. Witchcraft, human sacrifice, cannibalism. The list goes on and on. All across Europe, lots of people accused of being witches were being burned at the stake in the early sixteen hundreds, and the families must have decided they were all living on borrowed time. The Snows apparently led the diaspora. Nicholas and Constance Snow arrived in

Plymouth in 1620, then John and Anne Endicott in 1623. The Cabots were latecomers, probably because *their* reputations weren't quite as bad. They didn't make it to Massachusetts until 1700. And Antoine Cabot, he didn't come to New England, but took his family to New Orleans in 1753, because he—"

She was already boring the shit out of me, and I interrupted. "'And unto Enoch was born Irad: and Irad begat Mehujael: and Mehujael begat Methusael: and Methusael begat Lamech.' Can we skip the genealogy falderal?"

Selwyn seemed surprised I could quote Scripture. But, like they say, it pays to know them what want to put wooden stakes through your chest, decapitate you, and cut off your head, tiddley-pom.

"I thought you wanted to hear this."

I called for another beer; this time I skipped to the chase and asked the bartender to leave the bottle of Jack.

"Yeah, okay," I said and rubbed my temples; I was getting a headache. You'd think being dead, at least I'd be spared headaches. You'd be wrong. "I'm assuming this wasn't just paranoia, that these actually were dipping their collective big toes in the black arts."

She shook her head.

"No, it wasn't just paranoia. Sometime back in the fifteenth century, during the reign of Henry VI, during the Wars of the Roses, that's when it started. What with all that feuding from the nobility, you know, the power of the Crown was starting to erode. Rumor has it that the families were somehow involved in the deposing of the king by his cousin Edward in 1461. Edward was the first Yorkist King of England, you know."

I'll be the first to admit I know less than fuck all about English history, and give much less than two shits, and the Girl Who'd Lost Her Tail had also just lost me.

"The families, the men and women whose descendants would become the three families, they made a pact with the Ghūl. So long as one daughter was offered to them each generation to bear half-ghoul children, the families would prosper. The ghouls had been squirreling away treasures in the vaults of Thok and Pnath since they were cast down into the Underworld by the Djinn—"

I'm not making this stuff up. Neither was she. Lovecraft might not have known about the war—or he chose not to write everything he knew—but he got a lot of other stuff about the ghouls right.

"—and as long as the families kept their pledge, some of that plunder would be given to the patriarchs and matriarchs and so forth. Both sides were good to their word. And the families grew bolder. They started summoning demons and making deals with dark gods—at least this is what my mother had told Daddy. Even got in with one or two of the Great Old Ones. I'm not sure I believe that part. But maybe. Dad saw the Snow library once—long story—and he swore there were copies of both *Cultes des Goules* and the *Necronomicon*, possibly the Greek translation that had belonged to Richard Pickman.

"Also," she added, "except for the ghouls and maybe an occasional ritual tryst with worse things, the families don't breed outside the families. Which was one of Mom's terrible transgressions against them. In their eyes, of course, it makes me an abomination."

I sipped at my whiskey and smoked my cigarette.

"What a naughty bunch of shitbirds," I said. "Guess it's no wonder your mother tried to disown them. And these twins?"

"Isaac and Isobel," she said and pushed her watery old-fashioned away. The napkin had soaked through, and she smeared water across the varnished wood. "They were sired by a ghoul. See, that's how it is with the kids. The Ghūl send them back up into this world. Well, all of the ones who can pass for human."

She stopped talking, so I prodded her.

"And they send them back because?"

She looked at me again. But at least her eyes weren't bugging out over me being a werewolf.

"They're trying to come back. The Ghūl. They've been looking for a way since they lost the war. And the half-breeds give them a foothold. And they're looking for something . . ." She trailed off. Sitting there among the relics of a fallen Communist empire, trying to digest Selwyn's tale and wishing I was still capable of getting utterly cockeyed, I remembered my first impression of her from the night before. That she could have been a monster herself, hiding inside a glamour or some other sort of spell. That skin so damn pale I swear it almost glowed, but wasn't the waxy sort of pale mine is. Her black hair. The sapphire eyes I keep bringing up. And, voilà, turns out I wasn't too far off the mark, was I?

"So, this makes you?"

"Makes me what?"

I liked her, and I didn't want to come right out and say it. Fortunately, I didn't have to. It only took her a couple of seconds to realize what I was asking.

"My mother's mother was a half-breed," she said.

"Which makes you—"

I don't know why I couldn't seem to shut up and just let her talk.

"One-quarter," she whispered. "That makes me one-quarter." Which explained the tail, and if you buy into that shit about kids born with cauls being marked by demons, well, if the three families truly had made deals with demons and Yog-Sogthoth and what the hell ever, it explained that part, too.

End of infodump. Later, she'd tell me what happened to her parents, but that can wait.

"Is this why you specialize in ghoul artifacts and bones and stuff?"

"Quinn, I don't specialize in ghoul artifacts. I already told you that."

"Right," I said. "Coincidence. I forgot."

She checked her pocket watch again.

"You got some place to be?" I asked.

"I had some place to be twenty minutes ago." And she put away the watch and took out her phone. "Now I have to explain why I'm late."

"It happens," I said. "Another customer?"

"Yeah. Up in the Bronx. Maybe you'd better sit this one out." She took out her wallet.

"Who, me? Are you kidding? And miss you hawking the toenail clippings of the Earl of Weir or some shit? No way, baby girl."

I'm not gonna lie. All I wanted was to sit there with Marx and Engels and Stalin and finish off the bottle. But, hey, she'd just paid for it, and it was portable. And I might as well admit that I was beginning to feel protective, no matter how furious I still was over Aster the Faerie. It crossed my mind Selwyn might be a witch herself, and that maybe she'd cast some sort of hoodoo to make sure I'd become that special someone to watch over her. Besides, I'd conceded to myself while she'd confessed her sordid lineage, I was tired of being bored. Tired of playing it safe.

"And you'll behave yourself?" she asked me.

"As long as there are no fucking Faeries, sure, I'll be good." And I crossed my heart with my right hand and made the three-fingered Girl Scout sign with my left.

"It's not a Faerie," she assured me.

And that third stop of Selwyn's day, it was actually sort of anticlimactic. The customer was a crazy cat lady who paid five hundred dollars for dried-out trichobezoar she thought might cure her arthritis. And then Selwyn was hungry again, and I sat on the curb and smoked while she sat on the curb and ate two hot dogs and an order of fries.

She didn't say anything else about Isaac and Isobel Snow or ghouls or diabolical get-rich-quick schemes of yore. And I didn't ask.

CHAPTER THREE

QUARREL WITH THE MOON

How about let's call this bit comes next "Quinn's getting sidetracked or digressing or what the hell ever with some crazy and inconvenient werewolf hijinks." Works for me. Straight lines, all neat and tidy—from *here* to *there*—are for Aesop and los Hermanos Grimm. You'll keep reading or you'll stop. Also, it *is* what happened next, and while it's gonna leave you hanging for a bit as regards the Snow twins and ghoul conspiracies, it *is* what happened next. And it's relevant to what came later on. Patience, young Jedi.

Have I said all this was going down early in November? I'm pretty sure I mentioned that, but if I haven't, it was. October had been unseasonably warm, but the weather turned cold just after Halloween. The night I met Selwyn was the evening of the third, a Sunday night. New moon. The cleaners disposed of the CPA's corpse on the morning of the fourth, and that night I fed from Selwyn for the first time. Then came the three deliveries, KGB, and Selwyn's revelations on the fifth. Tuesday. The next two days were more or less unremarkable. Lots of sex. I fed from her again Thursday evening. Those two days, we didn't talk about her business, she didn't have any transactions to attend to, just some phone calls, and none of Mr. Snow's goons showed up. We watched movies, and she told me stories about her father's work in places like Egypt and Iran. I read. There you have it. That cliché calm before the storm.

Never let your guard down.

By Thursday night, mine was slipping. All that time in Brooklyn with Barbara O'Bryan I'd been pretty sloppy, I will admit. Spent less time looking over my shoulder than I should have. Selwyn knowing what I was, that should have been more of a wake-up call than it was. But that Thursday—well, after midnight, so it was more like the dark hours of Friday morning—I wasn't thinking about much of anything but the taste of her.

I'd noticed the first time that her blood had a faintly musky edge. I didn't think too much of it. Different people taste different. But some people taste more different than others. Now that I'd gotten the lowdown on her family line, I was pretty damn sure I was tasting just a dash of ghoul. I'd never sampled one before, and, frankly,

I'd planned to go the rest of my life without doing so. I mean, ew. Anyone who's ever seen one of the bastards, they can tell you last thing you'll have on your mind thereafter is wrapping your lips around any part of a ghoul's anatomy.

The strange edge to Selwyn's blood, it tasted a *little* like fried chicken livers. I've never come up with a better analogy.

That morning, I took less than I'd taken from her the first time, just enough I wasn't hungry anymore. I had just enough more self-control to manage that trick. And I managed not to make too much of a mess. Afterward we fucked. She had a pretty spectacular strap-on, one of those double-ended, silicone jobs salvaged from the effects of the CPA. That night, Selwyn was on top.

A few seconds after I came, which was a few seconds after she came, Selwyn slapped me. Hard. I wouldn't have guessed she could hit that hard. I've mentioned her being a sadist. Well, that was a turn-on. But the slap took me by surprise. I suppose it was meant to, right? She raised her hand for another strike, but I grabbed hold of her wrist and just stared at her. Whatever she saw in my eyes, it wasn't meant to make her smile, but it did. She smiled, and she said, "Goddamn, I wish I had teeth like those."

The sudden wave of anger that had washed over me was fading almost as quickly as it had arrived. But it left me jangling and on edge. That part of me that wasn't human, it didn't quite understand when being struck only meant your girl got off seeing her girlfriend in pain.

"Don't do that again," I whispered as she withdrew and lay down beside me. She didn't immediately take off the dildo, and the phallus, wet with me, drooped slightly towards the bed, cause gravity sucks and all.

"Oh, Quinn, c'mon. I hardly—"

"Just don't," I said.

She shrugged and slipped her right hand around the shaft of that pretend cock, lazily stroking it. Not sure if that was supposed to be for my benefit or not. I didn't ask. She had a mischievous expression.

"So, what? Now you're pissed at me?" she asked.

"No. I'm not pissed at you. But maybe we need some ground rules."

"That lady of yours in Brooklyn, she never hit you?"

"No, she didn't. But hurting people wasn't her thing."

"I've never understood that one-sided mentality," Selwyn sighed. "Making it all give and no take, or all take and no give. You're missing half the fun either way. Anyway, from a political standpoint, it seems more egalitarian, less like—"

"Come off it, Selwyn. You do not give a shit about being a politically correct pervert."

She shrugged again, tugged roughly on the dildo before letting it go. It flopped over sideways.

"Can you take that ridiculous thing off?"

"Sure," she said and began loosening the straps on the leather harness. "You didn't seem to think it was so ridiculous a few minutes ago."

I shut my eyes.

"I dated this girl for a while," she said, "and she was a pretty hard-core masochist. She'd let me do shit like sewing her labia together, run needles through her nipples, and so forth. But I could never get her to lay a hand on *me*, like I was some sort of china doll and was going to shatter into a million pieces. I'm pretty sure that's why we finally broke up. It got boring."

There's no denying that Selwyn would have made a goddamn wicked vamp. That one-quarter of her that came courtesy of ghouls getting their rocks off with human women (and, undoubtedly, vice versa), it had laid the foundations good and proper. If you're reading this, hoping for a likable, sympathetic character—and I just *know* you've already given up on me—well, you're not likely to do any better with Selwyn. I mean, not unless you're willing and able to rise to the occasion and overlook the ugly fucking truth of her inherited appetites. We can talk nature versus nurture until we're blue in the face, but I don't care how she was raised; in these matters, blood will out, and you can bet your bottom dollar on that.

But no, I didn't turn her. I've never turned anyone. That's one of the very few gold stars you'll find stuck up next to my name.

"She once had me sew her lips shut for two days," says Selwyn, my mean girl disguised as a mild-mannered geek. "I'm good with stitches, if I do say so myself. Oh, what happened to her, you ask?"

"I didn't ask," I said, my eyes still shut.

"Yeah, but you wondered."

"I didn't wonder, either."

"Well, too bad. She killed herself about six months ago. Drank a bottle of . . . Shit, I don't recall what it was, but it killed her dead."

"Usually, that's the way people *get* killed."

"Don't be an ass," she said and punched me in the

left shoulder, and I opened my eyes. The room was spinning, the way it does when you make the mistake of getting spectacularly shit faced, then lying on your back. Only, I wasn't shit faced.

Selwyn gently bit my left biceps; her teeth were as dull as pencil erasers. She was quiet a moment, then whispered, "Quinn, you okay? You look sorta ill."

I blinked my eyes, then rubbed them. The dizziness refused to pass. I gripped the edge of the mattress, with my right hand, you know. I felt, all at once, the need to hold on to something solid, anything at all. A wave of nausea swept over me. My arms and legs had begun to tingle.

"That's sorta the way I feel," I told her.

The vertigo, the nausea, it was joined then by tunnel vision. First thought, had Selwyn poisoned me somehow? Had she actually poisoned that ex-girlfriend whose lips and pussy she'd sewn shut? She hadn't. Poisoned me. I don't know about the ex-girlfriend. Still that was the first thing popped into my head.

My head had begun to pound. My chest hurt.

Vampires do not have heart attacks.

I sat up and went to get out of bed. When I tried to stand, my legs folded under me and I hit the floor. I was dimly surprised. I was beginning to have trouble thinking clearly.

"Jesus, Quinn," Selwyn said, alarmed. I heard the box springs creak.

I tried to stand again. No dice. So I crawled to the bathroom. By the time I got the toilet seat up, I was completely blind, and the headache was a jackhammer. I puked a stomachful of Selwyn into the dirty porcelain bowl. The smell of blood made me puke again. And again.

"Fuck, Quinn. What's happening?" She sounded scared. Her voice seemed to be coming from somewhere very far away. Like Hoboken.

I managed to croak, "Drugs?"

"Drugs?"

"Jesus fucking Christ. *Drugs*. Have you *taken* anything tonight?" I managed. Not that it should have mattered.

Fire bloomed in my rib cage, and that, right there, is when I knew, without a doubt, what was happening.

"I . . ." she started, and I realized she was kneeling and had her arms around me.

I shat myself. The smell made me vomit again, though there wasn't anything left to puke up. Note: Vampires also don't shit. Hell, after a few decades, our assholes and lower intestines just shrivel up and disappear (same with our genitals). I heard Selwyn scrambling away from me across the tiled floor.

"I just . . ."

"You just *what*, bitch?" I growled. No, I snarled.

"Wolfsbane," she whispered, horrified.

Okay, so my newfound blood doll wished she was a vamp, but she wasn't so keen on the *loup* thing. Not that I could *blame* her.

I laughed; then I had a bout of dry heaves. Then I laughed again.

"You're fucking kidding me."

"I thought maybe . . ." She trailed off again, and then she added, "Just a tiny, tiny bit, Quinn. Hardly any at all.

And it's the detoxified, medicinal stuff I get from . . . I mean . . . not even enough to—"

"—hurt *you*," I finished.

Garlic and holy water might not work on vampires, but werewolves have a vicious goddamn problem with *Aconitum*. Even hardly any at all. Here's what Wikipedia has to say about wolfsbane: *Marked symptoms may appear almost immediately, usually not later than one hour, and with large doses death is almost instantaneous. Death usually occurs within two to six hours in fatal poisoning. The initial signs are gastrointestinal, including nausea, vomiting, and diarrhea.* Oh, there's more. But I expect you get the idea. Of course, I wasn't gonna die. I wasn't that lucky.

Whee.

Except something else was happening. Selwyn had done more than poison me. She'd given the Beast a swift kick in the balls, and my puppy was waking up with the mother of all hangovers.

"Run," I croaked. "Run as far as you can. Get somewhere I can't find you."

"Quinn, I didn't know. How could I—"

"Shut the fuck up and fucking *run*!" I roared.

Roared. Snarled. Growled. I don't mean these words in the usual euphemistic sense.

Selwyn ran. Later, I'd learn she grabbed the bag with my weapons on her way out. I heard the door slam behind her. I heard her feet on the stairs on her way down to the lobby. I heard the lobby door open and slam. She hadn't even bothered to get dressed. I never did find out how she got away with that. What the hell. New York City, right? Enough said.

The pain was closing around me like a steel fist, taking hold and squeezing. My chest and belly, my skull, felt like they were trying to turn themselves wrong-side out. An apt enough analogy, as *loups* everywhere can attest.

I waited for the merciful and inevitable blackout. because that's what had always happened.

Always.

But not this time. Oh, no. I didn't fade out. Before, the change had always been accompanied by oblivion, a dreamless unconsciousness that lasted until I was only a vamp again. I still can't say for sure what made the difference, and what made the difference forever thereafter every time the Beast came to dance. I believe it was that one dose of wolfsbane, but I can't swear to it.

The pain was everything in the world. The pain was God. What do you do when the hand of God reaches down and touches you? Me, I screamed. At least what came out of my throat was *meant* to be a scream. I tried to stand, lost my footing, and careened into the wall beside the toilet. No. The Beast *slammed* itself against that wall. I heard the brittle crack of ceramic tiles, the crunch of old plaster, the tiny bathroom window shattering, the tinkling of glass scattering across the floor. The creature toppled backwards into the tub, pulling the shower curtain down on top of itself, on top of me, of us. While we flailed about in the small cast-iron tub, the blindness passed as quickly as it came. But what returned to me wasn't my vision. It's not exactly that I was color blind, but telling one color from another was just about impossible, and the bathroom was sort of a muddy emerald blur. I watched as the skin of my arms and hands split and sloughed bloodlessly away.

There was the fucking Beast underneath, like it had been waiting there all along, stuck inside a Quinn-shaped suit.

There wasn't much of the pain left. Mostly just a smothering, all-consuming frustration. Wherever the Beast wanted to be, Selwyn's tub was not that place.

The plastic shower curtain came apart as easily as my flesh, and for just a moment the Beast and I lingered at the medicine cabinet, its golden eyes staring furiously back at me, twin pits in its face packed with molten gold. Strips of me were still tangled in its black fur, hanging off its muzzle. Jesus, I'd killed my share of *loups*, and I'd never seen one I'd call anything less than ugly. Anybody's ever set eyes on one knows whatever joker coined the term *werewolf* was full of shit. But I suppose that's the sort of shit that happens when words fail, right? Anyway, there in the mirror was a special sort of gruesome, which I chalk up to the unholy marriage of the Bride of Quiet and Jack Grumet. Two nasties for the price of one. I'd never seen its face before.

There was confusion in those eyes, and fear, and more hate than I'd ever thought could be crammed into a glare. The hate, that was mostly the Beast's. I was the bitch who held her chain, who kept her locked away to rot in the prison of me. Ever been to the zoo and looked into the eyes of a wolf or a coyote or a mountain lion stuck there behind iron bars or Plexiglas? Ever seen that venom, that spite? Well, there you go.

One or the other of us, me or the Beast broke the mirror. I like to believe it was me who did it. But that's probably wishful thinking.

I say *one or the other of us* because that's the best I can describe what it was like. Like I said, my mind hadn't had the decency to take a powder, so there we were together at last. And speaking of the limitations of language, I'm not sure I have the language needed to describe the hours that followed. I doubt anyone does, anyone dead or alive or whatever. But I'm gonna try.

I don't remember leaving Selwyn's apartment or the stairs. Next thing I knew I was out on the sidewalk, and a woman was screaming bloody goddamn murder. You remember the end of *An American Werewolf in London*, after David Kessler's final transformation in the porno theater, when he's rampaging around Piccadilly Circus fucking shit up? Well . . . it wasn't like that. Just that one unfortunate woman. We, it, I reared up on two legs and towered over her, seven and a half, eight feet. She opened her mouth to scream again, and the *loup* picked her up and smacked her head once against a lamppost before dragging her away into an alley, leaving nothing behind but a gooey smear of brains. A great deal of what was to come would involve skulking through alleys and shit, because, turned out I was more than a reluctant passenger. Turned out I still had a modicum of control over the Beast. Which, you know, only pissed it off that much more. But that night I managed to teach it the value of caution.

Go me.

The screaming woman was the first person we ate that night. Whatever revulsion I might have harbored, I harbored it very briefly. It had been a long time since I'd known the simple pleasure of chewing and swallowing solid food. I found myself savoring every raw, greedy mouthful. Those razor teeth pulled her apart easy as you please, and between those jaws her bones might as well have been pocky. Whoa. Weird analogy. How about *her bones might as well have been pretzel sticks*, instead? No, that's really not much better. Never mind. Probably, you know what I mean.

And shit I felt strong. I felt motherfucking *alive*, which I'd never, ever dared imagine I would feel ever again. Here was how the other half lived. The Beast was seducing me, whether it knew it was or not. And I thought, *I could lose myself in here. I could just let it run on and on and on, and I'd never have to go back to being Quinn.*

Who was she, anyway? Some pathetic dead girl, good at being bitter and surviving, but nothing much more than that. She was a parasitic phantom who wanted with all her sour heart to be *truly* dead, but she didn't have the balls to make that happen. To grab that brass ring and get off the merry-go-round. But the Beast, it knew joy.

Nasties tend to look down on *loups* as the white trash of our psychofuck supernatural menagerie. Nothing lower than a *loup* but maybe a ghoul. Sure. That's the party line. Demons and Faeries on their lofty pedestals, vamps out on the street, and werewolves in the gutters. Except, at least if we're talking about the way bloodsuckers look down on *loups*, maybe that ain't nothing but envy. Maybe, somewhere down deep, it's obvious how living, how lycanthropy isn't a curse at all.

How maybe it's a blessing.

Not bad enough my very existence is a blasphemy in the eyes of Big Bads the world over. Not bad enough I'd become a traitor who hunted and put them down. I'd just become a heretic to boot.

When we were done with the screaming woman, there wasn't much left of her but a puddle of gore, and a stingy puddle at that. And I was still starving. My taste for blood has always been easy enough to temporarily satisfy. But this, this was a hunger that was utterly absolute and insatiable. I instinctively knew how the Beast could eat for days and never get its fill. And, honestly, crouching there in the alley behind Selwyn's apartment building, that would've been fine by me.

We, I, it glanced up at the sky, as if seeking a premature full moon. Not that the *loup*'s appearances have ever much synced up with lunar phases. I'd long ago written that off to superstition, and, hey and by the way, learning that the world is full of monsters and magic's real and all that crap doesn't mean that isn't still superstition. Everything isn't true, just because an awful lot of weird shit turns out to be. Yes, there are demons and vamps and unicorns and Faeries, but it ain't bad luck to walk under a ladder and black cats are nothing but cats that are black. And werewolves don't seem to care about the moon.

Where was I?

We howled, and I'd have sworn, for an instant or two, the night around us held its breath.

And then the *loup* ran, and I'd say that I was dragged along for the ride. Only it wasn't like that at all. I was *riding*. Oh, I could have fought, and maybe the struggle would even have made a difference, but I didn't. We went south, keeping always to alleys and side streets. I can't say which side streets and alleys, because it hardly mattered. Not like I was reading the signs. Lurching along on two legs, racing on four, our claws dug furrows in asphalt and scraped across concrete and cobblestones. Everything un-folded around me in a ghostly haze of night vision. Some-where, the Beast's left shoulder clipped a dumpster, and the dumpster skidded away, doing almost a full one eighty before smacking into a brick wall. We were briefly stunned. Or it was stunned, and I was aware of that fact. Which the fuck ever. It was knocked off its feet, but got right back up again. Jesus, I've never felt so invulnerable. Like . . . like what? Like that bullshit self-confidence comes along with the rush after a couple of lines of cocaine, but multiplied a hundred times.

Yeah, like that.

Car horns, car alarms, the squeal of tires and brake pads. Screams and curses. Dogs locked up inside going monkey shit at the smell of us and barking their heads off. The stink of garbage and rats and pigeon shit and . . . every smell of Manhattan amped up and off the scales. And we killed. Almost anything, anyone unlucky or dumb enough to get in our way went down and stayed down. Most barely had a chance to scream. Barely knew what hit them, or didn't know at all.

Probably the latter.

You're out for a stroll, or your walking your Pomera-nian, and this huge fucking brute lunges out of the shad-ows, in those final seconds, how likely is it you're gonna think, *Oh shit on me, a werewolf,* right? You're too busy being totally stupefied or with fleeting thoughts of just how screwed you are. I mean, I'm talking about regular people here, those not in on the great cosmic joke that monsters walk among them.

We barreled headlong, full-tilt boogie into the passenger side of a Volkswagen Beetle, and the car was tossed several feet into the air and landed upside down on a punk kid on a skateboard. Splat. I was dimly amazed. Dude, that was, I gotta say, one of the coolest things I've ever seen. Hey, I bet that guy on the skateboard would have agreed.

Unlike the dumpster, the Volkswagen didn't even slow us down. The Incredible Hulk? That snot-green son of a bitch has nothing on my *loup*.

Yeah, that night, that November morning, was when I began thinking of the Beast as mine. Or, no. Wait. That's not quite right, 'cause the Beast is without a doubt her *own* Beast. More like, I realized she's an integral part of me, an intimate part of me—of the *new* me that Mercy and Grumet had created—wedded inextricably to whatever miserable crumb was left of my soul. Suddenly, she was more than a bothersome fucking furball who popped up from time to time for the express purpose of messing with precious goddamn me. Might come off schmaltzy, but dashing helter-skelter about Gotham, decapitating and disemboweling and dismembering, I also found myself thinking of her as a *friend*. Yeah, right? Hell, I hadn't had too many of those when I was alive, and no more than a couple postmortem, Selwyn Throckmorton and Aloysius the troll. Oh, and a violet-skinned succubus went by the fine old Puritan name of Clemency Hate-evil before being my friend got her killed. Or got her worse. I was never sure which.

But it wasn't as simple as that. This epiphany, I mean. There was more to it. We hit the Volkswagen, and shortly afterwards I had . . . let's call it a vision, because I don't know what the hell else I'd call it. You got something better, be my guest. One minute I was all but drowning in the sound of the Beast's paws hammering at the pavement, tripping balls on the carnage, on a million noises, odors, sights, et cetera and fucking et cetera.

Jump cut.

And I was walking slowly through a forest. Dry leaves crunched under my bare feet, and the moon—a *full* moon, mind you—was shining down through branches that were mostly bare. Because wherever I was that was no longer Lower Manhattan, it was autumn there, too. Maybe it was even November. I knew right off those woods weren't real. They could have been a storybook forest, the sort of place dreamed up so wicked witches can build their gaudy gingerbread houses while Snow White lies in a coma surrounded by her seven dwarves. A forest built out of imagination. Yeah, that was the way it struck me, like it hadn't grown there, like it had been thought into being.

Regardless, I didn't want to be there. I wanted to be with the *loup*. I was *supposed* to be with the *loup*, wasn't I? By being hauled away to that soundstage forest, I was being cheated out of my half of our wild hunt. I stopped and looked over my shoulder, like maybe there was gonna be a flashing neon exit sign waiting behind me. But there was only more trees. Paper birch and oak trees and shaggy hemlocks. I cursed them and started walking again, because walking seemed to make slightly more sense than standing still. I don't know how long I walked. Everything about that place was so much the same it could have been a short loop of film, playing over and over. I could have been walking in tiny circles that I'd only mistaken for a straight line, some sort of Möbius strip . . .

I walked through the trees until there weren't any more of the trees to walk through. They came to an end at the edge of a field of tall yellow-brown grass. The woods had been still as my dead heart, but a cold breeze rustled the field, blowing the grass this way, that way. The forest had smelled like cinnamon and cloves, but out in the open, the air smelled like apple cider. And I was no longer alone. There was a blonde child and a huge black wolf staring out over the tall grass. The wolf was sitting on its haunches. She was standing, but, even so, she was hardly as tall as that wolf. It wasn't a *loup*. Except for its size, it was, you know, just a wolf. The child was stroking the top of its head. When I stepped out of the forest, they both turned and looked at me. The girl smiled. But it was a sad sort of smile. A pitying kind of smile that ought to have made me even more angry, because I cannot bear being pitied. But, for some reason, her smile was a relief. Could be anything would have been a relief after those trees.

"Hi," she said and waved.

"Hi," I replied. There were a lot of questions I wanted to ask. I picked one more or less at random.

"What's going on?"

The girl raised an eyebrow.

"What do you mean, Quinn?"

"I mean . . ." And I paused, uncertain for just a second what I *did* mean. "I mean," I continued, "where am I?"

Her smile returned.

"Oh. Well, you're standing between the forest and

the meadow. Do you know what's on the other side of the meadow, Quinn?"

"More fucking trees?"

She shrugged, and the wolf whimpered, so she scratched it under the chin.

"Could be. I don't know. We've never tried to cross the meadow. I think we're afraid to try."

I gazed out across the grass. Whatever was on the other side, it was too far away to see.

"Today," she said, "my name is Quinn."

"I should tell you, I'm not in the mood to be fucked with."

She just shrugged and kept scratching at the big black wolf's chin. It occurred to me that the wolf's fur was the same color as Selwyn's. It also occurred to me that the girl's hair was the same dirty blonde as my own.

"So, okay, what was your name yesterday?"

"I can't remember. Does it really matter? You weren't here yesterday."

"I'm going to sit down," I told her. "My feet hurt."

"If you sit, you won't be able to see anything," she said. "The grass is too tall, if you sit, to see over."

"In case you haven't noticed, there's not a hell of a lot going on out there."

"Not yet," she said, and stopped scratching the wolf.

"You're a strange one," I said, and she shrugged again.

"Said the vampire who's also a lycanthrope."

I let that go. She had a point.

"How long have you been here?" I asked her. I sat down cross-legged with the trees at my back. I discovered that several fat gray grasshoppers were watching me. If grasshoppers can watch something cautiously, then that's what they were doing.

"I'm not sure. But I guess it must have been a very long time. Long enough I can't remember. Unless, of course, I only got here yesterday and just can't remember I got here yesterday."

"Do you always fucking talk like a character from *Alice's Adventures in Wonderland*?"

She laughed. It was a totally creepy laugh.

The wolf turned its head and stared at me. Its eyes—the irises of its eyes—were so pale I'd call them white.

"Does he have a name?" I asked and nodded at the wolf.

"She," the girl said. "He's a she. And I've never thought to ask her, Quinn."

I grabbed at one of the grasshoppers and missed. It hopped away, and all the others wisely followed its example. My hand closed around nothing but a few yellow-brown stalks. Screw you, Mr. Bug.

"I'm not dreaming," I whispered to myself.

"No, you're not, Quinn."

"Isn't that what I just said?"

I didn't have to look to know the wolf was still watching me. I could feel its white eyes on me.

"Is she here to protect you? The wolf, I mean."

"Who else would you have meant? But no, I don't think so. I suspect it's a coincidence, that we both just happen to be here at the same time. Which is better than being alone. I would hate to be here alone. I don't like that field. Something about that field isn't right."

"It's just a field," I said, dropping the dead blades of grass.

"I know," she said very quietly. "I know."

And I wanted to tell her I didn't think her being there *and* the wolf's being there too, their being there together, was a coincidence, any more than, it had turned out, my being found by the Bride of Quiet the same night—right damned *after*—I'd been bitten by Jack Grumet had been a coincidence.

You ask me, which you haven't, coincidence is often a coward's way out of facing facts.

And please feel free, right about here, to become exasperated at my complete cluelessness. No, I didn't see what was right in front of my face. And I don't mean all that grass. I don't mean the forest for the trees. I didn't add up two and two and get four. Often, I'm not the sharpest knife in the drawer.

I said, "There's a bloodthirsty *loup*—my *loup*—tear-assing through Chelsea or the West Village or some shit, and I'm sitting here playing pretend and talking to a hallucination."

"Is that all that I am, Quinn? Pretend? A hallucination? Did you make me?"

"Didn't I?"

She sighed and stopped scratching the wolf's chin. "I really don't know. That's why I asked."

I shut my eyes. I shut my eyes very tight, and I saw—or at least thought that I saw—the *loup* working its way clumsily up a fire escape. The rusted metal groaned and creaked under its weight. Our weight. Or was she alone now?

All these fucking questions were becoming a stone around my neck.

"I have," the girl said, "thought sometimes there might be a peaceful place on the other side of the field."

The *loup* was about halfway up the fire escape when it gave way, when the bolts or whatever holding it into brick and mortar came loose, and the whole mess crashed to the alley below. I was wondering what would happen to me if the bitch got herself killed, and I was assuming that would be the end of both of us, when the monster pulled herself from the wreck. She looked like . . . well, a were-wolf that had fallen thirty feet and had a ton of steel dropped on it. But she hardly even seemed fucking fazed. Just shook her head a few times, then resumed her killing spree. Scary monsters, right? I could hear police sirens and ambulances now, rescue vehicles, whatever.

So much for caution.

Scary monsters. And, thank you, Mr. Bowie, because, I thought, and there she goes, opening those strange damn doors, and ain't no one ever gonna come along and get them closed again. And *she* might have been the porcelain demon who'd made me half of what I am. Or *she* might have been the girl with the wolf. Or my *loup*. Or, simply, *me*.

The girl's wolf whined, and I opened my eyes.

The girl's black wolf. My black *loup*.

Lightbulb. Duh and/or hello. Me, myself, *and* I.

"Sometimes," the blonde girl said, me talking to me, "people lose themselves in their secret selves. Once upon a time it happened in France. Have you ever heard of the Beast of Gévaudan? That was someone who lost herself and never did make it back again."

"Yeah, I've heard of the Beast of Gévaudan. But I didn't know it was a *loup*."

Between 1764 and 1770, a nasty attacked more than two hundred people in the Margeride Mountains of France. More than a hundred died. The nasty ate on most of those. Don't say I never taught you people anything.

"Sure you did, Quinn."

"If you say so," I told her, getting to my feet, wiping grass and dirt and crap off the seat of my jeans. There was a shiny iridescent beetle crawling on my leg, and I flicked it away. "I don't have time for this."

"You don't have to hate her, but you can't lose yourself to her," said the girl. "You always have to come back." Then she kissed the top of the black wolf's head, and it thumped its tail happily—at least I assume it was happily—against the ground. Goddamn heartwarming stuff. A girl and her carnivore.

I rubbed at my eyes. The sirens were getting louder, nearer. The sound of them only seemed to encourage the Rhode Island werewolf in Manhattan. It gutted a waiter who'd just gotten off work.

"Yeah, well, people die either way, whether it's the Beast or a vamp. What difference does it make?"

The girl narrowed her eyes, and for the first time she looked impatient with me.

"Quinn, if you lose yourself tonight, or any other night, you'll both be killed. That's the way it always goes when a *loup garou* surrenders to—"

"You're assuming I give a rat's ass."

She nodded very slowly.

"You're not a suicide, Quinn. Maybe that's what keeps you going, knowing it's an option, that you can always kill yourself if the world gets to be more than you can endure. But, personally, I think if you were going to do it, you'd have done it by now, don't you?"

Fuck it. Fast-forward. I'd figured out where that neon exit door was. First I broke the black wolf's neck with a single quick twist. It didn't put up much of a fight. The blonde girl didn't try to run. I'd halfway hoped that she would. I drove my right hand through her rib cage and breast bone and tore out her heart. It wasn't beating, and it wasn't warm. It was nothing but a shriveled lump of discolored muscle. And it was exactly as easy as that.

The forest and the field dissolved.

And I was looking out across the city from some high place, out across rooftops and the asphalt grid of streets, everything lit up like a Christmas tree.

You always see people saying that time seems to slow way down during, say, car wrecks or pretty much any other sudden, violent event. Those times when their lives are in danger, or the lives of a loved one. Those sorts of situations. Encounters with the unexpected, chaotic incursions. Well, what came next, it was surely fucking chaos, and it certainly could have ended with my going down for the count, once and for all. But it happened so fast it seemed to be over almost before it began. Looking back, I can only recall a series of images, like photographs or flashcards.

I'll use present tense here. Seems more appropriate somehow:

I see the city, from up there, and I realize *up there* is the High Line, that odd park on the Lower West Side that used to be a section of the New York Central Railroad. In the wolves' greenish night vision, I see leaves, gravel, rusted tracks. Sirens are screaming.

Jump cut.

There's a rent-a-cop motherfucker with a gun aimed at me, at the *loup*. He looks scared shitless. The streetlights glint off the barrel of the revolver. His hands are shaking. He's pissed himself.

Jump cut.

A figure steps out of the bushes, someone dressed up like the Unabomber, big, baggy hoody, face hidden in shadows. They're holding a crossbow in leather-gloved hands. My crossbow. It's aimed at the security guard's head. I'm thinking, *Don't you fucking do it*. Maybe that's meant for the *loup*. Maybe for the guard or the person holding the crossbow, or maybe it's meant for all three at once.

Jump cut.

The Unabomber shifts just so, and I can see it's Selwyn. She's so goddamn calm, as if she's done this a hundred times before. The rent-a-cop obviously doesn't see her. He's whispering "What the fuck?" over and over and over again as if it's a litany against death by werewolf. Or whatever he believes he's seeing looming up before him. The *loup* roars, and the gun goes off. I'd almost believe that bullet did a time-travel trick and hit me, us, the *loup*, before the man squeezed the trigger. There's fire in our left shoulder. All this is happening so incredibly fast. Selwyn fires a carbon-composite bolt, puts it through the guard's skull, temple to temple.

Jump cut.

I can't remember seeing the man fall. But now he's on his back, his body twitching, legs and arms doing a death-throe tarantella, right? I smell blood. The sirens are very close. My shoulder is burning alive.

Jump.

I'm staring up at Selwyn, her face still half obscured by the hoody. I know the *loup* is gone, and I'm alone now. And sweet Jesus on rubber crutches, I have never felt so alone as I do right now. Selwyn touches my face, and she whispers something I don't understand. I'm wondering where the hell she got those clothes, wondering how long she was on the streets in her birthday suit before she scored them.

Jump cut.

We're in a taxi, and I realize the blood I smell is my own. "Don't move," Selwyn says. "It's not much farther." I can't hear the sirens anymore. The driver smells like sweat and patchouli. I smell fake evergreen from the pine-tree-shaped cardboard swinging from the rearview mirror. I'm wrapped in a blue wool blanket. My shoulder throbs. It's not the first time I've been shot, and the pain's familiar. I want to tell her I'll be fine by dawn, but I don't. I'm dizzy, but it's not from the pain. I'm dizzy from the sheer weight of *color* werewolf us couldn't see. My vamp eyes are flooded with color.

Okay, I'm gonna stop with the damn "jump cut" device and the present tense. You get the point.

The taxi ride seemed to go on forever. The longest taxi ride of my life, though it couldn't have lasted more than twenty minutes. My face was propped against the window. On the other side of the glass, the world was a slow blur of nothing I recognized.

"Where'd you get the clothes?" I asked Selwyn.

"It doesn't matter," she replied.

"You really shouldn't have done that," I said.

"Well, I wasn't about to come looking for you stark naked, Quinn."

I laughed, and my shoulder ached worse.

"That's not what I meant, you pinhead. You don't throw down on a cop."

"He wasn't a real cop. And don't call me names, okay? I just saved your ass from a metric fuck-ton of real cops with *much* bigger fucking guns."

A few moments before, Selwyn had sounded concerned. Now she just sounded angry. I wasn't sure if we were talking quietly enough the driver couldn't hear. I also didn't care. Actually, I was considering having her drive to some deserted spot and having a snack to help my shoulder heal.

"You don't want me to call you a pinhead," I told her, "don't go around acting like one. Did you at least not leave the bolt back there?"

She didn't answer, which meant, of course, that she had left the bolt sticking out of the man's head.

"Where are we?" I asked.

"Almost there."

"Almost where, Selwyn?"

I saw a homeless man pushing two shopping carts tied together like boxcars and piled almost to overflowing with bulging Hefty bags. I thought how good he'd taste, and my mouth watered.

"I'm hungry," I said, and I wiped drool off my chin. There was a smear of it on the window.

"After everything you puked up back there?"

I never do manage to keep down what the *loup* eats. This body ain't so keen on solid food.

I closed my eyes. I wanted to be in a very, very dark place, away from headlights and taillights and sodium-vapor light. A closet would suffice. A subbasement would be wonderful.

"You have my bag? You didn't leave it on the High Line?"

"I have your bag, Quinn. Stop talking so much, why don't you."

Good advice, which is probably why I ignored it. The driver drove, and I rambled on. I asked if we were going all the way to fucking New Jersey, and Selwyn told the driver to ignore me, that I was drunk. That I was, in fact, an alcoholic who'd fallen off the wagon. She told the driver she was my AA sponsor.

"Liar," I said.

"You oughta know."

I oughta. Takes one to know one. The pot calling the kettle black.

That smudgy, alien blur of street rushed by outside the cab, and I asked her, "This isn't the way back to your place, is it?"

"No. You sort of trashed my place. And the cops have it cordoned off. It's like a crime scene or something now. I don't know how I'm gonna get my shit out of there."

"I'm sorry," I told her, but I expect I didn't come off especially sincere. Apologies are not my specialty.

"It's my fault. I know it's my fault. The *Aconitum*. I should have known better."

I didn't disagree.

"They're gonna know it's your place, Selwyn."

"Yeah, they will. So, we go to ground. We keep our

heads down. I know some people who'll help. But it's a mess. I'm not going to pretend otherwise. I'm too tired to pretend otherwise."

"B, he used to say I could cock-up a wet dream."

Selwyn laughed, and she sounded as tired as she'd said she was. She didn't argue with me, either. I didn't ask about these people she knew; figured I'd learn all about them soon enough. The taxi ride couldn't go on forever.

"There's stuff in there you need?"

"There is. Maybe I can get in later, but I'm not gonna count on it. And even if I do, I doubt the safe will still be there. You know that's going to be taken as evidence."

I didn't ask her as evidence of what. My head was too foggy. Everything was too foggy. I shut my eyes and listened to the wheels on the road until we finally got where we were going. The Village, MacDougal Street, an apartment three floors above a frozen yogurt joint. Selwyn paid the driver while I stood on the sidewalk wearing the blue wool blanket, wishing my old duster wasn't back in Hell's Kitchen or already tucked away in an NYPD evidence room somewhere. There was a woman waiting for us at the door.

"This is Jodie," Selwyn said, nodding to the woman. "Jodie, this is Quinn."

Jodie said it was good to meet me and offered me her hand. I shook it, and her skin felt very, very hot. Everyone alive feels hot when I'm hungry. Her skin was almost as dark as Selwyn's was pale, but her eyes were a startling, unexpected shade of green.

"You've made the news," she said, just before leading us upstairs. "But no one has any idea what happened."

"No shit," Selwyn muttered.

"The police aren't saying anything yet, but the most popular rumor is that a drug dealer's pet grizzly bear got loose and went on a rampage."

I couldn't help but laugh.

Jodie's apartment was bigger than Selwyn's, and it wasn't cluttered. It was furnished with pricy-looking antiques, and there were real paintings—not prints or posters—hanging on the walls. Real fucking art. Oh, and a stereo system I once would have done murder for. I wondered what she did for a living. I mean, Selwyn was making a small fortune peddling her junk, but you'd never have known it from the way she lived.

I caught Jodie staring at me. It was more a curious stare than a worried or frightened kind of stare.

"I'm your first?" I asked her.

"Yes," she said softly. Jodie said everything softly. "You're my first."

Right then, I caught a peek at myself in a mirror hanging in the hall. It was a miracle a taxi had stopped for us. Between the bruises and scrapes, the dried blood on my chin and cheeks and forehead, and the wet, dark splotch on the blanket from the seeping bullet hole that hadn't yet begun to heal.

"I need a shower," I said.

And Selwyn said, "You need three or four."

"The bathroom's just past the kitchen," Jodie told me, and she pointed down the surprisingly long hallway. "You'll find everything you need. Soap, clean towels, shampoo. If you need it, there's disinfectant and a needle and silk thread in linen closet. And gauze bandages."

I thanked her and said I could use the gauze, yeah, but there was no need for the rest of it.

Undead girls don't tend to get infections. It's one of the perks. No matter how much it hurt—and hurt it did—if I could get some sleep, by sunrise my body would spit out the slug, and there wouldn't even be a scar.

I stood under the hot spray of this Jodie woman's showerhead, letting the water hammer my chest, shoulders, my buttocks and face. I didn't want to be remembering anything at all. But I couldn't stop remembering the forest and the field, the blonde girl and her black wolf. I knew full well who they were. The *loup* was me, and they were also me. Me knock, knocking, knocking on my so often slow-on-the-uptake conscious mind. *Do you get the gist now, Quinn?* Yeah, I got it. I wasn't sure what I was supposed to *do* with the knowledge, but I got it.

While I dried, I took stock of my reflection in the mirror above the sink. My shark-black eyes, my waxy skin, my piranha mouth, me more naked than any absence of clothes could make me. Me without the makeup, contacts, the grille that hid my teeth. All that shit was something else trapped back at Selwyn's cordoned-off apartment, unless they'd also been confiscated as evidence. I'd have to find replacements, but I could worry about that later. After sleep. I could also worry about who the fuck Jodie was and whether there was any chance the cops could get any leads on Selwyn. I knew I was likely safe from any investigation, but she had a paper trail—her lease, just for starters. Shit knows how much else—identifying documents and shit. Truth be told, I'd been inconvenienced; she'd been screwed over good and proper.

There was a time I wouldn't have given her situation a second thought. There was a time my attitude would have boiled down to, *What's any of that got to do with me?* But she'd changed me. In less than a week, she'd changed me.

Which scared me bad, more than I was willing to admit.

I'd figured out long ago how dangerous it was allowing anyone to get close to you, forming emotional ties to the living. Or much of anyone else. Vamps aren't pack animals. Doesn't matter how lonely the isolation might be, it was a lot safer than the alternative. For me and for whoever found themselves the object of my affections. Maybe you've read shit about vamps and werewolves as guardian fucking angels. That's wishful thinking, ignorant fantasies. You may as well snuggle up to a leaky nuke.

We slept in the guest room, me and Selwyn. I don't know if I'd ever in all my life slept in a bed that comfortable. The room smelled like lavender and citrus, aging fabric woven before my grandmother had been born, old wood and Murphy's Oil Soap. My clean body and Selwyn's clean body, and the blood in her veins. Before I nodded off, she offered herself, and I almost refused. It was dangerous, drinking from her in the state I was in.

"You need it," she said. "I can see how much you need it, Quinn."

What else can this pale child see?

She didn't have to twist my arm. But I managed to take only a couple of mouthfuls. And then we slept. I had no dreams, not of the girl by the field, not of the *loup*. Nothing, just the bliss of oblivion.

Jodie didn't wake us until after three in the afternoon. She knocked lightly on the door. I lay blinking at the ceiling, but Selwyn told her the door was unlocked, to come in. Then she kissed me on the forehead. She smiled sleepily, looking way more refreshed than I felt. She looked . . . what? Relieved? Certainly not much like someone who'd lost all her worldly possessions the night before and had to put a bolt through a man's head to save the nasty she was shacked up with.

I sat up. Our host was standing in the doorway with a breakfast tray. If she cared that we were both naked, it didn't show in her face.

"I thought you should have a bite to eat," she said to Selwyn.

"I'm not going to turn it down," Selwyn replied.

There were also several newspapers tucked under Jodie's left arm. She brought the tray over and carefully set it on the bed in front of Selwyn. There were eggs, toast, some bacon, OJ, and a big-ass glass of Guinness. Them pretty blood dolls need their vitamin C and iron, right? Selwyn thanked her and wasted no time getting to work on the food. The sight and smell made me a bit queasy.

"I'm sorry, Quinn," Jodie said in that soft, silky voice of hers. She had an accent I hadn't noticed the night before. Haitian maybe. Or Jamaican. "I don't have anything on hand for you. I'll have something by this evening, though. I put out feelers."

She dropped the papers in front of me. The *Post* was on top, its cover-page headlines every bit as lurid as you'd expect: MYSTERY CREATURE'S ORGY OF BLOOD. Selwyn was reading over my shoulder.

"An orgy?" she mumbled around a mouthful of egg.

She washed it down with Guinness. "Jesus, lady. You get to have all the fun."

SEVEN DEAD

BEAST STILL AT LARGE

"One of those is mine," said Selwyn, pointing at the page. "They better not give you credit for all seven."

"Actually," said Jodie, "the body count's now at nine. They found two more after the papers went to press. They're still trying to figure out what to make of the security guard." She looked at Selwyn. "Is that the one you did?"

"Damn straight."

"Where did you even get a crossbow?"

I cleared my throat. "She can lay her hands on ghoul skulls and Hell merch, and you wonder where she got a crossbow?"

I was assuming Jodie knew all about the source of Selwyn's income.

Selwyn tapped me on top of the head. "It's Quinn's," she said. I swear, she was getting her rocks off on the mayhem and pandemonium. What was it I said earlier about how she'd have probably become a serial killer if she hadn't found me?

"It's in that gym bag I brought in with us last night, with all her guns and stuff."

"Fuck me running backwards." I sighed. Or something to that effect. There was a garish color photograph of a body beneath a bloodstained sheet.

Selwyn ate, and I read. The *Times* had a photo of the flipped-over Volkswagen, cops and paramedics crowded around it. ESCAPED COUGAR SLAYS SEVEN. There were quotes from eyewitnesses and exactly the sort of vague, noncommittal statement from the chief of police. On page two there was another photo, this time of Selwyn's building. The doors hung crooked on their hinges, what was *left* of the doors. Yellow crime-scene tape and plastic sawhorses were up to keep the looky-loos at a distance.

I tossed the papers to the floor.

"Hey," Selwyn protested, "I wanted to read those."

I glared at her. "Why don't you shut up and eat?"

Jodie sat down on the foot of the bed, where, by the way, she'd laid out some clothes I could wear, jeans and a Yankees sweatshirt.

"It seems to me no one has any clear idea what really went down last night," she said. "And no one's going to swallow the monster angle. But whatever was in your apartment, Selwyn, you'd best consider all that a complete write-off. No way you're getting back inside, and even if you did, well . . ." And she trailed off.

Selwyn stopped nibbling at a crispy strip of bacon.

"Fortunately, it wasn't much," she told Jodie. "Tuesday was a payday. I got lucky."

"And none of the safe-deposit boxes are in your name?"

Selwyn laughed and took a sip of Guinness. "Hell, no. No way they can trace those back to me."

"You hope," I said and lay down again. I wanted to go back to sleep. No, I wanted to feed again, then fuck, and *then* go back to sleep.

"Nothing comes with an ironclad guarantee," Jodie added. "You should not be so confident."

"Listen, the both of you. Don't sweat the damn safe-deposit boxes, okay? Jesus. I'm going to clean them out before anyone's the wiser, just in case."

Jodie clicked her tongue against the roof of her mouth. Not just once, but several times. For a moment I considered the possibility that she and Selwyn had worked out some sort of secret tongue-clicking Morse code.

"Regardless," said Jodie, "you may have bigger problems than the police."

Selwyn kissed me on the forehead. I gently swatted her away.

"How's that?" she asked.

Jodie looked at me, and then she looked back at Selwyn. She pointed at me.

"Does she know?"

"Shit, lady." I laughed. "I know she used to have a tail and that her mama wasn't exactly altogether totally human."

Selwyn nodded. "If you're about to say what I think you're about to say, yeah, she knows. How did he find out so fast?"

Jodie scowled.

"Dear, he's in Boston," she said. "Not on the moon. They do have newspapers, television, radio, and the internet in Boston."

Selwyn did that tapping at the end of her nose thing. Maybe their secret code involved tongue clicking *and* nose tapping.

"Yeah, okay. Shit," she said and tapped her nose again. I waited for Jodie to click her tongue and was disappointed when she didn't.

"Said the girl who didn't know poisoning a *loup* with wolfsbane was a terrible idea."

Selwyn punched me in the arm.

"I wasn't trying to poison you, you ass. Wolfsbane is supposed to guard against werewolves, *not* trigger their transformations."

I think I glared at Selwyn skeptically.

"Wait," Jodie said, and her scowl had turned into an expression of disbelief. "*That's* how this happened?"

"Pretty swift, right?"

Jodie shook her head and stood up.

"Quinn, our Miss Throckmorton there, she's resourceful. A pity she suffers these lapses in judgment."

Selwyn flipped her off. "I need to piss," she said.

Okay, I'm getting sick of the *she said, she said* blow-by-blow. I'm sure you are, too. Anyway, we lay low for a couple of days. Turned out this Jodie woman—Jodie Babineaux, and she was from Sierra Leone—was a halfway decent witch. You don't find many of those. The wards and shit she had erected around her apartment kept us off the radar just long enough for me to get my bearings. Selwyn got her hands on a cloned phone and made a bunch of calls, sussing out her predicament and trying to keep tabs on what Isaac Snow did and didn't know. We hardly left the building.

The *Post*'s headlines got weirder and weirder. They talked to a cryptozoologist at some university in New Hampshire who claimed the cougar attacks had actually been the work of a chupacabra.

Because, you know.

CHAPTER FOUR

PICKMAN'S MADONNA & GHOULS ON A TRAIN

We did go back to Selwyn's apartment. Despite what she'd said about there being nothing important there, nothing worth the trouble and the risk to retrieve, after three days of hiding out in the witch's safe house, Selwyn began to grow antsy, and she started to let on that there might, after all, be something worth going back for. Surely, she reasoned, the cops weren't keeping the place under surveillance. Now, if I was an NYPD detective, and I thought I knew the starting point of the "cougar" rampage, and if that place was full of bizarre and valuable books and gewgaws, you bet your fanny I'd keep my eyeballs on it. As I have often said, people are stupid. This includes people who keep dangerous wild animals locked up in Manhattan. Stupid people do stupid, sloppy, ill-advised things, like go back to apartments the PoPo have staked out because they probably have fuck all in the way of leads.

Selwyn was in a stupid mood.

And she badgered me until I agreed to go along.

We'd slip in and slip back out before anyone had any idea we were there. In and out, quick as a flash. No, we wouldn't use the front door. Obviously, we were smarter than that. Obviously. We'd take the fire escape.

That's what smart people do.

Looking back, never mind how it turned out, the way that night started off is pretty damn funny. Jodie brought us black pants and black turtleneck sweaters and versatile black ski masks, just like Tom Cruise in a *Mission Impossible* movie. Or Sterling Archer. Because that's what smart people would do.

When I asked Selwyn what, exactly, was so important that I was agreeing to allow her to put my ass on the line, she wouldn't tell me.

"You'll see," she said.

When I demanded that she tell me or I'd let her undertake this idiotic expedition alone, she said, "You'll see" again. So I went. Why? If Selwyn was in prison, I'd have to find someone else to fuck, and I'd also lose a willing donor of red sauce.

I am a smart cookie.

I took along the Glock 17 9mm I usually pack.

Jodie had a car she kept in a garage somewhere nearby,

and she drove us. Not like we could take a taxi or the subway in our styling secret-agent, ninja, cat-burglar getups. She pulled the car into an alley a couple of blocks from the building, and we walked the rest of the way. No sense in her getting hauled off to the pokey if we got ourselves caught.

Pause a moment to consider the fate of a vamp, who's also a *loup*—or vice versa—who finds herself in lockup. Standing next to a box where a homeless dude was sleeping off a couple of bottles of Thunderbird, staring up at the fire escape, I asked Selwyn to ponder that very scenario.

"No one's going to jail," she said, pulling the ladder down with a loud clank. The homeless dude didn't wake up.

"You bet your ass they're not, because I'm not gonna let it come to that."

"Then what's the problem?"

"The problem, Grasshopper, is the mess I'd have to *make* so that it didn't come to that."

"We're not going to get caught," she sighed and started climbing. I hesitated a second or two, thought about leaving her to the pissy gods of fate and heading to Port Authority and buying a ticket on the first bus anywhere far from New York City. And then I followed her.

Because that's what stupid people do. Even vamps.

Being dead has yet to boost anyone's IQ.

I did my best not to make noise, but the rusty fire escape had other ideas. We creaked and squeaked our way to the fifth floor and the apartment's single window. Which had, as noted earlier, been painted shut. But, super vampire strength, right? I tugged it open, which made,

115

probably, only slightly less noise than breaking it would have made.

"Five minutes," I told her. "That's all. You ain't done in five minutes, I'll leave you here."

She rolled her eyes and muttered and wandered away through the dark towards the bedroom. I sat on the windowsill, where I could keep my eyes on the door. The cops had tossed the place. At least, I assumed it was the cops. Someone had. The carefully ordered chaos had been reduced to simple, run-of-the-mill chaos.

I lit a cigarette and waited. Five minutes went by and I could hear Selwyn bumbling around in the dark. She had a Maglite, because even stupid people know better than to break into a crime scene and turn on the lights. I decided I'd give her a little extra time. So far, so good, after all. I told myself I'd been worrying over nothing. I smoked and listened to the night outside and the night inside and every other sound in the building.

And then the phone rang. Selwyn had this old avocado-green telephone that must have been new about 1970, and there in the dark, the ringer sounded at least as loud as a fire bell.

"Shit," I heard her whisper. By the second ring, she'd emerged from the bedroom carrying a soccer-ball-sized bundle, but I couldn't make out what it was. She shined the Maglite in the direction of the phone, perched on a stack of books, but nailed me square in the eyes instead.

"Jesus shitting Christ," I hissed. "Get that thing out of my face." She did, but the flashlight's beam left a swarm of giant fireflies in my head.

"Should I answer it?" she asked.

"Why? Are you expecting a fucking phone call?"

Third ring.

"No," she whispered. "Of course not. No one knows we're here, and I don't use the landline for business."

Fourth ring.

"Don't answer," she said. "It's no one."

Which is probably why I answered it.

It's *precisely* the sort of thing stupid people do.

I stood there, the handset against my ear, looking in Selwyn's direction, but still seeing nothing except all those orange-white fireflies. I didn't say a word. Well, not at first. Probably a whole minute went by, and I was just about to hang up, when the caller said, "Hello, Miss Quinn. I was so hoping it would be you who picked up."

It was a smooth and utterly sexless voice. I mean *utterly.* A voice entirely devoid of gender. Could have been a man or a woman or anything in between. Also, and I say this as a nasty, it was a damn creepy voice. The sort of voice puts a fucking chill in you, right? And it was a *jovial* voice. If a voice could grin, that voice was grinning ear to ear.

"Miss Quinn? Hello?"

The only question in my mind was whether the caller was Isaac Snow or Isobel Snow. Brother or sister?

"Is this a bad time?" it asked.

"Yeah," I replied. "It's a bad motherfucking time. What the fuck do you want, asshole?"

"Only what Miss Throckmorton is holding," the smiling voice said. "I can assure you she's been paid well, and I merely desire to conclude my business transaction with her. I dislike loose ends."

Usually, in situations like these, I have a snarky comeback at the ready, drawn from my all-you-can-eat buffet of gutter wit. This time, all I had was a sudden case of dry mouth. I swallowed and licked my lips.

"A pity," said the creepy voice, "the same cannot be said for you, Miss Quinn. It almost seems as if you take a perverse pride in leaving messes that others have to clean up. Your former employer in Providence would, I'm sure, testify to that."

"We're sort of in a hurry," I said. "I'm gonna hang up now. Fuck off." But I didn't hang up.

"Are we not, all of us, in a hurry, Miss Quinn? Isn't that a shame, that we rush about like ants, rarely pausing to enjoy the time given to us? Of course, some of us get more time than do others, some lucky, lucky people like yourself. Hardly seems fair, does it?"

"Hardly," I said. "But I've learned not to waste a lot of time worrying over what is and isn't fair."

Not witty, but oh so true.

"Touché. You know, I wasn't certain, at first, that it actually *was* you, the celebrated Twice-Dead, Twice-Damned, there in Manhattan, watching over poor lost Miss Throckmorton. But that escapade of yours Friday night, my sister heard the news, yes, and that removed any doubt we might have harbored."

So Isaac.

Chilling or not, the guy was starting to sound like a villain in an old Charlie Chan or Sherlock Holmes movie. Or one of the cheesier James Bond films. If his voice hadn't been so creepsome, he probably would have had me in stitches. But, you know, lots of the bad folk have that effect on me. The line between scary and hilarious is often no wider than a bug's dick.

"I was hoping we would have a chance to meet face-to-face," he said, "but, alas, that's not the way events are unfolding. My loss, I'm certain."

Actually, he was beginning to remind me a little of B.

"I'll give you a dollar to get to the point," I said.

Ah, *there* I was, back to my usual mouthy self.

"Miss Throckmorton knows why I'm calling. Will you please pick up, Selwyn?"

He knew her name. Her real name.

I wasn't even aware there was another phone in the kitchen. But in a second or two Selwyn was, in fact, on the line. I rubbed at my eyes, chasing off a few of the Maglite fireflies, just enough I could see her. She'd set the Maglite on the counter, but still held the bundle.

"There we are," he said. "Little Lamb, smile."

"I have it," she stammered. If he'd unnerved me, he was clearly scaring the bejesus out of her. "I have it. I was going to get in touch tomorrow."

"You possess fine attributes, Little Lamb, yes, but you cannot number among them being a good liar. We know that you were going to do no such thing."

"No, I'm . . . I mean, just had to be sure it is still here. The police . . ." She trailed off and glanced towards me. I squinted. She looked as if she was about to puke.

"Would never have seen it," he said. "You and I both know that. My sister and I, we thought you were dependable. You came so very highly recommended. We made this deal in good faith."

"Listen," Selwyn said, trying to keep her voice from trembling. "Just tell me where to meet you, where to make the drop, and we can make this right."

"How can we do that, Little Lamb, now that you've sold off the skull and *La Saignement de gorge*. We are, yes, rather amazed you still have the Madonna. No, as much as we would have liked to uphold our end of the bargain, you made that impossible."

"No, if you'll just—"

"We can no longer trust you. We've had to enlist the services of a third party."

I shut my eyes, trying to clear my head.

"Miss Throckmorton's going to hang up now," I said. My words came out like blocks of wood. "Isn't that right, Selwyn?" She didn't answer me.

Isaac Snow said, "We do hope, yes, that you'll understand with the position you've put us in, Little Lamb, that you left us with no other recourse. We hope you will understand it's nothing personal, dear. Isobel sends her love. *Qgi e'ia*, Selwyn Throckmorton. Walk in the light."

Fuck, I hate the sound of Ghūl. If a turd could talk, it would speak ghoulish.

"Isaac, wait, *please*—"

But he'd already hung up.

I put down the receiver, and I opened my eyes again.

"Selwyn," I said, "if you've got whatever the fuck you came for, I have a feeling we need to get out of here." She didn't reply. I said her name again, and she didn't reply again. I could see myself having to carry her back down the fire escape.

The cigarette I'd lit before the phone rang had burned down to the filter, scorching my fingers. I cursed and stubbed it out on the side of the avocado phone.

"Selwyn," I said, *did you fucking hear me?*"

She nodded her head, and she said, "I think it's too late." She was staring towards the window.

The first bullet didn't exactly miss me. It carved a deep furrow in the left side of my face. Selwyn screamed, and I dropped to the floor and rolled. Instinct kicking in and all, because it might have been stupid coming back to the apartment, but at least my sense of self-preservation was still intact. The red beam of a laser sight played across the wall near Selwyn, and the second shot almost hit her. From the way my face ached, I knew the slugs were silver. I also knew the gun was fitted with a silencer, a damned good one, too, probably metering at only 117 decibels or so.

"Get the fuck down!" I shouted at her. She didn't get down. Instead, she picked up the object she'd been carrying. I'd guessed what it was. I have my moments. Even a blind squirrel finds a nut, every now and then.

I glanced back towards the window. There was a figure crouched on the fire escape. The adrenaline seemed to have brushed aside the last straggling afterimages from the flashlight, and I could see that the shooter was a woman dressed in a black leather blazer and black jeans, plus safety goggles. Way more stylish than our outfits. The gun was a standard-model SIG Mosquito, double action, chambered for 22LR cartridges. I had to admit she had good taste in pocket rockets.

"If you don't get behind that counter right this god-damn minute," I whispered, but didn't have a chance to finish the thought. A third shot plowed into my left shoulder, shattering my collarbone. The bullet disintegrated, and the shrapnel chewed up muscle and opened veins. It hurt as much as you'd imagine it would. I howled and grabbed a dusty book from one of the teetering dusty stacks and hurled it across the room at the assassin. I missed the mark by several inches.

"Be still," Selwyn said, raising the bundle up to her chest.

"What the *fuck* are you doing?" I whispered about as urgently and angrily and totally stupefied as I have ever whispered anything.

"You'll see," she whispered back, and she didn't sound at all scared now, not like she had on the phone with Isaac Snow.

On the fire escape, the woman in black cursed. She didn't fire again, but she also didn't lower her pistol. The laser painted a bright red dot in the center of Selwyn's forehead like a bindi.

"You won't dare," Selwyn said. "You know it, and I know it." The tremble had vanished from her voice. The silly bitch was cool as a moose in snow.

"Selwyn, I swear to God, if she shoots you, I'm gonna fucking clap."

"She won't shoot me," Selwyn replied confidently.

"And you know that how?"

Selwyn nodded at the bundle. "I might drop the Madonna. It might break. Worse, she might miss *me* and hit *it*."

I looked at Selwyn, and then I looked at the woman on the fire escape. She still hadn't lowered the gun, but she also hadn't squeezed off another round.

"Sweet," I said and stood up, shooting the assassin twice in the chest. My gun didn't have a suppressor, and the Glock roared like thunder. The woman stumbled backwards, the SIG falling from her hands to the rusty metal at her feet. But she didn't go down.

"She's a vampire," Selwyn said. I could only just make out the words over the ringing in my ears.

"Fuck her," I whispered to myself. The next bullet was meant for her skull, but she dodged it and disappeared over the railing. I waited a full two minutes, counting off the seconds in my mind, before I lowered my gun. I waited another minute before I took my eyes off the window. My left arm hung limp at my side, and blood slicked my sweater and pooled on the floor at my feet. The silver shrapnel burned like white-hot embers buried in my flesh. I still have no idea how I'd managed to hurl that book.

"Selwyn, did informing me this son of a bitch uses fucking vamps for hired killers never cross your fucking mind?"

"I didn't want to make you any jumpier than you already were," she said, lowering the bundle.

"Oh, you did *not* just say that."

She shrugged and set the bundle on the counter. Her hands were shaking.

"Quinn, if I'd told you, you might not have come. You might have stopped me from coming. Am I right?"

"You bet your skinny white tailless ass you're right."

"Well, then, there you go," she said.

I was speechless. I do not deal well with being manipulated, though I've spent a great deal of my existence postmortem *being* manipulated. The undead make wicked good weapons, as Isaac Snow obviously understood. They also make good bodyguards, as Selwyn obviously understood. Being junkies, we're easy marks. More often than not, we'll do a lot of fucked-up humiliating shit and let people get away with using us to their ends if it means we don't have to worry where the next fix is coming from.

I stared at Selwyn and very, very seriously considered smashing whatever was wrapped up inside that bundle of hers myself and all parties involved be damned. It's a testament to my not inconsiderable shortcomings that I didn't destroy it. If I'd known what was coming, I like to think I wouldn't have pussied out, that I'd have acted on that impulse. Instead, I tucked the Glock back into the waistband of my pants, did my best to ignore the pain and blood, and went to the closet in the hallway. Selwyn had hung my duster there the afternoon before she'd poisoned me with wolfsbane. I was frankly a bit surprised it was still there. I yanked it off the hanger and draped it over my good arm.

"You don't know what's at stake," she said.

"Then how about you enlightening me?"

Not that, right then, I especially gave two shits.

"It's complicated," she replied.

"Seems pretty simple to me. You have something there this cocksucker wants. Something he paid you to find. But after you found it, along with that other junk, you decided to double-cross him. I won't speculate why you did it. I'm sure you had your reasons. Now, tell me, am I wrong?"

She didn't answer, one way or another.

"Darling," I said, "you do know what tends to become of stupid little girls who fuck over monsters?"

"I will not be condescended to," she said angrily, as if she had some say in the matter.

"I don't recall asking for permission," I replied.

I went to the window and peered down at the alley, then up towards the roof. There was no sign of the vamp anywhere. I hadn't expected there to be. By now she was holed up somewhere safe, licking her wounds and busy trying to decide exactly how she was going to explain having bungled the job.

I climbed out onto the fire escape. I could hear sirens. Maybe they had our names on them; maybe they didn't.

"Wait!" Selwyn shouted, the anger gone, replaced by . . . well, not quite panic. Let's say an attack of desperation. She quickly picked her way through the clutter to the window.

"Where are you going?" she asked.

And I said, "I've taken two bullets now because of your dumb ass, Annie Smithfield. I'm not sticking around for the third."

The sirens were getting louder, so I assumed they *were* headed our way.

"Come *on*, Quinn. Please. I'll explain everything."

And then I said, "I might have told you this already, but whatever's happening here is your mess. You got yourself into it, and you can sort it out on your own. Or not."

She reached through the open window and grabbed

my left elbow, the side with the shattered collarbone. I almost gave into reflex and punched her in the face. It probably would have broken her neck.

She'd tucked the bundle under one arm. I could see now that whatever she was carrying had been wrapped in a black Morrissey T-shirt.

Sirens.

"You hear that? The cops are on their way," I said. "I'm leaving."

"Quinn, *please*."

I stared down at the alley, at the spot on the pavement where, regrettably, there wasn't a dead vampire. Then I looked back at Selwyn. She was leaning out towards me, all twinkly, big, star-sapphire eyes. Sad puppy-dog eyes. I felt a flutter in my belly. And another flutter between my legs. Go me, sentimental monster, thinking with her cunt.

"Fine," I muttered. "Come the fuck on, then."

Because that's what stupid, horny people would say.

We found Jodie and the rental car waiting exactly where she'd promised to wait for us. Only someone—presumably the assassin—had ripped out her throat, slashed the tires, and punched a hole in the radiator. Scratch one getaway vehicle. Scratch one helpful witch. We'd have to beat our hasty retreat on foot, which wouldn't have been such a problem if I hadn't had Selwyn. On my own, I could have moved a whole hell of a lot faster. But I *did* have Selwyn. We headed towards the subway station at Fiftieth and Eighth. It didn't even occur to me until we were waiting on the platform just how fucking suspicious we'd look in our matching black outfits.

"Quinn, where are we going?" she asked.

"I don't know. You tell me."

"We can't go back to Jodie's."

Near as I could figure, she wasn't upset by Jodie Babineaux's death. Well, not unless it had made her more worried about her own skin. I could tell Selwyn wouldn't be mourning the woman anytime soon. Or ever.

The train pulled into the station, the doors slid open, mind the fucking gap, and we got on. Luckily, the car was empty. I sat down. Selwyn didn't. She held on to one of the shiny poles with her free hand and stared at the floor while we swayed and bumped along beneath the grimy streets of Manhattan. I watched her, waiting for an explanation. No dice. She clearly wasn't about to *volunteer* the lowdown she'd promised. Now that I'd decided not to leave here high and dry, probably she was hoping I'd just forget all about it, distracted by our daring escape, apparently dire predicament, and possible pursuers.

"So," I said, "what the fuck's going on?"

Warning. Next infodump ahead. If that sort of thing annoys you, might want to skip a few pages ahead. Of course, then you'll have no idea what's going on later. I know. Decisions, decisions. Whee.

Selwyn glanced at the bundle.

"You promised," I said.

"Have you ever heard of the Byzantine Ghūl?"

I shook my head and looked out the window at the blackness rushing by.

"I must have been playing hooky from the Monster Academy that day," I said. "You got me. What's the Byzantine Ghūl? Short version."

"I'm not sure there is a short version, Quinn."

"But it's got to do with Isaac Snow and why he's trying to kill us."

"Yeah," she said. "It has everything to do with that. Do you know anything about the church during the Byzantine Empire?"

"Hooky," I reminded her. "Monster hooky. Jesus hooky."

Selwyn showed me what was hiding in the T-shirt. It was a plaque, a bas-relief carved into a slab of dark gray stone. It was one of those mother and child things, good old Catholic idolatry. Only, with a twist. The artist had managed to give what I assumed was meant to be the Virgin Mary a hungry, leering smirk. And the Baby Jesus, well, he looked as if he'd fallen out of an ugly tree and smacked into every branch on the way down. He was also smirking, like the two of them were gloating over some awful secret, a secret that amused them no end. There was a fossil ammonite, about as big around as a silver dollar, set into the plaque, clutched in the kid's hands. It was some sort of glittering gold-colored mineral, the ammonite, and I guessed pyrite. Fool's gold.

"What the fuck, Selwyn?"

"It has a lot of names," she said. Just then the train lurched and she almost fell, almost dropped the carving. I wouldn't have caught it. It would have been a relief to see the thing break into a hundred pieces at her feet.

"Such as?"

She held the thing closer to her chest.

"Basaltes Maria Virgo, La Virgen negra de la Muerte, Unser Mutter von der Nacht—"

"Anything in fucking English?"

She sighed and frowned. Oh, the burden of having an ignorant vampire girlfriend.

"Well, in *Cultes des Goules,* François-Honoré de Balfour translated *Basaltes Maria Virgo* as *La Madone de basalte.* The Basalt Madonna. And mostly that's what it's been called ever since he published his book in 1702. The ghoul call it *Qqi d'Evai Mubadieb.*"

I couldn't take my eyes off that hideous plaque.

"Just how many languages do you speak?" I asked her.

"Only eight," she said.

"Right. *Only* eight. Go on. I'm listening."

Mostly, I was. I admit that chunk of gray rock was taking up a good deal of my attention. Especially the ammonite. There seemed to be something wrong about it, like the golden whorl of the shell went on and on and on, spiraling inward forever, never quite reaching the spot that should have been its center. *Neat trick,* I thought.

"I've heard of Balfour," I told her.

"Yeah. Not too many copies of *Cult of Ghouls* left. Right off, it made the Church's *Index Librorum Prohibitorum* and most of the copies were destroyed. Supposedly, Richard Upton Pickman, he had one, but it vanished with him."

I'd heard of Pickman, too.

"I thought that book was a nasty urban legend," I said. "Like the mad Arab and the *Necronomicon.*"

She was silent a moment.

I stared at the ammonite. It was beginning to make me woozy, the fucked-up optical illusion of it. At least, I hoped it was an illusion.

"Quinn, the *Necronomicon* isn't a myth," she finally said. "Lovecraft didn't invent it. Dad saw a partial copy when he was in Iran, back in the sixties."

"You're shitting me."

She shook her head. I definitely remember her shaking her head, though I *don't* remember looking away from the ammonite, which makes me wonder about . . .

Never mind. Let's not go there.

"It was under lock and key at the Jam'karān mosque just outside Qom."

"It was under lock and key, but your dad saw it?"

"An imam owed him a favor."

The woozy feeling was turning into genuine nausea, and I bit my lip hard enough to draw blood. Which ain't really very hard with teeth like mine. The pain was enough to break whatever hold the bas-relief was exerting over me. Thank holy fuck. You know how at the end of *Raiders of the Lost Ark* the bad guys' heads all explode? I'm pretty sure that was next, after nausea. Also, the Ark of the Covenant thing seems a good comparison, since Selwyn's father was starting to sound an awful lot like Indiana Jones.

"Wrap it up again," I told her, turning back to the dark tunnel walls outside the subway car. She did as I told her, and I said, "So this is what Isaac Snow's after."

It wasn't a question, because I already knew the answer.

"Yeah. This and the skull and the necklace. A couple of years ago, he thought he'd found the Basalt Madonna. A hack novelist woman named Aimee Downes made what was apparently a pretty convincing counterfeit, and she sold it to him. Didn't fool him for long, though. Right after that, she sort of went missing."

"Sort of?"

"I heard parts of her body turned up here and there," Selwyn said. "An eye. A hand. A breast. But no one knows if he actually had her killed."

Ghoul justice. Happy fun time.

"Anyhow, when he hired me to find the stuff, I didn't have any idea what it was, the Madonna, or, more to the point, why he wanted it."

"And what has all this got to do with the Byzantine Empire?"

"It's a long story," Selwyn said. "It's hard to make a short version out of it."

"Try anyway."

The train lurched and swayed, and she gripped the pole a little tighter. I could see her reflected in the glass. I was so regretting not having left her back in that apartment. In fact, I was regretting ever having met her. If I hadn't, I'd still have been shacked up with my CEO, safe and snug and bored.

"Sometime during the fifth century," Selwyn began, "though no one's sure exactly when, I don't think, a monk in Constantinople found a ghoul—only he didn't know it was a ghoul. He thought it was a leper, you know. That sort of almost makes sense—"

"Not really," I cut in. "Not if you've ever actually seen a ghoul, which—"

"—I have. I'm just telling you that's how the story

goes. The monk thought the wretch he found huddled in the shadows was a leper, and he led it back to the abbot, who saw that whatever it was, it definitely wasn't human.

"Father, look what followed me home," I said. "Can I keep it? Please? Pretty please?"

Selwyn didn't laugh like I'd hoped she would.

No, I admit it wasn't very funny.

She just tapped her nose and soldiered on.

"The abbot, he realized that the monk—and no one knows his name, or the abbot's—had discovered a subhuman race, and, what's more, a pagan subhuman race that had yet to be converted to Christianity. So, that's exactly what the abbot set out to do. He evangelized to the Ghūl," she said. "The abbot had the brothers lock the ghoul in a cell, so it was a sort of captive-audience situation. But they fed it, not cadavers or anything, but they fed it all the same, and they made it comfortable, and, in return, it told them stories of the Sunless Lands, of Thok and the Vale of Pnath, of the war with the Djinn."

Selwyn was now spouting stuff even the nasties take with a grain of salt. But I didn't interrupt her again. I was hoping we were coming up fast on the next station. I wanted off the train in the worst fucking sort of way. I needed not to be shut up in that claustrophobic metal tube with Professor Indiana Throckmorton's own beyond creepy Madonna of the Damned.

"Knowing ghouls," she continued, "the fucker was probably getting his rocks off horrifying them, shocking their monastic sensibilities. You can imagine those pious, ascetic men making the *signum crucis* and whispering prayers while the ghoul rattled off descriptions of the necropolises and the bone plains, while it introduced them to the likes of Shub-Niggurath, Nyarlathotep, Azathoth. Hell, some of them probably pissed themselves. Every now and then, the ghoul would lapse into its own language, and the monks slowly began to decipher some of it. Anyway, after a few months, they sent their pet off to spread the gospel to its fellows."

I snorted. "I bet *that* went well."

"I suppose it might have gone worse. The Hounds of Cain did listen, but you know how it often goes when the Church starts trying to fob its beliefs on other cultures. The ghouls picked and chose. Classic case of religious syncretism. They took what suited them. Invented new quasi-Christian deities and fused them with their existing pantheon. You know about the *Qqi*?"

I'd heard the word.

"Their word for god," I told her. "But that's all I know. I'm not exactly a goddamn Ghūl scholar, Annie Smithfield."

"Quinn, I wish you'd stop calling me that. I really, truly do."

Okay, by this time, we definitely should have reached the next station. Seriously. But between Selwyn's tale and getting a gander at her treasure, I'd been distracted.

"I'm still not sure it isn't your real name. Also, what with all those fake IDs of yours, I'm not so sure you could ever prove it isn't."

She sighed, and she let go of the pole and sat down next to me. She held the bundle in her lap.

"Fine, Quinn. Have it your way."

"I usually do."

She tapped the end of her nose and sighed again.

"The *Qqi*," she said, "which, in ghoulish, is the number Fifty, is their ancient pantheon. Their *prehistoric* pantheon, their version of the Elder Gods, Outer Gods, Great Old Ones, Nodens, whatever. When the australopithecines were still busy avoiding lions and leopards and hyenas, oh my, the Ghūl had already been worshipping the *Qqi* for a twenty thousand centuries. The *Qqi*, the Fifty, the Ten Hands, Fifty Fingers, that menagerie fitting together like a Russian nesting doll."

"*Matryoshkas*," I said, "Russian nesting dolls," because it was something to say, and I didn't want to admit I wasn't really following her little history lesson. I was beginning to worry more about why the train was still zooming merrily along as if the next stop wasn't until fucking Boston.

"Right. Like a *matryoshka*. Anyways, the ghouls latched onto this brand-new theology, incorporated it with their own cosmogony, and out popped a host of *new* gods and goddesses. A freshly reconsolidated pantheon. Not that the Ghūl gave up worshipping Claviceps, Amylostereum, or Paecilomyces, mind you."

Fairy tales for the eaters of the dead. The profane names rolled off her tongue like a rotten, off-key tune.

"But," she said, "they invented. They invented with a passion."

"I get the idea," I told her. "Archetypes, cultural contamination, corn kings." I was squinting at the doors to the car, squinting because the fluorescent lights were starting to hurt my eyes. I hate goddamn fluorescent lights. Forget what you hear about vamps and the sun. I'll take a sunny day over fluorescent bulbs every time.

"Have you read *The Golden Bough*?"

"No."

"Joseph Campbell?"

"No."

"Is something wrong?" Selwyn asked.

"Probably not," I replied. "Go on. Where does *that* . . . ?" I waved a hand at the thing in her lap. "Where does it fit into all this nonsense?"

"Well, you see, the ghouls didn't junk their many gods for monotheism, but they *did* take to the idea of a savior. They remade the Virgin and the Christ Child to fit their needs. Ever since they'd lost the war with the Djinn and been banished to the Dream Lands they'd prayed for deliverance. For a messiah who'd lead them back to the World Above. And that's where the Basalt Madonna comes in."

I got to my feet. Unlike Selwyn, I didn't *need* the pole for balance, but I sure as shit felt better hanging on to it with my good arm. I said, "Fascinating as all this is, you're going to have to save the rest for later."

She frowned and glanced up at me. She looked just the tiniest bit worried.

"*Is* something wrong?" she asked again, with a bit more oomph than before.

"I'm gonna err on the side of caution and say yes."

"But you just said 'probably not.'"

"I lied."

I drew the Glock and checked the clip, which is when

the doors separating the cars opened and four ghouls lumbered in, two from each end. They were big damn bastards, stinking of mold and shit and rotting meat, all four crusty with wicked cases of scabies. To my knowledge, no ghoul yet has ever been accused of good hygiene. Their hooves thumped loud against the floor, and they snarled and bared their yellowed fangs. That abbot in Byzantium shoulda spent his spare time proselytizing to the hounds about toothbrushes, not forgiveness and hellfire.

If anyone back then *had* toothbrushes.

Never mind.

Their manes bristled. Their rheumy yellow eyes were chock-full of a serious desire to dole out mutilation and death. Near as I could see, no one was holding their leashes. One of the sons of bitches jabbed a crooked finger at me.

"This does not concern you, Twice-Damned," it snarled. "Step aside, Siobhan Quinn."

"Make me," I said.

"Step aside," it repeated and took a step towards me.

"Selwyn, you might wanna cover your ears."

Which she did.

I squeezed the trigger and put a bullet through the nut sack's skull, right between the eyes, and it went down like a bag of rocks. I pulled back on the slide and chambered another round, wishing I could have covered my own ears.

"Who's next?" I asked, hardly able to hear myself. None of them volunteered. All three were busy staring at their fallen comrade.

"She shot Bustard," said a ghoul with a jagged scar across its short muzzle. It had been standing directly behind the one I'd killed, and now it was hunched over the bloody, lifeless body.

"Look at that. She *shot* him," said the hound. It didn't sound so much upset as surprised. "He's dead."

"What the *fuck* did you expect?" I asked, taking aim at Scar's face. To Selwyn, I said, "You watch those two behind me. Watch them close. If one of them so much as fucking twitches an ear, you tell me."

"Yeah," she said. "Don't worry."

"He only wants the Throckmorton," one of the ghouls behind me grunted. "Not you, vampire. We were not told to harm *you*. This is not your fight. You are not the one who has betrayed him."

It sort of had a point.

"He," I said. "That he would be Isaac Snow?"

"The *Qqi d'Tashiva*," it replied.

"You wanna translate that for me, Annie Smithfield?"

"The God-King of Rags and Bones," she answered. "Hand of the Fifty."

"Filthy vampire scum does not utter the name of the *Qqi d'Tashiva*," Scar said, looking up from the dead ghoul. Its eyes had gone more muddy orange than yellow. "Your foul phantom's tongue is not *fit* to—"

I shot it. Two down. The odds were looking better. I turned my attention to the remaining pair; they were clearly dumbfounded.

"You shot Chester," one of them said and scratched the tuft of coarse hair on its scabby chin.

"Guys, c'mon," I said. "You are seriously starting to

bore the shit out of me. Did you honestly believe you were gonna just waltz in here, pretty as you please, and take her without getting a fight?"

"Siobhan *Quinn*," growled the ghoul who'd scratched its chin at the death of poor deceased Chester.

"Right. You know my name, but you obviously don't have a clue what happens to weasely douche bag shitcicles without the good sense to stay out of my face."

I was standing there talking smack like I was the baddest of the bad, but to tell you the truth, I was amazed through and through that I hadn't yet found a way to fuck up and get me and Selwyn both killed.

"Quinn," whispered Selwyn.

"What?"

"The train's slowing down," she said.

Which is when both the surviving ghouls dropped down onto all fours and charged me. I had time to get off one more shot, but it went wild and punched a hole in the ceiling of the train. To her credit, Selwyn didn't scream. She was fast and got clear before four hundred or so pounds of stinking flesh and bone slammed into me. My gun went skittering away, and I heard bones snapping, all of them mine, natch, and the ache in my shoulder was drowned in a shimmering wall of fresh hell.

Their breath was almost as bad as the pain.

"*Kill you*," growled one of my attackers, just before I drove a knee into its crotch and pushed my thumbs into its eyes. The left eye popped, and the ghoul howled and stumbled to its feet. But the other ghoul pinned me, good and proper, and wrapped a hand tight around my throat, those talons digging into my skin. I knew it could yank my head off easy as brushing away a fly. And there we were, nose to nose. It grinned, as ugly a grin as any nasty ever grinned. A grin to impress a true demon. It's face lit up, and I knew the ghoul knew it had won.

"Finish you now, vampire," it said. "But finish you slow and hard. Make you beg and scream for the delight of the King of Bones."

I heard Selwyn racking back the Glock's slide. The ghoul, it was too busy savoring the thought of picking me apart limb by limb, flaying and disemboweling me, to notice shit. She blew the top of its head off, spraying me with brains and gore and specks of skull in the process. Small price to pay, right?

"More are coming," she said, not sounding half as scared as she had a right to be, and then I caught the tattoo of many pairs of hooves pounding steel. Yeah, ghouls also have hooves where their feet should be. The floor beneath me vibrated with the weight and force of them.

"They're *close*, Quinn."

"Tell me something I don't know," I mumbled.

I blinked and wiped at my face, trying to get dead ghoul out of my eyes. In a second or two, I could see well enough to see Selwyn was squatting next to me, still holding on to the Basalt Madonna. In the chaos, part of the T-shirt had slipped enough that one corner of the stone plaque was visible.

I told her to run.

And deep down inside me, the Beast opened her eyes.

Yeah, I said to her. *Sure thing, puppy. Let's party. Let's rock out with our cocks out.*

But it wasn't like it had been on wolfsbane. There was

the old fade-to-black routine. And, frankly, I was then and still am grateful for that. Sure, I'd have loved to feel what it was like, ripping apart the hounds who flooded into that subway car. I wish I could claim I have no idea what magical, mystical cosmic agency decides if I'll retain consciousness whenever the Beast arrives to paint the town red. If it's all up to me, that child and her wolf at the edge of the field, the forest at their backs, or if it falls to some secret sliver of my brain making nanosecond decisions. Or both. I don't really care.

I awoke on cold stone, and at least half the pain I'd felt in the instant before I'd blacked out was still right with me. Hell, the transformation into Beast would have seen to a sackful of ouch, without having first been shot in the shoulder and then pummeled by fuck knows how many of the Ghūl who'd jumped us.

I'd been dreaming of long-lost Lily—murdered by a ghoul, the first nasty I killed, even if it was an accident, beginner's fucking luck. Pretty, pretty Lily, my compatriot in Needle Park, Lily and the streets.

Not kind dreams.

I opened my eyes and lay still on my back a long time. Fifteen, twenty minutes. Half an hour. I don't know. I was disoriented, and I was trying to get *re*oriented. There was a growing urgency as the attack on the train came back to me, and as I realized Selwyn wasn't there with me. I called out her name a couple of times, but got nothing except my own voice echoing back to me. I was naked, and if I'd been alive, I'd likely have been freezing to death. Wherever I was, it was cold and dank and stank of mildew and ages of accumulated dust. Wherever I was, was dark.

Not that it much mattered to my built-in vamp night-vision goggles. It was just a matter of convincing the three of everything to get together and be the one of everything.

There was a tremendous whoosh of warm air and then the cacophony of a train rattling past. So, I knew I was still in the subway. But I was alone. Alone and naked. I rolled over onto my left side and there was my duster, neatly folded, and there were my pants, also neatly folded. A great what-the-fuck moment. No shoes, though. No shirt. And, I'd see soon enough, no gun. What kinda half-assed mercy was that?

My surroundings were beginning to wriggle into focus. It was a deserted station. There are a lot of those, though most people have no idea they even exist. Abandoned, shut-away platforms, trolleys, entire stations. I'd seen a few of them in my time in NYC, when restlessness had gotten the better of me, and I'd roamed the city without Barbara O'Bryan the CEO blood doll hanging on. This particular abandoned subway station, it was one I'd visited twice before. I'd found it a great place to be alone. It was the old City Hall Station, decommissioned back in 1945, shut away more than seventy years. There's nothing else like it down in the tunnels. Nothing else like it in the rat's maze below Manhattan, all decked out with stained glass, tiled vaults, Romanesque brick arches, and brass chandeliers. You know humans. They toss out the old and beautiful for the new and soullessly functional. Once upon a time, this station was the southern terminus of the Interborough Rapid Transit, which stretched from City Hall to Grand Central Station, across 42nd Street to

Times Square, and all the way north to 145th Street along Broadway. Sometimes the station is lit, and passengers who linger on the 6 after the Brooklyn Bridge can get a peek of that ghostly reminder of a more graceful age.

Listen to me, waxing all damn sentimental over a fucking subway station. Jesus.

I rolled over onto my back again, not even bothering to wonder how the Seventh Avenue line had dumped me a stone's throw from the Brooklyn Bridge station. I'd encountered pocket universes before, and sorceries used to wrap time and space to the needs of an elite few who wielded that brand of mojo. Certainly it hadn't been the doing of the ghouls. Isaac Snow maybe, which made him a much more formidable dude than I'd suspected from what Selwyn had told me. If he could pull shit like this, or if he had those who could on his payroll, he was way more than some power-hungry half-breed. He was the thaumaturgic equivalent of a goddamn thermonuclear bomb.

I groaned and sat up. I wanted to lie right back down again, but fuck that. For all I knew, I'd been out for hours, maybe an entire day. Selwyn could be anywhere. She could be fucking dead, for all I knew. And yeah, I cared, whether I *wanted* to care or not. Was I pissed at her dragging me into this cloak-and-dagger hullaballoo with the Snow twins? Damn straight, but that didn't change how I'd discovered I felt for her. I was past walking away, and more's the pity. Probably, I'd been past walking away since the first time we screwed, no matter what I might have told her to the contrary.

I sat there and stared at the mosaic of yellow and

green and black, brown and cobalt-blue glazed bricks that make up the stations walls, archways, and the vaulted ceiling, building blocks laid a century before. Those blue stained-glass skylights, and even through the haze in my head, I couldn't help but be amazed there was an age when people bothered to make a subway station so beautiful. Probably, I was recovering from a concussion, which would explain this gawking at Victorian architecture when I should have been dragging my sorry ass off to find Selwyn.

It was a fair bet the ghouls had taken her.

And if they had, they'd taken her to Isaac Snow, which would mean he had the Madonna, and . . . well, I still had no idea what he wanted with that rock.

My stomach suddenly rolled, and I cramped, then crawled on hands and knees to the edge of the platform and puked into the darkness where the disused track lay. This is what usually happens after the Beast comes out to play. My liquid-diet vamp stomach can't deal with all that shit the wolf wolfs down, and as soon as I'm this me again, I hork up all that meat and . . . well, too often, worse stuff than meat. The Beast is not a discerning gourmand.

So, there I am, huddled on the filthy platform of a forgotten subway station, naked as the day I was born, puking up my innards and cursing the indiscriminate appetites of *loups*. Hardly digested ghoul McNuggets spattering all over the place. Not a pretty picture. Not one I'd want preserved for posterity. What I would like very much to consider a private goddamn moment. Too bad. Not meant to be. I wiped my mouth on the back of one hand

and sat up, hoping there was nothing left in me wasn't supposed to be there.

I realized someone was watching me.

Vamps are extraplusgood at that. Probably I'd have figured it out sooner, if not for all the hurt and regurgitation.

And then the watcher spoke. He—it *was* a he—had a voice like a two-hundred-year-old chain smoker. But I could also hear the remnants of the same sort of old-money Boston accent I'd heard through the phone when Isaac Snow had called Selwyn's apartment. I have an ear for shit like that, accents.

"Poor girl," he said. "I trust you feel better now?" he asked. I turned around and gave the whoever it was a good look at my middle finger. Right hand.

The speaker was leaning against a tiled wall, puffing a cigarette. He wasn't a ghoul, not really. But he also wasn't human, not really. He was what you'd get if a mad scientist set out to make one, then decided, halfway through, to make the other. He was also naked, so at least I wasn't the only one. He had the scabby gray-purple skin of a ghoul, but his face was still more of a face than a muzzle, and his feet were not quite hooves. I could sorta make out a couple of toes. The son of a bitch had a schlong that dude porn stars would kill for, right? I mean, never before had I beheld a baloney pony of such prodigious dimensions. How do you *not* stare at something like that?

"Who—and *what*—the fuck are you?"

He didn't answer me, just took a long drag off his cigarette. The tip flared in the gloom.

"You're not Isaac Snow," I said. "I've heard his voice, and you're not him."

I spat, trying to get the throw-up taste out of my mouth. Didn't work.

"No, I'm definitely not Isaac Snow," said the nasty with the enormous dick. "But he's the reason I'm here."

I'd already sorta guessed that part, but I didn't tell him that.

"Is that so? Well, do you happen to have any idea where the rest of my clothes are?" I pointed at the duster and my pants. "And my fucking gun?"

He grinned, and his eyes glimmered. He for sure had the eyes and the toothsome smile of a ghoul—only different. I spat again.

"And what about Miss Throckmorton?" he asked. "Surely you've noticed she's missing, as well."

"Yeah, well, fuck her," I said. "I'm tired of getting my ass kicked on her account. She can go hang, for all I care."

And right then, I probably meant it.

"Fair enough," he said. "But the hour is late, Quinn, and how you feel about her has ceased to be an issue."

I crawled the few feet to my clothes, my legs still too wobbly to stand. He kept talking.

"She's made you a part of this, and it's unlikely you could, at this point, extricate yourself from the muck and mire of unfolding events."

I pulled on the duster. It was ripped and torn and the leather was still tacky from all the blood.

"Goddamn cocksuckers went and killed my fucking coat," I muttered.

The nasty laughed, a sound that made his *speaking* voice positively melodious by comparison. I glared up at him, and he smiled back at me.

"Dude, who the fuck *are* you?"

"Pickman," he said. "Richard Upton Pickman."

My turn to laugh. I dropped the ruined duster in my lap and shook my head, the way you shake your head when you can't decide between *That just fucking figures* and *No fucking way.*

"Well," I said, flipping a mental coin, "that just fucking figures."

"Then you've heard of me?" He sounded pleased at the prospect.

"Maybe I read a couple of stories once," I replied.

"Ah, yes. Those. I once had a bowl of strawberry ice cream with the Old Gent of Providence. He was never good about keeping secrets."

Smelling his cigarette, I started jonesing for one of my own. I needed the nicotine, and maybe it would help get the barf taste out of my mouth. However, I was not about to bum a smoke off the half ghoul.

"Fine, Richard Upton Pickman. Am I also supposed to ask what you're doing here?"

"It does seem a more or less logical next step in the natural course of events."

"Ain't nothing natural about the course of these events," I said, setting the late lamented duster aside and reaching for my pants, only to discover they were as much a mess as my coat. But I pulled them on, anyway. What else was I supposed to do? I was tired of giving Pickman a free coochie show. Though, from what I'd heard, the guy (and his astounding wonder cock) didn't swing that way.

"I'll not argue with that," he said and laughed again. "But to answer your question, I'm here because I needed you not to die back there. Or, I should say, we needed you not to die."

I zipped my pants and stared at him.

He asked, "We who, you'd like to know, yes?"

"If you say so. Frankly, I'd rather know where the rest of my clothes are. And my gun. My gun's been coming in especially handy lately."

Pickman produced a pistol, seemingly out of thin air, and tossed it to me. I caught the gun. It was a Browning Hi Power 9mm. Not my first choice, but beggars can't be choosers. I checked to see if the clip was full; it was.

"It isn't yours," he said, "but perhaps this will do for the time being."

"Thanks," I said, popping the clip back in. "Fine, so what are you doing here?"

"We have a common enemy, Miss Quinn. You do prefer to be called Quinn, or have I been misinformed?"

"By 'a common enemy,' you mean Isaac Snow and his sister?"

"I do."

"Then you're gravely mistaken, my ugly friend. I said I don't want anything else to do with Selwyn, and by extension, that *includes* the Snows. That most especially includes the Snows."

Pickman narrowed his eyes skeptically. He dropped the butt of his cigarette and ground it out under the thick sole of a deformed left foot.

"Miss Quinn, not to be presumptuous—"

"He said immediately before being just that."

"—but Isaac Snow has tried to kill you twice now. Even if you truly are washing your hands of Miss Throckmorton, you have a reputation for not letting people get away with such grave insults to your person."

"Don't believe everything you hear," I told him. "People exaggerate." And I aimed the Browning at one of the stained-glass skylights, sighting down the barrel. The heft of the pistol felt good in my hand. "Or maybe you caught me in a forgiving kinda mood. Shit, maybe I'm turning over a new leaf."

Pickman frowned and scratched his chin whiskers.

"Make no mistake, Miss Quinn. He may not kill her straightaway, because he needs her as a bargaining chip. But he will do her great mischief, he and Isobel. And if you do not bring him the Madonna, if that strategy proves futile, he will simply murder her. Well, not simply, as torture will surely be involved. Afterwards, he'll come for you again. And he'll continue hunting you until you're dead and he has what he wants."

I lowered the Browning.

"What do you mean, *Until I bring him the Madonna?* I don't have the thing."

Pickman cocked a mangy eyebrow.

"Oh, but you're very much in the wrong on that account, Miss Quinn." And then he nodded to a bundle at his feet. Selwyn's bundle, the black Morrissey T-shirt wrapped about the basalt atrocity. Jesus, Joseph, and Mary, I swear it hadn't been there a second before. My stomach rolled, and I gagged.

But let's say I didn't.

This *is* my story, right? And if I don't *want* to throw up again, I don't have to.

Let's say *this* happened, instead:

I aimed the 9mm at the bundle.

"Awesome," I said. "Then I can do what someone should have done a long damn time ago. And when I'm finished, I'll mail the gruesome twosome all the itty-bitty broken pieces. You might wanna step aside. And cover your ears."

"You go ahead and do that, Miss Quinn, and—assuming the Madonna *can* be undone with mere bullets, which I doubt—they'll send her back to you in itty-bitty broken pieces. Then everyone can play Humpty Dumpty and All the King's Men. Is that what you wish?"

"I told you I am *done* with Selwyn."

"Yes, Miss Quinn, you did, and you lied. That was obvious. I would think that someone who lies as frequently as you would be better at it by now."

"Fuck you, you fucking elephant-dicked freak."

I tightened my grip on the trigger, as if I actually believed, even for a second, that I *wasn't* lying. Holy goddamn dancing Moses in drag, I wanted to do it. I wanted to squeeze the trigger and empty that clip, reduce Mother and Child and that hellish pyrite whorl to a couple of handfuls of gravel and dust. I wanted not to give a shit what would happen to Selwyn. I wanted, as much as I've ever wanted anything, never to have met the quadroon psycho bitch.

Problem is, I wanted her back even more.

For the second time, I lowered the Browning.

"Fuck you," I said again, though this time I was addressing myself, not Pickman. I looked at him, and the bastard was grinning ear to ear.

"Good girl," he grinned. "Now, if we play our cards right, I honestly think there is some slim hope that we can get her back. But . . ." And he paused.

"But what?"

He scratched his chin again.

"*But*, Quinn, there's rather more at stake here than yours and your lover's lives. Very much more. The Snows mean to start a war. Right *here*, in *this* world. Your world."

I sighed and lay down on my back, staring up at the candy-colored kaleidoscope skylights. We must have been quite a sight, a fine fucking tableau, the topless werepire—blood and puke spattered—and Pickman standing over me, the man who'd ditched his human skin for life everlasting in a ghoul suit.

"They mean to see the prophecy fulfilled," he said, "at any cost."

"The prophecy."

"Have you ever heard of the *B'heil Djinna*? The war between the ghouls and the Djinn?"

I didn't answer him. Instead, I closed one eye, then opened it and closed the other. It was a sort of a game I used to play when I was a kid, alive and kicking, lying in the grass staring up at clouds or stars or whatever happened to be overhead.

"The Ghūl were not always as you know them," he said. "Once, they had a vast kingdom on this plane, in this realm, until they made the unfortunate and ill-considered decision to go to war against the Djinn. Almost four million years ago, during what human geologists refer to as the Pliocene Epoch, when mastodons and mighty chalicotheres still—"

"Bored now." I sighed. "Can we please fucking skip ahead to the point? As in, what prophecy?"

Pickman pulled a face like a goat eating a tin can. He was clearly a fiend who disliked being interrupted.

"I assume the clock is ticking," I said.

"The prophecy promises that there will be a savior," Pickman said. "The Ghūl call him the *Qqi d'Tashiva*, a messianic warlord, who will lead us back to our former glory. And Isaac Snow believes he is the *Qqi d'Tashiva*, and that his sister is the *Qqi Ashz'sara*, and together—"

"Yeah, but hold up," I interrupted again. "Way back in the Roaring Twenties, you went and cozied up to the ghouls. So, isn't this savior something you'd *want*? Let my people go? Psalm 136. By the waters of Babylon, and—"

"Quinn, we are not all dissatisfied with our humble lot," he said. "Many, indeed most, are content in the Lower Dream Lands and in those dim, funereal corners of this world we still inhabit. We've no desire to enter into the folly of a second war with the Djinn, or, for that matter, to see your civilization reduced to ash and—"

"Pickman, it isn't *my* civilization. It stopped being mine when I died. I'm just a blood-sucking parasite latched on to the armpit of this civilization. A leech. A tick. A goddamn bedbug."

"Truly, you've that low an opinion of yourself?"

"On good days? Yeah."

He made an annoying *tsk, tsk, tsk* noise through his bucked front teeth.

"Anyway," I said, "so Snow thinks he's the Second Coming, but you beg to differ. *That's* what you're telling me?"

"No, not exactly. The prophecy may well be genuine. The Snows might be precisely who and what they believe they are. Yet that doesn't change our desire to avoid this war and all its unpleasant, inconvenient consequences."

"It's a ripping good yarn, Pickman. You should write a novel, sell the film rights, retire to a nice little cemetery in Bermuda. But I still have no idea why you want to drag me into your Luke Skywalker partisan shenanigans. Except for this fucker having snatched Selwyn, it ain't my circus, and it ain't my monkeys. You don't need me."

"Quinn, you're something Snow didn't count on, something unforeseen. The dreaded fly in the ointment, as it were."

"Yeah, right," I said. "And if I had a hundred bucks for every time I've heard that line, I wouldn't be couch surfing with wannabe monsters like Selwyn Throckmorton. Speaking of whom—"

"Someone will be in touch," Pickman replied. "There are other factors, other variables to consider. The way things stand, we can't afford to be hasty."

"No, no, *no*. Fuck that 'someone will be in touch' crap," I muttered, and I shut my left eye, then opened it and shut my right. "They have Selwyn, and I have their holy grail. Everyone wants me to play this game so badly, then we're gonna keep it simple. We make the swap and get it over with."

"It's not that straightforward. We cannot allow you to actually give them the Madonna."

"Then what the fuck am I supposed to do with it, and how do I get her back?"

I opened my right eye and shut the left.

"*Someone* will be in *touch*," he repeated, more firmly than before, and right then, before I could say another word, a train rushed past. I shut both eyes tight, savoring the noise and whoosh and the rumble beneath me, wondering what the passengers would make of the two of us, if any of them stopped sucking at their various electronic iTeats long enough to even notice the pair of monsters on the abandoned platform.

When the train was gone and the station was quiet again, I opened my eyes. Pickman was gone, too.

CHAPTER FIVE

BAD PENNY AND POSTCARDS FROM HELL

The abandoned platform was only about six hundred feet south of the Brooklyn Bridge Station, and I'd walked the tracks before and a hell of a lot farther than a paltry six hundred feet. Just mind that third rail, natch, and keep a weather ear open for those racing conqueror worms of stainless steel and fiberglass that call the tunnels home. I was naked except for my pants and the torn duster, and I was starving. It takes a lot out of a dead girl, going all wolfish, getting her ass handed to her by a pack of ghouls, and then puking up her eyeballs. So, first things fucking first. Food and clothes, and, conveniently, the latter tend to come with the former, no added cost or effort. It was only a matter of slipping out of the subway and finding dinner topside. Or breakfast. I had no idea whatsoever how long I'd been down there, how many hours had passed since Selwyn and I had gotten on the train at Fiftieth and Eighth.

Anyway, fortune smiled, luck was a lady, and all that happy horse shit. No one spotted me climbing from the tracks onto the mostly deserted platform, and I made it through the turnstiles and up the stairs to City Hall Park without incident. There were a few sidelong glances, sure, but nothing any filthy, barefoot bitch slinking about the subway wouldn't have attracted. Aboveground, more good luck. It was night. Late. Though I wasn't sure if it was *still* night or if it was night *again*. I pulled the tattered duster about me and waited in the shadows beneath the trees. Oh, and I had Selwyn's bundle, of course.

I gotta admit, I was feeling better right about then than I probably had any right to feel. Most of my injuries from the previous chapter's misadventures had healed up nicely. And if I let myself go, there's a warm and fuzzy place the hunger can take me, all sizzling anticipation, like being horny for days on end and here you know that any moment you're going to get laid good and proper. Or, say, like savoring all the smells of cooking while you wait for an especially fine meal. Or, fuck it, Quinn. Be honest. Like watching H bubble in the spoon, waiting for the needle's sweet prick.

I squatted in the gloom beneath a huge oak tree and waited as the dry autumn leaves rustled overhead. I didn't have to wait very long. After only twenty minutes or so, a young Korean woman, maybe twenty-five and just about my size, wandered past. She was in a hurry, probably running late and taking a shortcut through the park. I called out to her with the voice of a lost and frightened child. It's a handy trick I'd learned since Providence. And she fell for it. I can't say that I was merciful. I was too hungry to be merciful. I *did* manage to be quiet. I held her down on the grass, one hand clamped tightly over her mouth, the other between her legs. She fought, but only until my teeth sank into the flesh just below her left ear and opened up her carotid. She poured into me, a hot red deluge, and if this sounds like porn, well . . . down here in the pit among the nasties, the genteel distinction between fucking and eating can get awfully blurred sometimes.

To my credit, I wasn't messy. After all, I needed her clothes as much as I needed her blood, and I needed them more or less clean. I was careful, and when all was said and done, there were only a few spatters on the collar of her coat. I quickly undressed the corpse and left the body propped against the roots and trunk of the oak. I went to the granite fountain in the square to wash away the grime from the subway, the dried vomit in my hair, and the Korean girl's blood that stained my sticky face. There were a couple of kids making out on a park bench, but they ignored me while I bathed. The icy water raining down on me felt like heaven. Afterwards, well . . . let's dispense with all this tedious blow-by-blow nonsense.

Thanks to the CEO, it had been a while since I'd needed to kill. Okay, discounting the Beast's recent rampage. What I mean is, it had been a while since I'd done what all honest, hardworking vamps do, finding an unfortunate mark—wrong place, wrong time, as they say—and then drinking until the well goes dry and the heart gives up the ghost. And, sweet Moses on a motorbike, it felt good.

I could have lain there until dawn, drifting in the crimson buzz and the soft orange glow from the gaslights ringing the fountain.

But then the seagull showed up.

It was perched on the edge of the fountain, staring down at me with its beady piss-yellow eyes.

"Hey," it squawked. "Nice tits."

I glared up at it. Jesus, I hate seagulls. Not as much as I hate Faeries, but still.

"Who the fuck sent *you*?" I asked.

"You know, lady," it said, ignoring my question, "people do sometimes tend to notice shit like vampires bobbing around naked in public fountains."

"While talking to shit-for-brains talking birds," I said.

The gull scowled.

"Nice to meet you too, Sunshine." It sounded genuinely offended.

"*Who* sent you?" I asked again, sitting up and pushing my dripping bangs out of my eyes.

"I mean," said the bird in its raspy seagull voice, "I know it's New York City and all, but . . ."

"Dude, am I gonna have to fucking pluck you to get an answer?" I splashed the bird, and it squawked and flapped its wings like it wasn't fucking waterproof.

"Just need to be *sure* you're really *her*," it said, shaking itself indignantly. " 'Be absolutely certain that it's her.' *That's* what he said."

"He who?"

"Him," replied the bird. "My employer. And I have a rep to protect, I'll have you know. I take pride in my work, and I'm not gonna get all slipshod and careless over the likes of you."

I splashed him again.

As I've said before, lots of the hoodoo and demonic types routinely employ birds as messengers. Spies, too. Owls, crows, sparrows, pigeons, ravens, ducks, and, especially, seagulls. Their profound lack of scruples makes them imminently useful. Dirty deeds done dirt cheap, right? Hell, a herring gull will sell out its whole family for a handful of cold McDonald's French fries.

"Show me your hand," it said. "Your left hand."

Which I did. You see, right after the Bride made me what I am, I lost my left pinkie and the second toe off my left foot. Well, no, I didn't *lose* them. I *sold* them to a bogle grifter named Boston Harry in exchange for— never mind. It's a long story. I held up my left hand.

The bird nodded its head, making a big show of looking all serious and shit.

"Okay, good," it said. "Now, show me your left foot."

"Tell you what, birdie. How about I put my foot up your lice-riddled ass and you fuck off back to whatever landfill or chum bucket you call home?"

The bird scowled again. Seagulls are masters of the scowl.

"Why you gotta be such a hater? You don't hear me running down bloodsuckers, do you?"

I stood up and looked about. The couple on the bench were gone; near as I could tell, it was just me and the bird. I leaned forward and wrung some of the water out of my hair. Then I held up my left foot, balancing on my right. I wiggled the four surviving toes.

"See, now, was that so damn hard?" asked the gull.

"If you only knew," I said, and then I climbed out of the fountain, wishing I had a goddamn towel. I considered using the black T-shirt the Madonna was wrapped in, but that would have meant having to see the thing.

"Ballard sent me," the seagull said.

I stared at it a moment. "Yeah, well, I don't know anyone named Ballard. So maybe you've got the wrong nine-toed, nine-fingered vampire."

"Nope, you're her, all right. You're Siobhan Quinn Twice-Damned, Twice-Dead. You're that epic hard-core BAMF went all Chuck Norris on a whole goddamn *busload* of *loups*, and, oh, never mind the—"

I reached down and grabbed the gull's hooked beak, squeezing it shut.

"You want me to break this off?"

The seagull's eyes went wide with panic. It made a strangled noise, beat at me with its wings, and tried to pull free. So I squeezed just a little harder.

"I asked you a question. *Is that what you want?*"

The bird rolled its yellow eyes, stopped struggling, and shook its head. I turned it loose, and the seagull immediately hopped safely out of reach.

"So, who's Ballard?" I asked it.

"The man who ain't paying me enough to put up with this sort of abuse to my bodily person," snapped the bird.

I retrieved my dinner's panties and bra from the pile of clothes lying near the edge of the fountain. Both were decorated with My Little Pony characters—a matching fucking set, and I shit you not. I decided I could make do without underwear.

"You used to work for the guy," the bird said. "He changes his name a lot, like every damn day, but it always starts with the letter *B*. Always, always, *always*. Frankly, he's sort of a douche, but don't tell him I said that, okay?"

I dropped the ridiculous bra and panties and sat staring at the seagull.

"B," I said. "B sent you?"

"Ain't that what I just said?"

If I'd been holding the Browning that Pickman had given me, I'd have shot the bird dead, right then and there, before it had a chance to say another goddamn word. Kill the messenger and the message and be done with both.

"He *said* you'd be glad to hear from him."

"Of course he did."

"Wants a face-to-face," the seagull went on, "this morning, uptown at the Museum of Natural History. Says it's important. *Real* important. Wants you there at ten thirty a.m., sharp and on the dot."

"Yeah, and people in Hell want hemorrhoid cream, too. You fly back to that son of a bitch and tell him I said he can go fuck himself. I was done with him three years ago, and I'm ten times more done with him now."

The bird made a sort of flustered, exasperated face, and I picked up the black turtleneck sweater my dinner had been wearing.

"He said tell you it's about the Snow twins. What's their names? Ishmael and Isis?"

Suddenly, I felt dizzy, and my mouth had gone dry.

Clearly, the cosmos had no intention to stop fucking with me anytime soon, and clearly I had yet to see the bottom of this mess Selwyn Throckmorton had gotten me into.

"Isaac and Isobel," I said, and I pulled the sweater on over my head. The wool smelled, not unpleasantly, of sweat, herbal shampoo, and vanilla oil. Then I sat, still naked from the waist down, staring south out across City Hall Park towards Broadway.

"Yeah, *them's* the ones," said the seagull. "Always been terrible with human names, I have. They all sound alike. Six of one, half dozen of the other. But you'll meet with him, right? I can tell him that?"

"What does B have to do with the Snows?"

"How the heck would I know? You'll have to ask him yourself. Now, how about you put your britches on. Not too long till sun*rise*, Sun*shine*."

"Wait, what day is it?" I asked, but the seagull didn't answer. It just giggled the obnoxious way that seagulls do, and then it flew away and left me sitting there.

Sitting there *alone*.

I pulled on my dinner's jeans, and her socks, and her shoes—a scuffed and down-at-heel pair of black cowboy boots with red stitching, so score. I sat thinking how, in the old days, I'd have struck out for Boston on my own, and fuck Pickman's "someone will be in touch" and his "there's more a stake" shtick. In fact, I'd have said fuck him, in general. If all that mattered to me was getting Selwyn back— and that *was* all I gave a shit about—I had the twin's precious gewgaw, didn't I? How hard could it be to find them?

But now there was this nagging fear that doing things

the old way, *my* way, might get Selwyn killed—or worse (because when dealing with nasties, there's always something worse than dying). I'd spent the past three years solving problems with brute fucking force, putting out fires with gasoline, as Mr. Bowie said. There'd never really been anything at stake except my own sorry hide and, occasionally, a paycheck. I'd always come out in one piece, more or less, no matter how close the calls. But now . . .

Now Selwyn's life was at stake. And the fact that I *cared* was paralyzing me. Hobbling my tried-and-true recklessness. Never mind that for all I knew she was already being ceremonially tortured, raped, or served up with an apple in her mouth as the main course at some ghoul fête.

I looked up, and standing a few feet away, there was a homeless man pushing a baby stroller stuffed to overflowing with garbage. He was just standing there in his filthy rags, staring. And I realized my true face was on display for anyone and everyone who wanted a look-see. So, this guy with his scraggly gray beard and ratty Sherpa hat missing an earflap, he was gazing into the abyss, and it was gazing right back into him. But from his expression, I got the feeling he'd spent a decent part of his life seeing monsters of one sort or another. Maybe he was a war vet, and maybe he was a schizophrenic. Maybe he was just a drunk or a fellow junkie. Whichever way it was, he didn't look particularly surprised. Well, good for him. Too many ignorant motherfuckers walking around with blinders on and no idea whatsoever what the world's really made of.

I winked at the man, and he smiled a smile mostly devoid of teeth, then went on about his day.

Overhead, the sky was growing lighter, the oncoming day—whichever one it might prove to be—dimming the stars. I pulled on the dead woman's black wool peacoat, turned up the collar, and left it unbuttoned. I checked the pockets and found an iPhone, half a pack of American Spirits, a disposable lighter, an unopened pack of Juicy Fruit, and a MetroCard. After checking for cash (there wasn't any), I'd left her purse with the body, back beneath the oak tree.

The phone told me it was, in fact, Tuesday morning, 5:55 a.m. So . . . I'd missed a whole damn day in there, presumably lying unconscious on that abandoned subway platform, healing from my wounds while Richard Pickman watched over me. Presumably. There are few things I find more unnerving, on general principle, than missing time. And in this case, it was missing time during which fuck knows what all had happened to Selwyn.

Anyway, I still had four and a half hours left until I was supposed to see Mean Mr. B, and since I didn't have money for a taxi, and since I'd had my fill of tunnels and trains, I figured the long walk uptown would be good for me, give me some time to think some of this shit through, consider my options. But on the *other* hand, let's say the hand that still had five fingers, what options? It was hard to imagine there was much *to* think through. I was along for the ride.

I was still about fifteen minutes early, despite having traveled in anything but a straight line and having passed some time poking about the Garment District and Times

Square and then the Sheep Meadow. Along the way, I'd shoplifted a head scarf and a pair of cheap black wraparound sunglasses, because nothing screams "I'm not a vampire" like wraparound shades. As long as I didn't smile and was careful when I spoke, I could almost pass for a normal person. It was a sunny autumn day. Too damn sunny. One of those wide carnivorous skies, right? The blue like the blue of a demon's eyes? The sun a white-hot hole punched in Heaven? I kept my head down. When I reached the Central Park West entrance of the museum, there was someone waiting on the granite steps to greet me. The constant reader will not have to be reminded of B's tastes in ass, the parade of pretty young boys and drag queens and transsexuals he wears like cuff links. That day, the pretty young boy who met me couldn't have been much older than seventeen, and he had hair the color of pomegranate seeds and eyes such a startling shade of green I knew he was wearing colored contacts. His fake fur coat and lime-green patent-leather go-go boots looked like something stolen off a dead Russian hooker.

"You're early," he said.

"You're observant," I replied. "I'm guessing you're the welcoming committee?" I glanced back over my shoulder at the park, all the trees gone red, yellow, brown, gold beneath that bleak November sky.

"Barrett figured you might not have the price of admission," the boy smiled. He was wearing way too much makeup for a cold Tuesday morning.

"Well, he figured right. But I thought Ballard was the *nom du jour.*"

"That was yesterday," said the boy. "Gotta stay current, girlbaby."

"Fuck you," I said, and he laughed.

"You're her," he said. It wasn't a question. "You are really and truly her."

I held up my left hand, all four fingers.

"Oh," the boy said, "you don't have to prove it to me, girl. I ain't no blindtard. All that wicked coming off you like thermonuclear fucking radiation, that shit's cray. I'm the one oughta be wearing the hater blockers, not you." And he made a V with his right index and middle fingers and aimed it at my face.

"Yeah, but do you speak English?" I asked, and he laughed.

"Charlee," he said. "That two *e*'s. The pleasures all mine, undoubtedly." He offered his hand, but I didn't shake it. Never been a big fan of shaking hands.

"He's inside?" I asked, and climbed a couple more steps so I was standing above the boy.

"That he is," Charlee with two *e*'s replied, and he pointed at the bundle in my arms. "Is that what I think it is? Is that the Very Unpleasant News the weirdlies got such a hard-on for?"

"The weirdlies?"

"Yeah, you know. Thing One and Thing Two. The diabolical duo. Heckle and fucking Jeckle."

I looked down at the bundle, then back up at Charlee, trying to decide if the kid was getting on my nerves, or if maybe I'd finally met one of B's mollies that I liked. Or, hell, both.

"You wanna see?"

He laughed a nervous laugh and shook his head.

"Fuck no," he said. "Not in a million years."

"Then how about you lead the way to Mr. Ballard—"

"Barrett," he corrected.

"Which the fuck ever."

A mother shepherding her two brats passed us on their way down the steps, and she glared at me, silently admonishing my potty-mouthed ways.

"Hey, listen," Charlee said, and he reached out and—very gently—laid a hand on my left elbow. Now, I'm not accustomed to being touched by strangers, and I don't like it. Truth be told, it makes my skin crawl. But this time, well, this time I let it slide. There was something unexpected in Charlee's unnaturally blue eyes, and whatever it was, it caught me off guard. It sent a bit of a chill up my spine.

"You're here to help him, right?" Charlee asked.

"Whatever gave you that idea? I'm here because a rat with wings interrupted my bath."

"But—"

I frowned and pushed his hand away, climbed a couple more steps towards the heavy brass doors leading into the museum.

"But nothing," I said. "Listen, you seem a lot brighter than most of B's fuckbunnies, so I'm assuming you know how shit went between me and him."

"That was almost five years ago, Quinn."

"I don't care if it was *thirty* years ago. As far as I'm concerned, it was fucking yesterday."

Charlee stared down at the scuffed toes of his lime-green go-go boots.

"He speaks fondly of you, girlbaby," he sighed. "Just try not to make it any worse for him, okay?"

My patience, never exactly worth bragging about, was a frayed bit of kite string, pulled way too tight.

"What's the story, Charlee? Are we gonna stand around out here all day? 'Cause if we are, I'm gonna sit down and have a smoke. My feet hurt."

He looked back at me, and whatever I'd seen in his eyes was gone, replaced by a practiced indifference meant to keep all the world at arm's length. But I knew what it had been, that glimmer. This kid actually gave a shit about B, beyond the drugs and the money and all the other various and unsavory perks of being the bad man's toy.

"Gotta admit," he said, "hard to believe you're the notorious badass bitch people go on about. Well, what the fuck, right? You like dinosaurs?"

"Not especially," I told him.

"Then you're sadly SOL, sister dick. Follow me."

Which I did. We threaded our way through the noisy crowd, the school groups and tourists, and took the elevator up to the fourth floor, where we found Mean Mr. B waiting beneath the *Tyrannosaurus*. And I thought then, and I still think now, that if I hadn't been expecting him, I might not have recognized the man sitting there. To roll out a cliché, he was a ghost of his former self. At best. Had I passed him on the street, I might have had no idea whatsoever that *he* was *him*. I looked at Charlee, wishing now that I'd taken time to hear him out back on the steps. No, strike that. Wishing I'd ripped the seagull's head off its neck before it had a chance to utter a single goddamn word.

"What the fuck?" I whispered.

"Please, Quinn. Just don't make it any worse," Charlee whispered back. "You just promise me that."

I didn't promise him anything.

I can think of a lot of words to describe how B looked that Tuesday morning: wasted, broken, diminished, et cetera. But none of them seem quite up to the task. It was like seeing someone who'd folded in upon himself. I'd never known the man to be anything except fastidious, a seedy sort of dapper, but he appeared not to have shaved for days, and his gray pinstripe suit was wrinkled, like he'd been sleeping in it. On a park bench. His black hair, usually swept back and pomaded, hung limp and stringy. And he seemed to have aged far more than three years since the day I told him I'd had enough and walked away; B looked like an old man. He was slightly hunched over, sort of hugging himself. I looked at Charlee again and shook my head, and then I got it over with.

"She's here," Charlee said, clearly trying to sound happy about it. B looked up and squinted at me. His eyes were the color of dirty dishwater.

"Kitten," he said, "lose the scarf. You look perfectly ridiculous."

"You don't look so hot yourself," I said and sat down on the bench next to him. Charlee remained standing. I left the scarf on.

B smelled like cheap aftershave, sour sweat, whiskey, and stale cigarette smoke.

"How'd you find me?" I asked him.

"Are we trying to be funny now?" he asked me. "Do you read the papers or watch the news? Have you heard of the internet, kitten? You're a star, after a fashion. Next time you want the whole world to look at you, hold a press conference."

"The wolf? It was an accident," I said.

"It usually is, isn't it?" He managed a weak, unsteady smile and pointed up at the *Apatosaurus*. "They've ruined this place," he said.

"What?"

"The museum. Used to be like going to church, it did, coming to visit the ol' *Brontosaurus*. Now . . ." and he motioned to the shiny, brightly lit displays, the funhouse clutter of glass and chrome. "It was solemn. Put a right sense of awe into a bloke. Don't know when the arseholes decided to cock it all up, but this, this is so . . . cold, yeah? Sterile, yeah? And the rug rats, *they* knew how to behave themselves back when. But that was before your time." He stopped pointing at the dinosaur and waved his hand at a group of kids giggling over a computer terminal.

"Jesus, B. Never knew you to be the sentimental sort," I said.

"Yeah, precious, well, there's a lotta me you ain't ever seen."

Neither of us spoke for a few moments. There was just the noise of all the rowdy children, echoing about the crowded exhibit hall.

"B, what's going on?" I asked finally.

He laughed a tired laugh. "Good day to you, too, Quinn. Long time no fucking see, yeah? How is every little thing?" Then he looked up at Charlee and nodded at me. "Didn't I tell you? This cunt, she's all fucking business, through and through. Don't give a tomtit for pleas-antries, our Miss Quinn."

I wanted a smoke. I considered lighting up. Then I'd be thrown out of the museum, and I wouldn't have to talk to the shade of Mean Mr. B. I'd be free to careen into the next brand-new and improved flavor of What the Ac-tual Fuck.

"Sorry," I said, not meaning it in the least.

"Nah, you're not, kitten. But that's your charm, as they say. Fine, let's cut the pleasantries and *auld lang syne*, shall we?"

And that's when I saw the stump where his left hand had been. What remained of his forearm was encased in a plaster cast, but—oddly, I thought—he wasn't wearing a sling. He *saw* that I saw, saw that I was, I won't lie, star-ing. He held up the stump, as if I needed a better look and he was willing to oblige.

"Jesus, B . . ."

"Yeah, Quinn," he said. "What about that? Ain't it just the dog's bloody bollocks? Always fancied I'd stay two or three steps ahead of my just comeuppances, slip-pery as an eel in jelly and the devil take the hindmost. But will you just have a gander at that? Bastards didn't even have the common decency to kill me. See, they're the sort to take trophies and leave a man alive to contemplate his indiscretions and misdeeds."

"Who?" I asked, though I already knew full fucking well who.

"Same fucking berks you've gone and gotten yourself tangled up with, kitten. Isaac fucking Snow and that minjer sister of his, that's who."

I turned away. I reached into the dead girl's coat, the pilfered peacoat of my last square meal, and took out a cigarette. I didn't light it, just held it between my fingers and stared at the polished stone floor. I noticed how scuffed and dingy B's calfskin loafers were. Before, I'd always been able to see my vamp's reflection in them.

"Small damn world," I said.

"About as big as a canary's willy," he replied. "Just about that big and no more."

"What'd you do to piss them off?"

"That how it is, then?" he asked. "Guilty until proven otherwise?"

"Yeah, B. That's how it is. This ain't no tearful reunion, all is forgiven, and oh, hey, let me kiss your fucking boo-boo."

I glanced up, and Charlee was glaring daggers at me. I figure, if he'd had a stake right then . . .

"Fine," said B, "I might have antagonized Mr. Snow a bit more than was strictly sensible. He was looking for something, something he was of the belief was hidden somewhere in Providence."

"He hired you to find it for him," I said.

"That he did, love."

"Some sort of ghoul artifact?"

"Ain't polite, beating me to the punch like that. How about you tell me what's in your lap?"

Of course, what was in my lap was the Basalt Madonna, still wrapped in one of Selwyn's T-shirts.

"I have a hunch you know perfectly goddamn well what it is, B."

He sighed and nodded his head, brushed some of his oily hair back from his face.

"Unser Mutter von der Nacht," he whispered. *"Das Herz der schmutzigen Lektion, Gegrüßet seist du Maria, voll der Gnade."*

"I don't speak German, you asshole," I muttered, and he laughed that raggedy, tired laugh again. "Is this what he had *you* looking for?"

B didn't answer right away. He chewed at his chapped lower lip, and I realized then that he was also missing a couple of teeth up front. He kept his eyes on the bundle—and fuck it but I'm tired of using that word, *bundle,* but what the hell else would I call it?

"No," he said finally, and went back to watching the dinosaurs. "Not that, precious. I like to think I'd have had the cobbler's awls to tell them to sod off, if they'd come to me to find *that* horror. But here you are, just strolling around with it tucked snug under your arm. How's that work, kitten? Are you of a mind you keep it safe, hand it over to those two, you'll get your lady friend back?" he asked, then scratched at the stubble on his cheeks.

"Pickman said—"

"Pickman?" B asked, and there was a spark in those gray eyes, half a second when I almost saw the old B. "And you believe *that* old devil's porky pies?"

"B, way I see it, I don't exactly have an overabundance of options, do I?"

He shrugged and glanced up at Charlee. "Will you be a sweetheart?" he asked. "My mouth's gone dry as a hag's Morris Minor."

When we first met, B's penchant for cockney rhyming slang had yet to manifest. I'm not sure exactly when he'd decided to add it to his repertoire of mannerisms, his slipshod persona. I still don't believe he was even British.

Charlee fished half a roll of spearmint Life Savers from a jeans pocket and passed one to B.

"Why am I here?" I asked.

"Come after a ball of fire, did we?" B mumbled around the spearmint Life Saver. He clicked it about in his mouth, then scratched at his stubbled face again. "Might be," he said, "I want to *help* you, Quinn. Lend a hand, as it were. Mind you, not out of the goodness of my heart."

"No offense, B, but . . . you don't even look like you're in any shape to help yourself, much less me. You want my advice, cut your losses and sit this one out."

"Did he say he wants your advice?" Charlee asked, and the way he asked it left no doubt that he was getting angry. I began to wonder if maybe this kid was more than arm candy. Maybe. Or maybe he only had aspirations.

Either way, he was pissing me off.

I said to him, "Charlee with two *e*'s, you want to remind me how this shit's any of your business?"

"Now, now," said B. "Let's all be friends."

"I didn't come here to make friends, and I think your twink needs a shorter leash."

Charlee made half an admirable stab at shooting me a withering glare, and I showed him my middle finger. Nice try, boy, but no banana. B sighed, sucked on his Life Saver, and checked his wristwatch.

He said, "You and me, kitten, seems like we've per-fected the fine fucking art of finding ourselves between a rock and a hard place, Scylla and Charybdis, demons and the deep blue sea. And this time, well, here you have those inbred albino lunatics up in Beantown, got it in their col-lective fucking loaf they're gonna see some ancient proph-ecy come to fruition, yeah? Believe they're the chosen ones, gonna lead all the wee little downtrodden ghouls to the pearly gates of Kingdom Come."

He stopped talking just long enough to spit what was left of his Life Saver onto the floor.

"While on the other hand, you've got the venerable Mr. Pickman and his merry band of counterinsurgents, the agnostics in this right holy Barney the Snows are try-ing to incite, and that lot figure what they got now is bet-ter than reopening old wounds and picking a losing battle with the Djinn. *Id est,* the plonkers you appear to have aligned yourself with, my darling dear."

"B, I haven't fucking aligned myself with anyone. I'm just trying to get Selwyn back. And I'm gonna assume you know who she is."

"Indeed, I do. Your aforementioned heart's desire and lady love," he replied. "And do let me pause to con-gratulate you on having found that special someone. I was tickled pink at the news, I was."

Right then's when I realized there were a couple of kids, a boy and a girl, watching us from just a few feet away. They looked to be seven, maybe eight. Eight at the most. Small wonder they were the only ones giving us the hairy eyeball.

"I haven't taken a side," I said again.

"Why didn't Pickman hold on to the Madonna?" B asked, and now he was staring back at the two kids.

"Beats the ever-loving shit outta me. Why'd the twins cut off your hand? You get greedy and try to pull a double cross with them?"

"I had unexpected expenses," he said, speaking very softly now, still watching the two children who were watching us. "It happens. I'd underestimated my out-of-pocket, tried to renegotiate the terms."

"Yeah. That's what I thought."

Then B leaned forward a bit, towards the two kids, and he rolled his eyes back in their sockets until only the whites were showing. Actually, the whites were a little yellow, like possibly B's liver was reaching the end of its rope and jaundice was setting in. Also, he smiled. For a human, B's got a creepy fucking smile. I have, on occasion, speculated he might have a dash of infernal blood from a few generations back; it would explain a lot. Like that smile.

The two kids promptly stopped staring and melted into the crowd flowing by between the dinosaurs.

"Neat trick," I said. "Though, I do wonder why you thought meeting here was a good idea."

"Lately," he replied, "I've sort of developed a fondness for crowds, if you get my drift."

"Well, hey, then that makes one of us. What do you want, B? You're charming as ever, but I'm getting tired of sitting here."

He took a deep breath and rubbed at the bridge of his nose. And when he answered me, he almost sounded like his old self.

"What I *want*, precious, is my fucking hand back. But seeing as how that's not in the sodding cards, I'm looking to settle for revenge. I want those two freaks dead."

I glanced at the *Tyrannosaurus* looming over us, and though it was stripped of flesh and its bones turned to stone all those many tens of millions of years ago, it sure as shit still looked hungry. Ravenous, Mr. Dinosaur with those grinning jaws and petrified teeth long as my hand, like B, it wanted vengeance. And, I thought, like B, it's shit out of luck.

"I'm not for hire," I told B. "And if I were for hire, I still wouldn't come back to work for you."

He laughed, a quiet, sour laugh. A laugh that gave me goose bumps.

"I don't want to hire you, Quinn. Tell me, have you even seen them yet?"

"Who?"

"'Who,' she wants to know," he said to Charlee. Then B jabbed me hard in the ribs with his cast. "The mongrel berks, that's who. Have you *seen* them?"

"No," I said, rubbing my right side. "Talked to the brother on the phone. He called Selwyn's place looking for her and got me instead. But I haven't seen either of them. I'm beginning to think they don't like being seen."

"It's a right bitch, ain't it, treacle tart?" he asked, staring at me now as if he were challenging me to disagree. "Trying to face off against fucking gits when you ain't even got a face to put with the toil and trouble they've brought down upon you? Like boxing with your own shadow, wouldn't you say?"

And for just a second, Mean Mister B's gray eyes had

a hint of their old fire back. Just a spark, sure, but still enough for me to see that—no matter the damage the Snows had done to him—he was still in there.

"I just want to get Selwyn back," I said. And if we were playing chicken right then, well, I'm the one who blinked first. It was easier to watch all those anonymous faces filing past than the hate bubbling up from B's soul.

"Fuck what the fuckers look like," I said.

"Remember when I tried to get you to read *The Art of War*?" he asked.

I said no, because I had no recollection whatsoever of B ever trying to get me to read so much as a take-out menu.

"Right, well, you see, Sun Tzu, that wily sixth-century Celestial cocksucker, yeah, well, he wrote—and do forgive my paraphrasing, kitten—he wrote, if you know yourself and know your enemy, you can fight a hundred goddamn battles and always emerge the victor. But if you ride out into the jaws of death, into the mouth of Hell—like Lord Tennyson's six goddamn hundred cavalrymen in eighteen hundred and what the fuck ever—and you *don't* know your enemy, then, kitten, you are, make no mistake, righteously fucking *fucked* every goddamn time."

"Which means?"

"It means you're blind," he said, raising his voice. "It means you're in the dark, as the poets say. And the time's come to have those scales fall from your blinkered eyes, just like Saint Paul on the road to Damascus. Time for you to see your enemy, them two mad as a bag of ferrets with teeth just as sharp. If you really want her back, that is. You still got that much fight left in you, Siobhan Quinn? You still know how to dance the dance?"

They didn't wait for me to answer.

I say they, because it was Charlee who placed a hand on my neck, two fingers at the base of my skull. I didn't even have time to be surprised. There was a flash, as much pain as it was light, as much light as searing pain, and the sensation that I was falling. But that only lasted . . . well . . . it was pretty much over before it began.

Boom.

And I opened my eyes, though I didn't remember having shut them.

And I didn't need anyone to tell me who I was seeing.

I was seeing Isaac and Isobel Snow. It was night, and I was standing beneath a full moon in a grove of trees on a hill crowned with a weathered stone altar, the whole scene a cliché straight out of a tale of New England witchcraft, a Roger Corman film starring Vincent Price. The twins had their backs to me. Each was wearing an identical velvet robe the same shade as the night sky. I leaned against one of the trees, feeling queasy and weak, trying to ignore my discomfort and focus on nothing but those two. Their white hair had been twined together into a single ivory braid that hung between them, down past their hips. Something lay on the altar, but I couldn't quite make it out. One of the twins raised a crude dagger, a blade chipped from flint and set into a wooden handle. A fucking caveman's Neolithic knife. It rose up almost high as the moon, and both twins were calling out to "gods" even fouler than the things ghouls worship.

"Shub-Niggurath!" they cried in unison. "Iä! Mighty

Shub-Niggurath! The Black Goat of the Woods with a Thousand Young, accept this oblation in thy name!"

And the flint knife came down.

Whatever was on the altar screamed, and I heard the crunch of bone, and the whole fucking night suddenly smelled of blood.

Then I got hit by both barrels of Charlee's flashbulb again: *boom, boom.* I'd been right; there was way more to that kid than questionable fashion sense, a wicked pretty face, and a headful of idiotic slang.

"Where the hell did you find him?" I heard myself ask, without ever having moved my lips.

"Where the hell did I find *you*, precious?" B replied.

In the motherfucking gutter, B.

Down in the motherfucking gutter, a needle in my arm.

There was that pell-mell tumbling sensation again, but it went on longer than before. When it ended, I felt like I was being splashed with icy water, jolted awake from a nightmare. But the truth of it, I was being jolted awake *into* one.

I was underground, and I knew where, even if I didn't know *how* I knew. A tunnel below Mount Auburn Cemetery in Boston, a secret path the ghouls had scratched out centuries before. There was orange torchlight flickering off the damp walls, off moldering heaps of bones and skulls, off rubbery fungi growing in fleshy clumps on the exposed granite. I took a step, and mud sucked at my boots.

Ghouls crouched on either side of me, dozens of them, squatting in filth and half-devoured corpses. Their bristling hides seethed with lice and fleas, with maggots, and their eyes shimmered iridescent gold in the gloom. The air was cold, dank, and stank of mushrooms, rot, blood, shit, and wet dogs. I took a step backwards, just wanting to be anywhere except fucking right fucking there, but I tripped over my own clumsy feet and landed hard on my ass in the mud. I looked up, and the Snow twins had entered the passageway. They stood together, hand in hand—Isaac on the right, Isobel on the left—and the creatures crowded into the tunnels averted their gaze and murmured incoherent prayers.

I didn't look away.

I'm sure there are those who'd have called them beautiful. There's never a shortage of people in the world ready to look at the grotesque and the warped and call it lovely. I just don't happen to be one of them. Isaac's and Isobel's skin seemed to have been dusted in flour, it was so pale. Their irises could have been cut from the reddest rubies ever mined. They were tall, lanky, long-boned, and thin, *frail*, and I couldn't help but think that one good, hard shove and they'd have both shattered like antique porcelain dolls. They were completely naked, save for the mud and decay caking their pale bodies.

"Well," said Isobel, looking directly at me, "from somewhere and somewhen, somehow she's finally found her way to us." She grinned ear to ear and flashed a crooked mouthful of stained teeth filed almost as sharp as a vamp's or a *loup*'s . . . or, hey, a goddamn *Tyrannosaurus*'.

"Clever bitch," her brother whispered. "So, she's a sorceress after all."

"No, brother. No, it's not *her* magic. She *has* no magic

to call her own. Only curses. There is another guiding her. *Pushing* her."

Some of the ghouls were watching me now.

Oh, and I had to piss.

Funny how I remember how badly I suddenly had to piss. But, see, vampires do not actually pee, so I suppose that part was, by definition, rather memorable.

"Where is she?" I heard myself ask, taking myself my surprise. "Where is Selwyn?"

Like cartoon villains, the twins exchanged curious, amused glances.

"She believes we have the traitor," said Isobel to her brother. And, "So, that's how we'll get your attention, Twice-Damned," Isaac said to me. "I believed as much, but one can never be certain what will work."

"Never," said Isobel. "Never certain." And she leaned down and forward, reaching towards me with her long white fingers. Her nails reminded me of broken acorn shells.

"No," I heard myself say, and then, whatever Charlee was doing, he did it some more. The tunnel dissolved around me, swallowed up by the fall, the flash, the sonic fucking boom, and I felt my bladder let go.

I hit the floor like a sack of potatoes.

A sack of potatoes that had just pissed itself.

Warm urine trickled down my thighs as this Third Circle of Fuck All swam into focus. My mouth tasted like blood, and I realized I'd bitten my tongue. I was lying on my right side, staring out across a hardwood floor so dusty and gray it might well have been the surface of the moon. The buckled floor of a room in a rotten old house, that floor and walls defaced with chalk pentagrams and seemingly random letters from the Enochian alphabet. Here and there were clusters of white candles burning on the floor. You know, I can ladle on description and adjectives all damn day, all damn night, but it really won't say jack shit about how evil that place felt. How *evil* it smelled. Worse even than the tunnels, somehow worse than the summoning of good ol' Shub-Niggurath. The pitched roof of a garret room rose high above me, impossibly high it seemed, and I wondered if maybe this wasn't a real place at all. It struck me more as a carnival funhouse abstraction of a spooky old garret room than the real McCoy. Another page ripped from freaking Poe or Lovecraft or Stephen King and splashed across my frontal lobe. A wave of nausea swept over me, but I managed not to puke. Pissing myself was plenty bad enough.

I lay at one end of the garret, and far, far away at the other end, what seemed like fifty miles off, was a sagging canopy bed. The canopy itself had rotted long ago, and nothing was left but cobwebs and tattered strips of fabric hanging from the head and foot posts, from the vaulted crisscross of rusted metal rods suspended above the bed.

The twins were in the bed.

In a corner not far from the footboard, a woman sat in a chair, watching them. Her fingers were steepled, echoing the inverted V of the garret roof, and her chin rested on her fingertips. She wasn't young or old, beautiful or hideous. She was somehow completely unremarkable and entirely loathsome. Her hair was salt-and-pepper, and her eyes were golden. Amber. Eyes like honey. She wore a tailored pantsuit, black shirt, pants, vest, a stark white shirt with a ruffled collar. Her clothes were immaculate, despite the dustiness of the garret. She was barefoot.

On the bed, the twins were fucking.

"Who is she?" I whispered, and the woman in the chair looked my way, but only for a moment. The scene on the bed was far more important, more urgent, it seemed, than the vampire who'd just appeared on the attic floor *ex nihilo*.

"Hera Snow," Charlee answered, from someplace deep inside my brain. "Their mother."

"No way," I whispered.

"Yes way," said Charlee. "But they're hers by a ghoul father. Once in each generation, a daughter is sent down to the—"

"Selwyn already told me that story," I interrupted. "I absolutely do *not* need to hear it again."

There on that filthy mattress, Isobel was down on her hands and knees, her ass raised in the air, and Isaac was mounting her from behind. They both had ugly vestigial tails sprouting from the base of their spines, bent and hardly as long as my pinky finger. He growled and leaned over her. In response, she spread her thighs farther apart, just before he sank his teeth deep into the meat of her left shoulder. The smell of dust and candle wax took a backseat to the reek of blood and sex. Just before he entered her, I got a glimpse of Isaac Snow's cock. There were bands of backwards-pointing hooks, like those on a cat's penis. The sort of shit you see and can't ever *un*-see, right? There was not even the faintest hint of love in that lovemaking. It was more like witnessing a consensual rape, which is exactly the sort of nonsensical phrase that comes of trying to apply human sensibilities to the mating of hopelessly inhuman beings. Isobel screamed when he pulled out, when those spines tore into her. Hera Snow practically beamed, proud as proud can be.

"My pretty, pretty, pretty boy," she cooed. "My sweet, sweet baby girl."

I expected the bitch to applaud.

Isobel, sweat soaked and panting, turned her face towards me, and she smirked and said, "Hello there, little voyeur. Want to come out and play? I'll share."

There was blood leaking from her nostrils.

"Play with us, Quinn."

And my stomach rumbled.

Suddenly, all those candles flared in unison, and the room grew much, much brighter. Painfully bright to *my* eyes. I instinctively shut them, but not before I saw the *shadow* looming over the twins and Hera Snow, the shadow of something both voracious and infinitely impatient. Yeah, I shut my eyes, but not before I saw it, and not before *it* saw *me*.

Bring me back, I prayed to Charlee with two *e*'s. *Whatever the fuck it is you're doing back there, you fucking make it stop and bring me back, right fucking now.*

Not yet, he replied. *I apologize, but we're not finished yet.*

There's more.

What was. What is. What's coming.

What might *come.*

The garret room broke apart around me, the world collapsing into splinters and shards, spilling me ass over tits back into the void. Wham, bam, thank you, ma'am, and down the goddamn rabbit hole with you, Quinn Alice.

For a time, there was nothing at all.

Nothing.

That was nice. I'd have gladly spent several eternities drifting in that limbo, if it meant I'd be spared any more visions of the twins' depravity.

But you know what they say about all good things.

I heard the mutterings of ghouls.

And I smelled incense—myrrh, vetiver, frankincense, turmeric—cloying smoke from smoldering braziers.

And once again I found myself in some subterranean place, but not the narrow tunnels hollowed out beneath Mount Auburn. This was somewhere cavernous, a veritable goddamn underground cathedral stretching away on all sides, its ceiling so far overhead not even my fancy undead eyes could find any trace of it.

I'm in the belly of the world.

No, whispered Charlee. *But you're in its maw.*

I was crouched on my knees, my clothing in rags, the clothes I'd taken off the girl in City Hall Park only hours before. My hands and face were bleeding from dozens of fine cuts, paper cuts, razor cuts. My magical mystery tour was taking a toll on more than just my mind.

When I breathed, my breath fogged.

Before me was a wide dais carved from rough ebony stone shot through with veins of scarlet crystal. There must have been two or three hundred ghouls crowded into the cavern, a grunting, restless mass of muscle and fur, all of them jostling for a spot nearer the edge of the dais. They snarled and spat curses in their guttural excuse for a language. Here and there, skirmishes broke out. I saw one big silverback motherfucker, three hundred pounds if he was an ounce, pop the skull of a scrawny ghoul who'd shoved him—inadvertently, I think. I mean, the brute just *literally popped* the little guy's head in his hands. Then he licked his gnarled fingers clean of brain and gore and went back to watching the dais. They were, all of them, waiting on something. And I supposed that Charlee and B had seen to it that I was waiting, too. There was another dustup, not ten feet from me, and it ended in a spray of blood and the victor dancing with a garland of intestines draped merrily about his shoulders.

In the three long years since my untimely death, I'd smelled a lot of rancid shit, but nothing that quite compared to that gathering. I didn't care what B's boy had said; judging from the funk, I was lodged firmly in the world's goddamn descending colon.

Where is she, B? Where's Selwyn in all this?

Patience, kitten.

The twins appeared on the dais—just *appeared*—and, as they say, sports fans, the crowd went wild. A howl rose up from the throat of every ghoul in the place, and you didn't have to be wise in the ways of the hounds to know it was a *joyful* noise. The crowd surged forward, and I heard bones crack. Bodies were crushed to pulp against the sides of the black dais, and talons scratched desperately at the edges of the stone. But not one of the ghouls tried to climb up onto it. They wouldn't dare.

There *were* rules here, and the price for breaking them would, I suspected, be worse than being squashed and trampled to death.

My eyes stung, and my vision blurred. When I wiped at them I realized there was blood trickling into them from a deep gash across my forehead.

What the fuck, Charlee?

The twins were dressed in the same midnight robes they'd worn when I watched as they summoned the Black Goat of the Woods, and, same as that night, their long white hair was plaited into a single braid. They stood there hand in hand, eyes downcast, their expressions just shy of solemn. It was Isobel who spoke first, and *when* she spoke, the rabble fell quiet as—if you'll excuse the pun—the grave. She didn't lift her head. She didn't look at the congregation. But . . . she smiled. She smiled an awful smile.

"Long ages ago," she said, not raising her voice, not needing to raise her voice, "we walked freely beneath the sun. In immemorial nights, we lived beneath the moon. We did not fear the day. Nor did we have cause to fear the sky and stars. We did not skulk in graveyards, subsisting off the withered corpses of apes. We were a great race, until we were betrayed and cast down into the Sunless Lands, exiled to the peaks and plateaus and necropolises of Thok, lost to the Lower Dream Lands where most of our race now dwell. Before the Djinn made their war upon us."

At this, the ghouls once again began to howl and hoot and snarl, and the twins let them. The twins held their leashes, that much was plain as fucking day. I was watching a puppet show, and the two mongrels on the stage were pulling all the strings.

I tried to stand, discovered that I was too dizzy, and sat down with my back against a stalagmite.

Minutes passed. I can't say how many. It was all a blur of goddamn yodeling ghouls and snapping jaws. But eventually they fell silent of their own accord, and now it was the brother's turn to speak. Isaac kept his head down, same as Isobel had done, and he wore the same smile she'd worn.

"My sister," he said, "recites the sorrowful and cruel history of our fallen race. She speaks it true, yes. But remember that it is *but* history. It is *only* history. The crimes done to us in antiquity have gone unanswered for three *thousand* millennia while human men and woman— usurpers favored by the Djinn bastards—have risen and stolen all that *should* have been ours. But I stand here and tell you, there is a path back, long promised us, and this wrong will no longer be endured, these unspeakable indignities, this . . . captivity."

Pretty lame as "Let my people go" speeches go. But, once again, the ghouls raised their cries for justice, and again, the twins let them howl and slam themselves against one another and the sides of the black dais. I watched as more of the faithful went down, casualties of the frenzy, ripped apart, stomped to jelly under the hooves of their fellows. Once or twice I even looked away.

No kidding.

"I get the point," I muttered. "I've seen enough."

I didn't bother whispering. It's not like the ghouls could possibly hear me over the ruckus they were raising.

Not just yet, the boy with pomegranate hair replied.

"*Yes* yet. Fuck you. Stop this *now*, right *fucking* now, or B's gonna be window-shopping for a new favorite pillow biter."

Charlee didn't respond.

I can't exactly blame him.

The ghouls had all fallen silent once more, and I looked back at the dais, the stage for Isaac and Isobel Snow's own private Altamont, this carefully ordered chaos good as their own DIY Nuremberg Rally. All eyes were on them, every fucker there waiting with fetid breath for the next proclamation.

For the plan.

For deliverance.

"What has *any* of this shit got to do with me?" I growled, and maybe I ought to have been keeping my voice down after all, because Isobel's ruby eyes went right to me. Finally, she raised her head. She licked her lips and nodded once, a nod that seemed to be something more meaningful than a mere acknowledgment of my presence, though what that might be I had no goddamn way of knowing. But neither her brother nor the ghouls seemed to have noticed what *she'd* noticed. None of them turned towards me, and Isobel, after a few seconds, looked away.

Free of her gaze, I felt as if a concrete block had been lifted off my chest. I heard myself gasp.

On the dais, the twins turned to face each other, and behind them appeared—just *appeared*—a contraption that looked a bit like what might happen if an indecisive metalworker set out to create a torture rack, then changed her mind and started work on a cross, only to change her mind a second time and attempt the sort of cage that could be hung from a gibbet. In places, the iron bands still glowed red hot.

The twins opened their hands.

"What rough beast—" said Isaac.

"—its hour come round at last," finished Isobel.

They opened their hands again, or maybe I'd only thought they'd opened them the first time.

They held, between them, the Basalt Madonna, and where the pyritized ammonite had been was a spiraling emptiness. A hole in space and time and the consciousness of everything that has ever had a halfway coherent thought, a hole in the universe, spinning around and around and around.

They kissed.

And the ghouls wailed, and their hoofed feet hammered at the travertine floor of the cavern.

We're almost done, said Charlee.

For just an instant, like a few frames of film spliced into the wrong movie, I saw a squalid room where two hulking figures held B still while a third used a butcher's cleaver to take off his hand a few inches above the wrist.

I saw Charlee watching.

I heard Mean Mister B scream.

Isobel reached into the hole where the ammonite had been, and now there were tears flowing down her cheeks as a sticky blackness poured out of the Madonna and up her arm. Isaac Snow watched, eyes wide—but not with fear and not with horror for what was happening to the woman who was both his twin sister and his lover. That expression, it was glee. It was jubilation. The bastard was ready to cream himself. All his sick fucking dreams were coming true, right there before his eyes, and Isobel, I saw, was a price he was more than ready to pay.

Power.

Greed.

A thirst for violence that would never be quenched.

And, suddenly, right then, all I wanted was to see him dead. I struggled to my feet, shoving back against the dizziness and supporting myself against the stalagmite. I reached for the gun that should have been under my tattered peacoat, tucked into the waistband of the dead girl's jeans. But it wasn't there. Not that it much mattered, because an instant later I saw what was suspended from that device that was not exactly a rack or a cross or a gibbet's cage.

What rough beast.

I'd never seen its face so clearly.

My face. My wolf's face.

I'd never imagined she could be in agony.

On the dais, Isaac was letting the Basalt Madonna devour Isobel, while the *loup* in me watched on, while I tried to remember how to shut my eyes.

"Okay, Quinn," said Charlee. "Hang on. Time to come home."

I cursed him, and the scene in the cavern began disintegrating around me, and I let go.

CHAPTER SIX

NOT A ROAD MOVIE

I didn't come to in the Hall of Saurischian Dinosaurs, surrounded by petrified bones, tourists, and noisy children. In fact, I didn't come to anywhere in the museum. I opened my eyes, after all that falling and the whirling black stars and the void, fucking Carcosa, and I was sitting on a bench in the park. I couldn't even remember crossing the street. Not that it mattered. I opened my eyes, and B was sitting on my right and Pretty Boy Charlee was sitting on my left. Charlee was holding on to my arm, just above the elbow. And the Basalt Madonna, still wrapped in Selwyn's Morrissey T-shirt, it was right there in his lap.

I gasped, sucking in air like I'd never tasted the stuff before. Like I was a breather. It smelled good, clean. Well, as clean as November in New York City gets. It was, in fact, the best goddamn air I'd ever tasted. But there was a chill, too, in the afternoon breeze rustling the leaves, and I pulled the stolen peacoat tighter.

"You're okay," said Charlee, and he gave my arm an encouraging little squeeze. "You're just fine. The disorientation, that'll pass really soon."

But it wasn't the Tilt-A-Whirl wooziness—apparently a side effect of Charlee's magical mystery tour—that I wanted gone. It was the twins, their grotto, the altar and the garret, Mama Snow, the frenzied ghouls, the Madonna, all *that* shit, Isobel Snow looking me in the eyes—*that* was what I needed to pass really fucking soon. But I knew better.

Some stains don't come out, no matter how hard you scrub.

"Quinn, if you need to throw up—" Charlee started, and I cut him off.

"No, I'm fine," I lied. "I'm not going to throw up," I added, though I felt like that was a distinct possibility.

"So you see," said B, speaking so softly that his voice was almost drowned out by the buses and taxis on Central Park West.

"Yeah, asshole. I see."

He was sipping a bottle of peach Snapple through a pink bendy straw, and he glanced at me. Out in the light of day, Jesus, he looked even worse than he had in the museum. Haggard. Broken. Empty. The swaggering pansy thug who'd bullied and haunted me so long reduced now to a dry shell and not much fucking else. Just a few hours before, nothing would have pleased me more than seeing this man so completely undone. But a lot can happen to a dead girl in a few hours, and all I felt, looking at him, all I felt was revulsion and pity. And that made me angry. It made me *very* angry, feeling sorry for B after all the shit he'd visited upon my person. But there you go. Sympathy for goddamn devils, indeed.

"You're going to Boston?" he asked, then took another swallow of Snapple.

"What the fuck for?" I asked him right back.

B cleared his throat and set the Snapple bottle on the ground at his feet.

"She wasn't there, B. Yeah, I saw a lot of shit, but I didn't see Selwyn. I need a cigarette."

Charlee took a yellow pack of American Spirits from an inside pocket of his faux fur, shook one out, lit it, and passed it to me; he left lipstick stains on the filter. The smoke tasted even better than the crisp fall air.

"Doesn't mean a thing," said B. "In your heart of hearts, whatever's left of it, you know she's with them."

The fucker had a point.

In the tunnel, I'd put the question to Isobel.

"She believes we have the traitor," she'd said. And Isaac, he'd chimed in, "So, that's how we'll get your attention, Twice-Damned."

I took another drag on the cigarette and held the smoke for a couple of minutes before I exhaled. Such are the questionable benefits of not needing oxygen.

"Charlee, what you showed me, it was past, future, everything all scrambled up together. I get that part, but the way it turned out, that last bit in . . ."

"Nothing's set in stone," he said. "What you saw, think of it like you would a weather forecast."

I managed a coarse laugh.

"Wow. As accurate as all that?"

"As *mutable* as all that," he replied.

"Yeah, well . . . I didn't see anything that convinced me going to Boston was any sort of good idea." Then I turned to B. "I do understand," I told him. "The whole vendetta thing you've got going with the Snows. They fucked you up hard, and you want them dead, and they have it coming a hundred times over. But that's *your* fight, old man, not mine. When Pickman contacts me, then I'll—"

"You'll what, precisely?" asked B.

He fixed me with his bleary gray eyes, then asked Charlee to light a cigarette for him, too. The boy took out a silver case filled with rainbow-colored Nat Shermans.

"All they want is the Madonna," I said. "All I want is Selwyn back. Pickman said—"

"Oh, kitten." He sighed and shook his head. "You disappoint me." He accepted a baby-blue Nat Sherman from Charlee. He took a puff and shut his eyes.

"And how the hell's that, exactly?"

He exhaled and scratched his whiskered chin.

He sighed again. "You've never missed a chance to remind me I'm a liar, have you? And it's true; a liar is what I am."

"Among other things," I muttered.

"Exactly," he said and nodded his head, smoke leaking from his nostrils. "I'm a liar, a killer, a cheat, a bugger of anything what stands still long enough. I'm a goddamn heel and a miscreant; that's me. A right and proper arse. A villain. So, when I tell you how I stand in awe of Pickman's perfidious ways, you ought to know I'm telling you the truth."

Ever heard of the liar's paradox? No? Well, it goes something like that.

"Every single word I utter is a lie," I said, "but right now? Right now, I'm telling you the truth. Is that the gist of it, Mr. Barrett?" I glanced at Charlee. He was watching a squirrel perched on the lowest branch of a sugar maple. The squirrel twitched its tail—once, twice, three times. Its black eyes stared warily back at Charlee, like he was just the sort of monster who eats squirrels.

"After what you've seen, you still don't comprehend," Charlee said, speaking very softly, as if he was trying not to frighten the squirrel. "You're still willing to hand over the Madonna to the twins."

"Not that Pickman's ever going to let *that* happen," said B. "But we've been over all this, and I've never been one for repeating myself."

The smoke from the smoldering tip of my cigarette coiled into an almost perfect question mark.

And I said, and, in that moment, I meant what I said, "I'm not your avenging angel, B, and I'm not a hero. I'm not Pickman's ace in the hole. I'm not motherfucking Frodo Baggins willing to walk into the Land of Mordor to stop Sauron from covering all the world in shadow. I'm not Dorothy Gale, and I'm not here to get rid of anyone's wicked witches.

"You say there's a war coming? Well, ain't there al- ways? I'll find Selwyn, and we'll go to ground, and every one of these assholes can murder each other for all I care. They can burn this whole rotten world to the ground."

I flicked ash into the grass and took a long drag.

"Well, well," said B. "If I only still had me other hand, I'd applaud."

The squirrel in the maple tree chittered angrily. Charlee told it to shut the hell up, and it did. For a few minutes, none of us said anything else at all, and there was nothing but the noise of traffic, the breeze in the branches, and the chirping birds.

Now, as you'll see shortly, I *did* go to Boston. But here's the weird thing: I cannot for the life of me remember exactly why, what argument swayed me. Or if there was some card B had yet to play that put me once more in his pocket, behind his damned eight ball. Way back at the beginning of Chapter Four, I mentioned how, writing all this down, lots of time I'm fully aware I'm just making shit up.

That might have annoyed a few of you.

Well, if someone's telling you a story, and they claim to be a *reliable* narrator, as trustworthy as the length and girth of the night, they're lying to you, sure as shit stinks. And it's just as bad, you ask me, if they simply neglect to address the question and let their readers buy into some unspoken myth of total recall. So, yeah. Most of the time, I remember the broad strokes, whether I want to or not. But that's about it. If this sort of confession rubs you the wrong way, then you're not paying attention.

Every word I say is a lie. Fuckin' A.

But I digress, and the time for digressions in this

story has probably come and gone. As I was saying, whatever swayed me to throw in with B that afternoon, that's a blank. Sometimes I suspect it was an ugly little smudge of magic on the part of B or his pomegranate-haired molly, because all I needed was a slight push out the door, right?

So, right *here* we have a perfect blank.

And *then* here we have Charlee talking to someone on his iPhone, and Mean Mister B's standing hunched a few feet away. The Madonna was in my lap, and I'd smoked my cigarette almost down to the filter. B had his back to me, and he was peering through the trees towards the museum. Right then, the man looked a hundred years old if he looked a day, and he was gnarled as the roots of the cranky squirrel's red maple. Whatever they'd done to him, it went deeper than amputating a hand.

There was a crooked man, and he walked a crooked mile.

He found a crooked sixpence upon a crooked stile.

"It's all set," Charlee said, putting away his phone.

B nodded, and I dropped my butt to the ground and crushed it out under the pointy toe of my most recent meal's cowboy boot. I left the bundle lying on the bench with Charlee and walked over to where B was standing.

"So, Mr. Barrett," I said, "do you know any more than I do about this much coveted unholy of unholies?" And I nodded towards the bench.

"La Virgen negra de la Muerte?" he asked.

"I don't mean the pretty boy in the go-go boots."

"He's a right wonder, is Charlee. I've never wanted to

tell my boys the secrets. You know what I mean, Quinn. Those secrets keep us tossing and turning at night. But now *he* tells *me* secrets."

"About the Madonna?"

"Among other things," said B, and he managed a tired smile.

"What is it? Just fucking tell me, if you know. And if you don't, say so."

He glanced over his shoulder at the bundle, then back at me. He nodded once or twice.

"What *is* she? She's the whore that tilts the world, kitten. Pretty much a hydrogen bomb you don't even have to aim. Fission and splitting and a chain reaction that starts small until Her Magma Highness tears a hole in the world."

"What the fuck does that even *mean*?" I asked.

He squinted, and the briefest flash of the old B drifted across his face. He reached out and pressed the tip of his index finger hard against my forehead. It made me think of Selwyn, tapping her nose.

"She's the Anti-Mater, Quinn. She unbirths."

All at once then, the day seemed too bright, too loud. All the edges seemed drawn too sharply, and every sound was just a little bit louder and shriller than my ears could bear. In another life, I might have thought it was exhaustion, of head, body, *and* spirit. In this *after*life, fuck only knows. I rubbed at my eyes. How long had it been since I'd last seen Selwyn? Less than thirteen or fourteen hours? It felt like days had passed.

B's finger was no longer pressed against my skin.

My mouth was dry, and I wished I had a few sips of a peach Snapple of my very own.

"And the *ghouls* made a thing like that?" I asked him, my voice sounding distant and pinched and skeptical.

I looked back at the bench, and Charlee was gone. The Madonna was still there, though. He hadn't taken the bundle with him.

"Perhaps they were the architects and perhaps not," replied B, half thoughtfully, half wearily. "I've heard tales told, and I've read some others, but I'm right cream crackered on what's de facto actual."

"Fuck, last I heard, the hounds were still struggling with Tinkertoys."

He coughed and cleared his throat, then spat in the brown grass.

"Quinn, the ghouls you know, they're the surface dwellers, the outcasts, as it were. Degenerates."

Now, the fact of the matter is I'd never yet seen a ghoul out and about beneath the sky, night or day, cloudy or clear, stars, moon, or sun, not even once, and I told him that.

B smiled, flashing uneven, tobacco-stained teeth. "Well, then, let's just say, love, that your concept of *subterranean* is impoverished and insufficient to the task at hand, *id est* comprehending the true depth of the world and, more precisely, the complex strata of the cosmos, both waking and sleeping, conscious and unconscious, as it pertains to the history and social mores of the venerable race of the Ghūl."

I rubbed at my eyes again, wanting to go back to the

bench and sit down. The day stubbornly remained excessively everything. I tasted new fillings, and a catbird in a nearby holly bush screamed like the sky was falling down.

"You've hardly even glimpsed beneath the flinty rind of the world," said B. And then he reached into his jacket and took out a few yellowed typewritten pages and handed them to me. They were rolled up tight and tied together with green velvet ribbon.

"Read this," he said. "When you two are out of the city and on the road, read this. It might help, if only a sconce."

"What the hell is it?"

"A missive produced *anonymia, incognito,* so forth and what have you. People write things down and set them free, and that, pumpkin, is all I know. But it's a damn interesting read."

"And it explains this unbirthing business?"

"Not in the least."

"But you were *coming* to that, right?"

"Was I?"

If patience is a virtue, which I doubt, patience isn't a virtue of mine. And it was clear that, even now, B was fucking with me for no other reason than it pleased him to do so. I considered a hastily conceived Plan B: Snap the motherfucker's neck and leave town. Leave the bundle on the park bench for some unlucky passerby to find. Forget Selwyn; forget the twins and the threat of total all-out ghoulpocalypse; get the fuck out of Dodge and don't look back.

I'd never been to Mexico.

Or London.

Both seemed like a better idea than Boston.

But then B said, "It's fairly self-explanatory. Unbirthing. Erasure. He . . . *or* she . . . who wields the Madonna, they hold the power to take something from this world, from our dimension, to subtract from reality. Well, *if* you Adam and Eve the tales. Let's say . . ." And here he paused, leaning nearer, lowering his voice to a conspiratorial whisper.

". . . that your neighbor's Chihuahua barks all night, *every* goddamn night. And this neighbor, he's a real twat, all right, and the tosser won't do shite to keep his wee ugly mutt quiet. So, you take up that hunk of stone, and by the power invested therein by beings not to be named, click the heels of your ruby slippers, and, voilà, it's bye-bye, poochie wanker. Abracadabra, presto-chango, alakazam, nothing up your sleeve, and Bob's your uncle. No trace remains. And I mean *no trace remains*, kitten. You wouldn't even remember there'd been an annoying yappy Chihuahua that you had to get rid of, because, thanks to ye olde *Unser Mutter von der Nacht*, poof, there never was."

He laughed and stared at the plaster stump where his hand had been. And you know those little cartoon lightbulbs? Right then, one blinked on over my head.

"Your name," I said. "You've seen the Madonna before."

And he smiled that dingy smile again.

"Well, it's not as simple as that. Not quite, anyway, and it's a dreadfully long story," he said. "But maybe I'll have time to tell it someday, should we live to see the far side of this commotion."

"So, what are Isaac and Isobel Snow planning to unbirth?" I asked.

"I don't know, and I think that it hardly matters. Whatever or whomever they've decided will give them what they want, which is this globe remade as their own personal charnel house."

"I think I need to lie down," I said.

And . . . I'm really dragging this out, aren't I? Yeah, so . . . cut to the chase, already. I didn't leave the Madonna lying on that bench in Central Park. Ten or fifteen minutes later, B and I met Charlee at the corner of Central Park West and West 77th. He was driving a shiny cherry-red Porsche 911, and he told me to get in. I got in. I was too tired and too confused to argue. I tucked the bundle snugly beneath my seat. B whispered something to Charlee and gave him a kiss, and then we pulled away and left the raggedy old man standing in the shadow of the American Museum of Natural History. I honestly thought that was the last I'd ever see of him.

"Fasten your seat belt," said Charlee with two *e*'s, and I did.

"You know," I said. "I don't need a chauffeur. I could have done this on my own."

"Don't be a braggart," he said, and so I shut up as Charlee weaved his way through the traffic with as much disregard for red lights, stop signs, pedestrians, and other drivers as any cabbie ever born. In no time at all we were on FDR Drive, headed north at twenty or so miles above the speed limit. I had a feeling Charlee didn't have to worry much about cops and tickets. I took out the pages B had given me back in the park, and I started reading.

Some of it I'd already heard before, from Selwyn. Some of it completely contradicted what I'd seen and been told. The rest, well, it sure as shit didn't make me any more eager to find myself face-to-face with Isaac and Isobel Snow. It was titled simply "A Prophecy," and the last page was signed KPK:

In the perpetual twilight of the Lower Dream Lands, the twins stand at the precipice, with the desolate plateau and peaks of Thok stretching behind them. Far below the precipice, lost in shadows, stretches the bone-littered vales of Pnath. They have imagined, these two from Above, that if they shut their eyes and listen very carefully, they can hear the rattle and rumble of gigantic bholes plowing through those jackstraw heaps. No one has ever set eyes on those creatures and lived to tell the tale. But, from time to time, the noise of their busy habits rises up the high cliffs of slate to the ears of any who are listening.

The twins, though partway human, are neither guests nor tourists in the abyss. They belong here as much as any ghoul. They may travel awake down the seven hundred steps to the Gates of Deeper Sleep. They may pass freely; none dare bar their way.

His name is Isaac, and her name is Isobel. They were born, not by chance, in the final minutes of an All Hallows' Eve twenty-two years ago. One look at either and anyone at all would appreciate the aptness of their surname: Snow. Their skin is milk, and their corn-silk hair is white as white can be. But their eyes are the deep crimson of rubies, eyes that see as well in this gloom almost as any eyes may see. Their birth was not an easy passage, and it took the life of their mother, Hera. She saw them briefly, and then death came and delivered her from the blood-spattered crypt where the two were dragged out of the amniotic peace of Womb into the clamorous purgatory of the World. Had Hera Snow survived, herself only one-third a true Daughter of Eve, she'd have loved them and been proud, for the twins grew to be all that would have been expected of them by the three families and their Ghūl father.

Hera Salem Snow, a Boston Brahmin Yankee born to the fortune and power her family bargained for centuries before. Deals with the ghouls and with dark gods, obligating each of the three families—Snow, Cabot, and Endicott—to offer once in every generation a daughter for the Ghūl to do with as they see fit. And as they see fit is almost always the birthing of half-breed children. Hera was herself the child of such a pairing, and was also such an offering, when the moon decided it was her time to bleed. She was neither fair of skin nor hair, but she shared the twins' red eyes, and she shared their hungers. However, she could only ever have aspired to the ferocity of their terrible appetites and desires, for the son and daughter have excelled in the expectations of their father.

Long before they were finally shown the way down through secret tunnels beneath Mount Auburn, they'd stalked and killed. They'd taught themselves the arts and sciences of torture, how to prolong the suffering of their victims as long as possible before the mercy of a killing stroke. It began—with kittens, puppies, song-

birds, a hutch of rabbits—before their fifth birthday.
As teenagers, they moved along to adult dogs and cats,
a horse from the Snow stables, before, finally, they
graduated to the cook. When they were done with her,
they, appropriately, butchered the corpse and stewed
the finest bits. They shared that meal, and then, for the
first time, fucked beneath a full moon, upon an altar
they'd fashioned to honor Shub-Niggurath, the All
Mother and consort of the Not-to-Be-Named. That
night they first tasted one another's blood, and that
night they became truly intertwined. They were
wedded beneath and by the darkness between the stars,
the void that watched on as they consecrated unholy,
unspoken vows.

Now.

Here they stand, hand in hand, above the black gulf
of Pnath. They have brought with them, in a burlap
sack, the dry skeleton of their mother; they drop the
bones, one by one, over the cliff, saving her skull for last.
Isaac kisses its forehead. Isobel does the same. And then
she releases Hera to her final resting place among the
bholes. The twins drew lots to see which of them would be
afforded that honor and responsibility. Isaac did a poor
job of hiding his bitterness at losing the roll of a single
soapstone die. Isobel has always found his sour moods
especially endearing and particularly exciting.

Their sacred duty done, the two walk together
along the narrow, cobbled road leading back to the
great necropolis of Zin, a city once held by the race of
gugs until two years ago when the twins led an army
of ghouls to shatter the ramparts and breach the walls

*and rain hellfire. For the twins have become what was
never suspected any half-*modab *beings ever could
become. Together, by bold and secret sorceries, they
unseated the King of Bones, the Queen of Rags—Qqi
d'Tashiva and Qqi Ashz'sara, respectively—and took
for themselves the thrones of Thok. They put to death
any who dared oppose them or question their right to
rule, all traitors and rabble-rousers. These public
executions were accomplished by such cruel and un-
sightly means that very few were necessary to quiet the
dissidents. And they made the kingdom anew. No
longer did the ghouls cower in mold and offal, gnawing gristle and marrow from withered, pilfered
corpses. Isaac and Isobel raised them up, and made a
proper army. The gugs were enslaved, and the night
gaunts, as well. Within the Lower Dream Lands every
foul thing that slithers, flies, hops, or goes about on two
legs fell under their domain.*

The forever twilight became a new twilight.

*Rarely now do the twins bother climbing the seven
hundred steps back to the Gate of Deeper Slumber and
the cavern of flame beyond leading up and up and up
to those catacombs beneath Mount Auburn. Never
except when returning cannot be avoided. Those times
come, as Isobel and Isaac are still the rightful matri-
arch and patriarch of the Snow clan. Too, there are
other occasions when their duties force their return, as
was the case with the exhumation of their mother. As
was the case when the location of the Basalt Madonna—Qqi d'Evai Mubadieb—was discovered in a
cave in the Sultanate of Oman, a hole in the Selma*

Plateau long known locally as Khoshilat Maqandeli and to the Arabs as Majlis al Jinn. Since the "death" of an artist named Richard Upton Pickman, the idol had been lost, as Pickman neglected to bring it with him when he made his own descent into the Underworld of the Lower Dream Lands. It disappeared in 1926, taken from the painter's effects by some unknown woman or man or something that was neither. How it came to be hidden below the sun-blasted canyons near the southeastern coasts of the Arabian Peninsula no one knows. But the answer to that mystery is hardly important. All that matters is that it is no longer lost. The twins know well enough not to question the winds of Fortune, but only accept her boons when all too rarely they are handed down.

The cobblestones twist and turn, coming at last to the towering gardens of fungi and more unspeakable vegetation. They've spent many wonderful private hours here alone in one another's company. Beyond the gardens rise the fantastic archway framing the entrance to Zin, fashioned of obsidian, chrome tourmaline, and green fluorite. Isaac and Isobel cross the bridge above the moat, and she pauses a moment to observe a ring of bubbles rising from the inky waters. The trumpets of the Guards of the Wall announce the arrival of King and Queen, and the mighty doors to the city swing open on copper hinges. Isobel points into the moat, and her brother is quick to look for himself. It wouldn't be the first time the moat has whispered a portent. This time, though, the disturbance seems to be no more than gases of decay escaping from the bottom.

He looks a little disappointed, and she whispers promises of consolation. Then they pass into the royal city, and the doors draw shut again.

"What if the preparations are not complete?" Isaac asks his sister. They've left the gatehouse fortifications behind and come to the first gloomy avenues. Per their standing orders, none have come to meet them, and at the sound of their approach, every ghoul falls to his or her knees, head bowed.

"Then there will be a feast in the dungeon," she says and smiles. Her smile, like his, is an unpleasant thing: uneven yellow teeth that she had no need to file to cannibal points because she and Isaac were both born with those teeth. "But don't worry. The preparations will be complete."

For a reply, he only nods. Isobel is correct more often than she is wrong.

When they reach the palace, there are more trumpets, ordering all within earshot to drop at once to their knees.

The twins stroll hand in hand through the lightless corridors, acknowledging none of the supplicants.

"Are we hungry, brother?"

Isaac doesn't answer her straightaway, so she asks again.

"Well, are we?"

He laughs and kisses her right cheek. "When are we ever not?"

"There is time before the hour," she tells him.

"There is," he agrees.

So she calls for a meal to be prepared, and servants

get to their splayed feet and rush off to the larder and busy themselves at the dining table in the Great Hall.

So far as is recorded, the Basalt Madonna first appeared sometime in the fifth century Anno Domini Nostri Iesu Christi. *Well, not the lord of any of the inhabitants of the city of Zin or, for that matter, in all the Lower Dream Lands. Nor even the* Upper *Dream Lands. In Constantinople, a monk happened across one of the Ghūl who, in those days, slunk through the alleys and abandoned buildings of so many cities. The few ghouls still inhabiting the World Above were bolder than they are today, and they didn't confine themselves to graveyards and to sewers. So, the pious monk encountered what he mistook for a wretched leprous man gnawing on something in a gutter (he wisely did not look too closely at what it was the ghoul gnawed), and he led the wretch back to his abbot. The abbot, being sharper of wit than the monk, was quick to realize that the man from the gutter wasn't any sort of man at all, and thus did the "Hounds of Cain"—as they were* christened*—come to the attention of citizens of* Christendom. *As assimilation is inherent to that system, the abbot (his name and that of the monk are lost to history, and just as well) sent his monastic agents out to evangelize to and convert these misbegotten creatures, regardless of their foul habits and appearance and dubious origins.*

The effort was met with somewhat less success than the abbot would have wished.

For, of course, ghouls have their own gods. When humanity had yet to move beyond their australopithe-

cine progenitors, already did the ghouls worship their pantheon of Fifty, the Qqi. Ages before their fateful war with the Djinn, they had come to know the Hands of the Five, the Ten Hands, the fifty fingers. They weren't about to cast aside their veneration of Great Amylostereum or Mother Paecilomyces, Camponotus the Tireless Maw or eyeless, all-seeing Claviceps, in exchange for one god who'd not even seen fit to send his martyr down to the Lower Dream Lands. Still, there's always a gullible element in any assemblage, and a tiny but strident number, while not abandoning the Qqi, did engage in a notable act of syncretism. They wove their own rough patchwork of holy entities from the teachings of the monks. They brought into being the Maghor Rostrum (patron of the starving and tooth-less), Mortifien the Crypt Mason, Mistress Praxedes the Many-Limbed (midwife to the transformed who once were only women and men), bat-winged Pteropidion, and the maimed bride Saint Lilit (invoked for the endurance of exile and pain). These names and many others besides were set down in 1702 for the prying eyes of brave and foolish seekers after mystery by François-Honoré de Balfour in his infamous Cultes des Goules, a volume almost immediately consigned to the Church's Index Librorum Prohibitorum.

It is not known precisely how François-Honoré de Balfour learned the names, though his association with a handful of Jesuits would be sagely blamed.

And those ghouls who so cleverly fashioned these new "gods" also fashioned for themselves a new idol, their own Pietà, a Beáta Maria Virgo Perdolens to fit

*their needs, and among men it became known as the
Basalt Madonna, id est Basaltes Maria Virgo.*

*When Isaac and Isobel Snow have finished their
raw meal of the tongue, kidneys, ovaries, and heart of
librarian, a woman lately of Providence, Rhode
Island, they lick clean each other's faces and hands
before proceeding to the chamber where the priests have
erected—to their exacting specifications—an altar of
stacked skulls and blocks of volcanic rock mined from
the quarries of Thok. The altar rests on a wide dais,
and before the dais the priests have lain a bed of
mammoth furs and tanned skins peeled from off half a
hundred embalmed corpses. The smoky candles that
illuminate the room have been made from the fat of
both humans and ghouls.*

*"Are we ready?" asks Isobel. Before Isaac answers
her, he examines the brass contraption near the altar.
A single shaft of pale moonlight is shining down
through a hole in the high domed roof of the chamber,
and it falls across the contraption. It looks a bit like a
sextant, a bit like a sundial, yet also suggests an
elaborate clock.*

*"We are," he says, and she smiles. It's been a long
and arduous path to this hour.*

*What they are about to do cannot ever be undone,
which, obviously, is what makes what they are about to
do sublime. The twins stand at the hairline threshold of
the realization of a prophecy first uttered more than
four million years ago, in the days after the end of the
war with the Djinn, well in advance of the ghouls'
exposure to the tenets of Christianity and what they*

made of it. The teachings of the abbot were only—to those who understood—a means to an end. A means to fulfillment of a prophecy that might never have had a chance of fulfillment had not a monk found a ghoul in a gutter and led it back to a monastery. There can be hope, and dreams, and the illusion of design, but it's the accidents of history propel *history, for history is no more than innumerable tangled strands of happen-stance.*

Isobel spares a glance at the well that opens just a couple of feet behind the bed that has been prepared for her and her brother. Even a mind as gleefully, unapol-ogetically wicked as her own feels a slight shiver at the sight of the well, hewn from the native rock and eight feet across, the candlelight making no dint whatsoever in its implacable darkness. A mouth like that needs no teeth to be taken seriously. It was here long before this chamber was built, long before the city of Zin.

"Better, sister, that we don't look at it." He is thinking of basilisks and the gorgon Medusa, but he doesn't tell her that.

"Yes," she says, turning her face away from the well. "But—"

"It's better," he says again.

She undresses, and he follows her example. Their robes of yellow silk and wool damask form pretty puddles at their feet.

It is a shame, *she thinks,* this could not have been our wedding bed.

"It's a shame," says Isaac, "that this *couldn't have been our wedding bed," and she smiles and nods. Isobel*

smiles far more than Isaac; she sometimes thinks him far too serious for their own good. In all matters, it seems to her, a little levity is advisable.

The Basalt Madonna has been placed on the altar.

Half hidden in the ten arms of Mother Hydra rests the slain body of the messiah. Not the one that the monks of Constantinople hoped the Ghūl would come, in time, to venerate. This is a messiah fit for the Lower Dream Lands. It might be the graven image of almost any ghoul, from its vaguely canine face to its hooves. Which is the point. It might be any ghoul, were any ghoul made perfect. There is no describing perfection; it is seen and it is understood. Or it isn't. Over the centuries, many forgeries of the Basalt Madonna have surfaced. Some arose from within the blasphemous sect sometimes referred to (as in Balfour's book) as the "Byzantine Ghūl." Others were created by charlatans and also by occultists hoping a copy might prove as powerful as the lost (or only hidden) original. They were wrong, for without the blessings bestowed upon the first, the true Basaltes Maria Virgo, these counterfeits were no more than unnerving chunks of igneous stone. Here, in this place, at this appointed time, Isobel Snow lies in her twin's embrace, watching as the candlelight plays over the angles and curves of the idol. The pyritized nautiloid crowning Mother Hydra, her golden gloriole, only the geometry of its spiral are wholly an expression of any known mathematics. That organic manifestation of the golden curve, circular arcs connecting the opposite corners of squares in the Fibonacci tiling—1, 1, 2, 3, 5, 8, 13, 21, and 34. That *lone Paleozoic shell, pried from Turkish shale, is a comfort to any eye that lingers on the idol. Only it is not somehow alien to the sight of one born in the World Above or in the Dream Lands. For the hands of those who exist Outside had too great a hand in the conception and sculpting of the Madonna.*

In their defeat and humiliation, a hierophant of the Ghūl foretold of the coming of a mighty warrior priest who would lead them in a second war against their ancient foes and fully restore them to the waking world. The father and mother of this savior would be twins born of a mongrel bitch. And now the tribulations are ending, passing with the sacrifice of Hera Snow, grandmother of God. With the birth of Isobel and Isaac Snow.

In the shadow of the altar, he enters her, and she wraps her legs tightly about him. A distant piping music rises from the well, and the candles burn the sickly blue of the giant phosphorescent mushrooms in the garden beyond the city walls. There are no other words passed between the twins. There never will be. Once he's come and is asleep beneath her, she gazes at the obsidian dagger waiting on the altar. It will cut her hands when she wields it, that her own blood will mingle with her brother's when she slices his throat from ear to ear. She'll be alone when their child is born, but Isaac always understood that he'd never live to see the exodus from Zin and the deliverance of his people and the Age of the Second Kingdom.

"I love you," she whispers, knowing that she will never love another. Not even the daughter who will

grow within her to be born before another year is out.
Soon, she will cast his bones upon the vales of Pnath, to
join their mother's.

"You'll not ever be forgotten, Isaac," she whispers.

Somewhere in the twilight that hangs always above
the city, there's the rumble of thunder and the sound of
vast wings bruising the air. She kisses him, then rises to
take up the knife.

When I was done reading, I rolled the pages up again,
opened the Porsche's glove compartment, and stuffed
them inside. Charlee hadn't said a word the entire time
I'd been reading. The radio was on, tuned to a country
station. Neko Case was singing about ragtime and snow.

"Where are we?" I asked him.

"Connecticut," he replied, as if that said all that
needed saying, then added, *"Qui Transtulit Sustinet."*

"What?"

"He who is transplanted still sustains. Apparently, it's
the state motto."

"You speak Latin?"

"Girlbaby, this tongue of mine, you may live to learn
that it's no end of talented."

To this day, I have no idea if he was making a pass at me.

"Connecticut already?" I asked, more than a little surprised. It would have taken me half an hour, at most, to
read the story of Isobel and Isaac. We should have still
been stuck in traffic in the Bronx or some shit. Instead, we
were on a narrow two-lane highway, heading east, racing
along between fields and patches of forest. At our backs,
the sun was going down fast, and I glanced at the clock on

the dash. It was ten past four, when it shouldn't have been much later than two in the afternoon. Had I nodded off? I'd lost hours and fuck knows how many miles.

"What the hell, Charlee?"

"Well, I cheated," he smiled. "I took a shortcut. You'll find I know a lot of those." He smiled and turned the radio down a little. Neko Case seemed to fade into the distance.

"Where the did B *find* you?" I asked him and began going through the pockets of the dead woman's peacoat. I took out the pack of Juicy Fruit, the cigarettes, and the lighter. I opened the yellow pack of gum. I hadn't tasted Juicy Fruit since I was a little kid. So far as I knew, there was no rule against vampires chewing gum.

"He didn't," Charlee replied. "I found him."

"Now, that's gotta be a tale," I said, unwrapping a stick of gum and popping it into my mouth. I offered Charlee a piece, but he passed.

"I'm afraid it's not especially interesting," he said, glancing at the rearview mirror. "I was in Scotland— dreadful fucking country, by the way—studying the utter messtasrophe Miss Crowley made of Boleskine House when he ran off to Paris in 1934, because McGregor—"

"You're a witch?"

Charlee frowned slightly.

"I'm a *magician*," he said and glared at me with his too-green eyes. "An accomplished, disciplined practitioner of the true science of the Magi, *not* some neopagan Wiccan wannabe waving crystals at trees."

"Touchy, touchy," I muttered, then spat the pale wad of Juicy Fruit out into my palm. It was much sweeter than

I remembered, or, more likely, my ramped-up taste buds made it seem that way. I rolled my window down and tossed the gum out. Cold, fresh air and autumn smells flooded the car.

"All right, so what was B doing in Scotland?"

"He never told me, and I never asked."

"You're right; this isn't a very interesting story." I rolled the window up again and checked under the seat to be sure the Madonna was still there.

"All right," I said. "Forget how Mean Mr. B met Charlee with two *e*'s the magician. Here's another one. How the fuck did he get you to volunteer for this suicide run?"

"You think that's what it is?"

"Let's say that I do. And let's also note that I have more experience in that department than I care to admit."

"You'll get no argument there," said Charlee. "First the Bride and then that whordeal up in Old Lady Drusneth's place of business, you going all Arnold Schwarzenegger on her ass like that."

"Whordeal? Did you just make that up?"

"Oh," he went on, ignoring the question. "Plus, walking in on Capital E Penderghast the way you did, uninvited. Totally effing bravelicious, that one, or else an act of unbridled stuphoria."

"You got it right the second time," I said.

He had the headlights on now, and the scenery along the sides of the highway was beginning to fade into the gloom of twilight. I lit a cigarette and watched the speedometer; the needle hovered just below eighty miles an hour.

"We're coming up on Waterbury," Charlee said. "I know it's probably not something you have to worry about anymore, but I'm about ready for good long pissaloo."

"No, I don't piss." *Well,* I thought, *not usually.* I don't think the vision piss counted.

"Lucky you."

"Not especially."

Yeah, okay, this is turning into a scene that could put a rock to sleep. Note to aspiring writers: Steer clear of long scenes in which your characters are stuck in automobiles. Anyway, as we sped along towards night and Boston, the twins and maybe worse things than the twins, I was beginning to find it difficult to think about much of anything but Selwyn. I knew that if I cut the crap and was honest with myself, I'd have to admit that the odds were she was dead or soon would be, and there probably wasn't jack all I could do about it. Honesty was a goddamn rabid honey badger perched on my shoulder, whispering bitter nothings in my ear. Meanwhile, my old friend Denial was busy cowering beneath the seat with the Madonna.

"Also," said Charlee, "I need more cigs."

"I don't have a plan," I confessed.

"I know," he replied. "Me, either."

"Dude, we are so utterly screwed," I said, and Charlee laughed. I shut my eyes, listening to the hum of the wheels against the road and the twang of the country music coming through the radio, and I tried to clear my head, focus, take stock of my situation, weigh my options (assuming I had any). On the one hand, from a certain angle, it almost seemed straightforward: I had the secret ingredient to Thing One and Thing Two's nefarious plan for global domination, even if I had no idea whatsoever how they planned to use it to put the smackdown on the Djinn and usher in the endless fun and games of Babes in Ghūland. They had Selwyn, and apparently I was, fuck me sideways, in love with her lying, conniving, cute-as-fuck, one-quarter-ghoul ass. It could all come down to a simple exchange, the Madonna for Selwyn, and never mind Charlee and B's hard-on for vengeance. Maybe there was a stingy speck of honor in the twins, and they'd take their loving cup and send us on our merry way. Then we could beat a hasty retreat and . . . what?

Wait out the end of the world as we knew it in a ghoul-proof fallout shelter somewhere?

Or, contrariwise, it wasn't simple at all. To start with, what the fuck was Pickman playing at, and what did he have planned for me? You'd think that the one thing he had to want *most of all* would be to keep the Basalt Madonna out of the grubby paws of the Snows, and yet . . . when I'd proposed the swap, all he'd had to say is, "Someone will be in touch." He let me walk, knowing perfectly well where I'd likely, probably, almost inevitably be walking *to*. He'd told me all about how I was the fly in the ointment of the twins' plans, but he hadn't bothered to elaborate.

I shut my eyes, struggling to tie it all together, as if the days and nights since I'd met Selwyn were nothing more than the plot of some ill-conceived paperback. Death had not severed me from that all-too-human need to see patterns and solutions. If I squinted at it long enough and hard enough, wouldn't all the pieces finally fall into place, free of plot holes, unanswered questions, and inconvenient loose ends? Wasn't I the clever, well-prepared author, a master of resolution and foresight?

No, I wasn't.

I wasn't any of that.

And the bloodthirsty, lunatic world around me was not a book written to entertain . . . well . . . anyone.

"Someone will be in touch," I whispered.

"What's that?" Charlee asked.

"Nothing," I replied, not bothering to open my eyes. "Talking to myself, that's all."

"Maybe you should get some rest," he said. "How long's it been, anyway?"

"Since?"

"You slept, Quinn."

I tried to remember, but that nugget of information was as elusive as everything else, a tangled strand of cheap plastic beads ready to snap between my fingers. Did however long I was unconscious after the ghouls jumped us on the train count as sleep? No, probably not. So, the night before the night Jodie had driven us both to Selwyn's apartment, *that* was the last time I'd slept. But . . . hadn't I missed a day in there somewhere, after the attack and before Pickman, and . . . ?

"A couple of days," I guessed.

"Well, then, you should get some shut-eye, girlbaby," said Charlee. "We're both gonna need you bright eyed and bushy tailed much sooner than later."

And then it hit me, and I opened my eyes.

Someone will be in touch, Pickman had said.

I opened my eyes and stared at Charlee, there behind

the wheel, Charlee with his fake green eyes and Moscow-hooker fake fur coat and the red of his hair that was as unnatural as a werewolf who is also a vamp.

"Does B know?" I asked.

"He's beginning to suspect," answered Charlee.

"You're working with Richard Pickman," I said, feeling just a tiny bit pleased with myself, a teensy bit less clueless than usual.

"Not exactly," Charlee replied. He smiled for me, and I was treated to my second revelation in as many minutes. His teeth, like his eyes, were simply too perfect, a mask worn to disguise the truth. "But you might say we work for the same people."

"You don't need to take a piss in Waterbury."

His smile widened, and he winked at me. Then he reached into his mouth and slipped out the dental prosthetics, uppers and lowers. I tried to remember where I'd lost my own, but couldn't.

"And does B know about *that*?" I wanted to know.

"That I'm a vampire? Yeah, he knows."

I laughed and shut my eyes again. "Jesus fucking shitting Christ on a Greyhound bus," I muttered. "How the fuck did I fucking miss that?"

"It's a kind of magick," he said and winked again. "With a *k*, naturally."

"Naturally."

"Charlee, you were planning on telling me this when?"

He looked back at the road, at the twin beams of halogen light picking out the path ahead of us.

"I'd have told you before we got to Mount Auburn. I just wanted to see—"

"If I could figure it out."

"No. I wanted to see how mad my skills are up against the infamous Twice-Damned. I think I didn't do so bad. Now, get some rest."

I had a million questions. Anyone would. But suddenly I was almost too sleepy to keep my eyelids open. I suspected that was probably yet another stunt from his bag of tricks. But I didn't protest. Either this was some sort of double cross, or it wasn't. Either Charlee was here to help me put down the twins and get Selwyn back, or he wasn't. I'd find out soon enough, and if he was more foe than friend, there was only so much, at this late date, I could do about it.

The headlights and the oncoming night, the purr of the Porsche's engine and my exhaustion, it all melted together, and I let go.

I slept.

And somewhere in my sleep I found myself once again stepping out of a fairy-tale forest and coming back around to the edge of that vast field of yellow-brown grass. And same as before, there was the blonde-headed child and her wolf companion. Never mind that I'd brutally murdered them both the last time I'd come this way. The girl and the wolf watched me for a while, neither of us speaking. They didn't seem anywhere near as wary as I would have expected.

Finally, the girl said, "We didn't expect to see you again."

"Which makes it mutual," I said, peering out across those amber waves of grain towards the whatever that lay, unknown and unglimpsed, on the Other Side.

"It wasn't kind of you," said the girl, "and it wasn't

necessary, doing what you did. It certainly wasn't very productive."

The wolf's eyes were, if anything, even paler than they'd been before, and the fat gray grasshoppers were everywhere. The sky above the swaying grass was uncomfortably low, as if at any second it would scrape its belly against the field. The wolf blinked, then glanced up at the girl. Its tongue lolled half out of its mouth.

"What do they want with us?" I asked.

"Who, Quinn? What does *who* want with *us*?"

I took a step backwards and sat down, my back against the trunk of one of the trees at the edge of the forest, the edge of the field. The bark crunched loudly and gave beneath my weight, which is when I discovered it was only papier-mâché and chicken wire.

"It's not real," I said, and the girl shrugged.

"Real enough," she said. "What does who *want* with us, Quinn? Do you mean the twins?"

"Who the fuck else *would* I mean?" I asked her. "Don't all you dreams ever bother to talk to each other?"

The girl frowned, and the black wolf with the white eyes lay down at her feet. She scratched behind its ears for a moment or three, then sat down beside it, looping one arm about the animal's neck. The wolf was a brute, at least twice her size—larger, I thought, than it had been the first time I'd dreamed of the pair. She buried her face in its fur and began to sing, very softly, for the wolf. And the song she sang was the song that Mercy Brown, the Bride of Quiet, had sung to me the night I'd died.

Oh, where are you going, my pretty fair maid? Oh, where are you going, my honey?

She answered me right cheerfully, I've an errand for my mummy.

"*Stop* it," I hissed. She did stop. Singing, that is. She raised her head, narrowed her blue eyes, and glared at me, angry, confused.

"What did I do now?" she asked petulantly, defensive.

"You know goddamn well. You know perfectly god-damn well." I shifted my weight, and a handful of construction-paper leaves rained down from the pretend tree, red, orange, brown, yellow.

"That song," I added.

"It's just a song. It's just a song I heard somewhere, a long, long time ago." She went back to scratching the wolf behind its ears.

"The night she killed—"

"—us," said the blonde-haired, blue-eyed girl at the edge of the dream field. She kissed the wolf on the top of its head and it gratefully licked her hands. "I do guess that sort of ruins it," she said. "A shame. It's such a pretty song."

"Fuck you. I have enough ghosts without haunting myself." And I stood up, dusting off the seat of my jeans and scattering startled grasshoppers.

"Quinn," said the girl, looking up at me. The wolf, she was looking up at me, as well. Her eyes seemed damp, like she was about to cry. I didn't want to see her any-more, and I stared out across the field again. For the first time, I did see something on the other side. There was a wall of smoke, and there were flames, and the sounds of battle drifted in the cold breeze blowing through the stalks of tall grass.

"You saw," said the girl. "You saw us in a cage, an

awful sort of cage. You saw that the twins had locked us up inside a cage."

"I did," I said, unable to take my eyes off the advancing inferno. Something was coming, and it *might* not be the worst thing I'd ever come up against. But, then again, it *might*. It might be the worst times ten. I heard the cries of men and women. I saw the sun glinting off swords and shields and the banners of war whipped about the heads of soldiers like flying serpents.

"And I heard a voice," said the girl, "in the midst of the four beasts, I heard a terrible, terrible voice saying to me 'Come, child, and see.' And behold, in the midst of the whirlwind I looked, and I saw a pale horse."

The fire beyond the field was spreading, driven and fed by the wind, and an enormous white stallion was charging towards me, a white horse bearing not one, but two riders, a man and a woman, brother and sister. Their armor was as white as snow.

"And their names who sat on him were Death," said the girl at my feet, "and Hell followed after."

The sound of the horse's hooves was thunder.

The sky had filled with smoke and crows.

"We won't die in a cage," said the blonde girl.

I looked down, and where the girl and the wolf had been, there was only the skeleton of something that was neither exactly a girl *nor* a wolf. The bones were charred, as was the earth all around them.

I could feel the earth coming apart beneath me.

And then . . .

"Time to wake up, girlbaby," said Charlee. "We're almost there."

And I opened my eyes. The Porsche rolled along a darkened street, past darkened storefronts and restaurants and bars that were shut up tight for the night. I coughed and rubbed at my eyes. I could still smell smoke and scorched flesh. I reached for the pack of cigarettes and the lighter in the pocket of my peacoat. I asked Charlee what time it was and he tapped the clock on the dash.

"We were being followed," he said. "I had to take a serious detour after Hartford, and another at the state line. I wasn't in the mood for escorts."

"So we're late," I said.

"Don't you fret your pretty head, sweets. You were invited, remember? More importantly, you've got the life of the party, the main attraction, right there beneath your ass. We're not late."

"So, magician, how are you with dreams?" I asked him and lit a cigarette.

"Better than most. But you don't need me to tell you what you already know. Now, get your war face on."

CHAPTER SEVEN

OPEN THE DOOR

When we reached the cemetery at just past two in the morning, the gates were standing wide-open—Howdy! Come right in!—and there was no sign whatsoever of Mount Auburn security. Neither of us was surprised, and at least we wouldn't have to scale any walls or chain-link fences. Charlee shifted the Porsche into park, letting the engine idle, and we sat in the shadow of the strange Egyptian Revival archways that greet the dead and the grieving and the merely morbidly inclined. Until recently, I had no idea that *cemetery* is taken from a Greek word that means "a sleeping place." I certainly didn't know it that cold November night. And *that* night, *that* particular cemetery didn't feel the least bit like a sleeping place. In fact, it felt totally fucking awake and watchful, thank you very much. The air was, as they say, thick with expectation. Or anticipation. Whichever. Both. I rolled down my window and flicked the butt of my smoke out onto the asphalt, and it bounced away in a shower of sparks. Then I reached for the Browning—Pickman's gun—still tucked into the waistband of my pants. The weight and solidity of it was, it should go without saying, reassuring.

"Well," said Charlee, gazing up at the gates, "we *were* invited."

I knew, as I'm sure he did, that anyone else passing by the cemetery—anyone who'd not received an invite to the evening's festivities—would see the gates closed and locked, everything just exactly copacetic. All the little duckies in a row. The spell that made the difference for us was strictly kindergarten motherfuckery, so far as glamours come and go, but sometimes the most elementary tricks are all that're needed. Keep it simple, stupid. Fuckin' A.

I started to open my door, but Charlee stopped me.

"No," he said. "We'll drive in as far as we can. Just for shits and giggles, right? By the way, did you ever see any of Mr. Pickman's artful handiwork?"

"Nope," I replied and lit another cigarette. "Wait. We're calling that bastard *mister* now?"

"There's this one painting," Charlee said, "it's titled *Holmes, Lowell, and Longfellow Lie Buried in Mount Auburn*. Bunch of ghouls squeezed into a mausoleum reading from a Boston guidebook by candlelight, laughing their silly heads off."

I wasn't sure I got the joke, but I didn't say so.

"How long?" I asked him.

"How long what, Quinn?"

"How long since you died, pretty boy? That's how long what."

He didn't reply immediately. Charlee was busy looking up through the windshield at the night sky. When he did answer me, he sounded . . . different, you know? Far away.

"I saw the Doors play the Whisky a Go Go. I was at Woodstock. So, well before your time, girlbaby. Well before your time."

"So, you ever done anything like this before?"

Charlee shook his head and put the car into gear again. "Not lately," he replied and let it stand at that.

I exhaled and squinted through my own cigarette smoke.

"Before the fireworks start," I said, "I want to be clear on something. I'm not here for B. I don't care how badly they've hurt him; that's not why I'm here."

"I know that, Quinn. He knows that, too."

"Just so we're clear, okay?"

I popped the clip from the 9mm, checked it, and popped it back in.

"I'm also not here because I believe Pickman and his comrades in arms—of whom I've actually not *seen* warty hide nor mangy fucking hair—are necessarily the lesser of two evils."

"You're here for her," he said. "Were it not for Selwyn—"

"How about let's not get started in on 'were it not for Selwyn.' I'm tired of that game."

"But she's why you came."

"Looks like," I told him, and then I held up the Browning Hi Power. "Please be a sweetheart and tell me this is *not* our only gun."

"As it happens . . ." he said and trailed off.

"Oh, you are fucking shitting me."

"I don't like guns. B doesn't like guns, either. But I suspect you're already aware of that."

The Porsche crept slowly past the visitors' center and along a narrow, winding road leading us into the heart of the cemetery. We passed obelisks, a gaudy little chapel that would have been right at home in my storybook dreams, a goddamn sphinx, and all those headstones like warning signs we were too stupid to heed. But nothing moved.

"You know where we're going?" I asked.

"I do," he said. "It's not much farther."

And it wasn't. At the crest of what I took to be the highest point in Mount Auburn, we came to a granite tower. The thing, at least fifty or sixty feet tall, looked like someone had plunked one of the rooks from a giant's chess set down onto that hilltop. Clearly, subtlety wasn't something Isaac and Isobel were overly concerned with.

"Here?" I asked, and he killed the engine.

"Here," he said. "The hill's hollow. Well, if you know the way, the hill's hollow."

"And you know the way?"

"And I know the way. Are you ready?" he asked.

I looked at him, and then I looked back at the tower.

"So," I said, "we are seriously just going to stroll into the Snows' not-so-top-secret lair of unspeakable fucking evil, Madonna in hand. No backup, no escape plan, no contingency plans, no plans whatsoever. One gun. Don't you remember what Boromir said about just walking into Mordor?"

He turned and looked at me, and right then, I couldn't imagine how I hadn't realized, right off, that he was a vamp. Right then, there hardly seemed to be anything human about him.

"Quinn, do you want to save her, or do you want to see her cut down in the crossfire?"

I didn't bother answering him. Instead, I tucked the pistol back into my jeans, then reached under the seat and retrieved the Madonna.

"Who gets the honors?" I asked, holding out the bundle.

"You, I'm afraid. That's what they're expecting. Let's not disappoint our hosts."

I nodded, opened my door, and got out of the cherry-red Porsche. From the hill, the lights of Cambridge and the Boston skyline were spread out below us, and overhead there was only the waxing crescent moon and a handful of stars bright enough to shine through the urban light pollution. There was just one entrance to the tower, a gaping lancet-shaped archway at its base. A line of stairs led from where we'd parked straight up to that black hole.

What are you waiting on, Quinn? Come and see!

I looked across the roof of the car at Charlee. He'd pulled a small shoulder bag from the backseat. It was bubblegum pink, and the fabric was decorated with an assortment of Sanrio characters.

"I do have something for you," he said, reaching into the ridiculous pink bag.

I laughed and rubbed at my eyes.

"What the fuck could you possibly have in there, Charlee with two *e*'s? Maybe a handful of deadly, explosive chocolate-flavored Bad Badtz-Maru pocky? A sawed-off twelve-gauge over-and-under Hello Kitty charm bracelet?"

He smiled, and his own set of piranha teeth glinted dully in the faint moonlight. He took out a corked bottle and tossed it to me. I held it up and saw there was water— or some clear liquid—and a few shriveled, discolored leaves inside.

"I assume you know what it is?" he asked.

Fuck me, but I did.

"*Aconitum*," I said. "Monkshood. Wolfsbane."

"When Selwyn accidentally poisoned you—"

I lowered the bottle and stared at him.

"How do you know she—"

"—you changed, but you also remained lucid, for the first time ever. And please don't start asking questions now, girlbaby, because we don't have time for explanations. They are presently a luxury we cannot afford."

I looked at the bottle again.

"I didn't bring guns," he said, "but that doesn't mean I came unarmed. Grim as all this might seem, I intend to live through tonight."

"So to speak." I shook the bottle.

"Exactly."

Back at the museum, under the *Tyrannosaurus*, when Charlee had barged into my skull and put the zap on my brainmeats, I'd seen my Beast hanging helpless inside a cage. So, you can probably understand why the last thing I wanted was to go getting fuzzy in the presence of Isaac and Isobel and all their gang of groovy ghoulies. Never mind the fucking dream.

And Hell followed after.

"It's a last resort," he said. "That's all."

Or it was one last way that B could dream up to make me into a weapon, this time the Red Right Hand of his vengeance, set loose on the psychos who'd mutilated and crippled him. Ghouls can be scary monsters, sure. But next to a *loup* bitch with all her senses about her? Well, there are nasties, and then there are nasties. I came very close to smashing the bottle on the pavement. Instead, I stowed it in the pocket of the peacoat.

"Well, fuck it," I said. "Let do this thing." And together we climbed the stairs, a brief ascent before the plunge.

One of the first lessons I learned after my rude awakening to the world of monsters and preternatural mayhem was that, more often than not, there are at least two of everything. Any given tree, or street, or interstate underpass, or, in this instance, the entrance into a granite tower at the center of a one-hundred-and-eighty-two-year-old Massachusetts cemetery. Most people, and I mean mortal, living, human people, they'll only ever see one-half of the binary.

To grasp the true multiplicity of objects, one needs these dark-adapted eyeballs. Anyway, yeah, there was the entrance to the Washington Tower (as it's properly known) that Dick and Jane Mundane walk through in their visits to Mount Auburn, and then there's the one that Charlee and I stepped through that night. I almost didn't see the paper-cut-thin division between Door Number One and Door Number Two, though I certainly *should* have been expecting just that sort of sleight of hand.

The entrance we took, instead of leading us up to the tower's two observation decks, led us *down*. And down. And down a very narrow and very steep spiral staircase that had been carved out of the native stone of the hill. The steps were uneven, tilting this way and that, slick with groundwater and slime. In a Hammer horror or old Roger Corman picture, a passageway like this probably would have been lit with guttering torches, right? Well, the ghouls were content with the phosphorescent mushrooms that clung to the walls and low arched ceiling in thick, rubbery clumps, glowing a sickly pale blue. I'd seen those fungi in my vision, back at the museum. Me and Charlee, our eyes would have been just fine in complete darkness, and, truthfully, it would have been preferable to the damn, disgusting mushrooms. The air stank of mold and mud and wet rot. There were strange insects living among the mushrooms and spiders and slithering things I decided were some sort of underground salamander.

Charlee had taken the lead, and he was counting off each step out loud—one, two, three, twelve, thirteen, forty-seven, eighty-three, and so fucking forth. It was irritating, but I didn't tell him to shut up. For all I knew, he had good reason for keeping count, the sort known only to accomplished, disciplined practitioners of the true science of the Magi. I clutched the Madonna close to my chest and watched my step and tried to think of nothing but Selwyn. Keep your eyes on the prize, dead lady, and all that malarkey.

I followed Charlee.

And I followed.

And followed.

"Maybe we took a wrong turn back there some-where," I said, hoping for a laugh, anything to break the stillness. But he just kept on counting.

One hundred and twelve.

Two hundred and five.

"It's a trick," I said, my voice echoing flatly in the stairwell. "Probably, it's also a trap."

"It's not a trick," Charlee replied. "Trust me. Just chill, okay?" And then he went right back to counting. He didn't bother denying it could be a trap.

Trust me. Yeah, well, maybe B had neglected to mention to Charlee how me and Ms. Trust had never exactly been on the best of speaking terms. I looked back over my shoulder, and what I saw stopped me cold.

"Don't do that," he said.

"Don't do what?" I whispered.

"Don't look back, Quinn."

"Too late . . ."

The way we'd just come, there were no steps. There was no narrow passageway, no glowing mushrooms. No nothing. The stairwell was being erased as we moved deeper into the hill, and in its place there was only the pure velvet blackness of space. I mean *interstellar* fucking space, a forever void lit only by icy white constellations of stars hundreds of millions of light-years apart. It's one thing to stare into the face of a demon capable of eradicating you with the twitch of a pinkie or a stray thought; it was another thing entirely, standing on that precipice, the entire cosmos yawning before me. I felt myself being pulled towards it, and I thought of the moon pulling on the tide, dragging the sea ashore. I heard a flute, and its music was insanity and chaos incarnate, the piper at the gates of lunacy.

And behold, in the midst of the whirlwind I looked . . .

Then I felt Charlee's hand on my shoulder, yanking me roughly back from the mouth of that abyss. He cursed and muttered something in a language I'd never heard. The star field shimmered and quickly melted away until there was only the stairwell again.

"*That's* a trick," he said. "*And* a trap. They want you rattled, Quinn. They want you scared shitless."

I dropped to my knees and puked.

Yeah, not my proudest moment.

Charlee held my hair back from my face while I coughed up what little was in my belly, the dregs of that unlucky girl from City Hall Park. I spat and wiped my mouth on the back of my hand, and then I spat again. Dark globs of half-digested blood spattered the stone.

"We're stronger than them," Charlee said firmly, speaking with all the conviction I did not presently possess, and he kneeled beside me. "Whatever happens next, whatever you see down here, that's what you have to keep telling yourself, girlbaby. We're *stronger* than they are, and they *know* it. They're just trying to freak you out."

"Well, it's working," I told him.

"She's down there," he said. "Selwyn's down there waiting for you. No one else will come for her. You know that."

On the one hand, yeah, that helped get me up on my feet and moving again. On the other, it made me want to punch him in the balls. I totally grok the utility of that sort of manipulative shit, okay, and I'm as susceptible to it as the next nasty who only wants to be a real girl again. But, in a way, it was as cheap a shot as the Snows' counterfeit Azathoth.

"It's not much farther," Charlee said.

"How the fuck can you know that?"

"Jesus, don't you *smell* them?" he asked.

I sniffed the dank air, and he was right. Past the stench of mushrooms and wet earth there was the unmistakable reek of ghoul. Just think wet dog crossed with a Port-a-Potty that's been baking in the summer sun and you're halfway there.

Moving right along.

There were more steps . . .

. . . and then there weren't.

In fact, there was pretty much nothing at all, just a wrenching, sinking sensation in the *pit* of the pit of my stomach, *below* my stomach, all the way down in the subbasement of my bowels. My legs gave out from under me again, and I shouted for Charlee, because suddenly I couldn't see him anymore. The stairwell was folding back upon itself, and, for just an instant I was looking *up* towards the night outside. The dim blue light from the fungi seemed to bend, warp, twist itself inside fucking out and outside fucking in. The bugs creeping and crawling across the swollen caps and stems of those mushrooms imploded in silent puffs of spores, and the spores hung and drifted in the air, milky clouds coalescing into dazzling psilocybin spirals.

The dear Mr. Timothy Leary himself would have wept, I'm sure.

Me, I just wanted a fixed point, anything real and solid to hang on to.

For half an instant, I heard that awful fucking flute again, and I had just enough time to wonder exactly what sort of deals those two shitbirds had cut with their dark elder gods. "*That's* a trick," Charlee had told me, but now I wasn't so sure. I'd seen their altars and their offerings, and maybe, I thought, Isaac and Isobel had been plenty naughty enough to get the attention of the Big Bads that even the Big Bads don't like to talk about, the names we do not say aloud and try to avoid even thinking to ourselves. Maybe those primordial, alien not-gods that old HPL liked to go on about, maybe they had some vested interest in seeing the tables turned and the Ghūl sent topside again, with all the bells and postapocalyptic whistles. Fuck, maybe those fifth-century Byzantine god botherers, so hell-bent on making Christians out of sows' ears, had been in league with—

You think a lot of crazy-ass shit when you're stuck mind-surfing non-Euclidian hallways.

"Open your eyes, puppy," said Isobel Snow. I wasn't even aware that I'd shut them.

I met her halfway and opened *one* eye. I was relieved to see the world had decided to go back to being solid. I was down on my hands and knees on dusty flagstones. The air smelled of smoke and burning meat. And ghouls. I reached for the pistol in the waistband of my jeans, and someone or something kicked me in the ribs.

"*No,*" growled a voice I recognized as Isaac's. "Be still, corpse."

I heard whimpering and whining then, like whipped dogs. I opened my other eye and sat up, hugging my throbbing side, wondering if anything in there was broken and, if so, what the chances were that I'd be around long enough for it to heal. The Basalt Madonna lay a foot or so away from me, still wrapped up snug in Selwyn's T-shirt. I reached out, winced, and picked it up. Then I raised my head, and the twins stood nearby, hand in hand. As in my vision, their long white hair was plaited together into a single braid that dragged behind them in the dirt, and they wore the same long blue-black velvet robes I'd seen in the museum. Their feet were bare and filthy, their toenails dirty and cracked, and their eyes burned like molten rubies.

"Welcome, Twice-Damned, Twice-Dead," said Isaac Snow. "As it was written, yes, as it was foretold, you've come to us in these last, desperate hours of our captivity, bearing the *Qqi d'Evai Mubadieb,* hallowed instrument of our deliverance."

So much for my being Pickman's ace in the hole, an

unknown variable the twins knew nothing about. I wondered what discount bin he'd scryed his information from.

"We are more grateful," said Isobel, "than mere words ever can express."

My head was still spinning, and I rubbed at my eyes and tried to blink back the disorientation and queasiness. I glanced down at the bundle in my hands, then up at the twins. My surroundings were beginning to swim hazily, slowly, into focus. Wherever the fuck I was, it wasn't that great fancy cave from Charlee's vision, though it was clearly some sort of underground chamber. There was no ebony dais laced with red crystalline veins. But there were ghouls, a goddamn sea of doglike faces and gangly, hunched backs. And they'd been whipped into a mad frenzy, presumably by my arrival. Or, more likely, the Madonna's arrival. After all, I was nothing but the reluctant delivery girl. But the ghouls were hanging back, keeping a healthy, respectful distance between themselves and the twins. They yapped and gibbered and laughed the grating, barking way that ghouls laugh. They flailed and clawed viciously at one another, pushing, shoving, slamming their bodies together. It was impossible *not* to be reminded of a mosh pit.

And then I saw what was behind the twins.

A cage.

Again, Charlee's vision had embellished and missed the mark. It was nothing elaborate, not the amalgamation of gibbet and rack he'd shown me; its iron bars didn't glow red hot, either. And what was inside, it wasn't the Beast in me. It was Selwyn.

It was what had *become* of Selwyn.

Behind me, someone cleared his throat, and I turned away from the cage.

It was Charlee, standing there in his lime-green patent-leather go-go boots and Russian-hooker fur, looking as silly as it's possible to look in a pit of fiends, and I made the mistake of being glad to see him. He smiled and held up the pink Sanrio backpack he'd taken from the backseat of the Porsche.

"My Lord and Lady," he said, "*Qqi d'Tashiva* and *Qqi Ashz'sara*, ruthless and indomitable hands of the Fifty." And he bowed to them.

"Why, you lousy son of a bitch," I snarled. "You cunt."

Charlee smirked, but he didn't look at me.

"You've brought them?" asked Isobel, cocking her head to one side. "What the traitor Throckmorton stole from us, you've returned those treasures?"

Charlee nodded his pretty pomegranate head. "Precisely as you asked, my Lady."

One of the ghouls, a skinny little shit so thin it looked like it hadn't eaten since Pong was the next big thing, scuttled out of the shadows on all fours and snatched the backpack from Charlee's hands. Charlee, he kept his cool and kept his eyes on the twins. The skinny ghoul carried the pack to Isaac, groveled and slobbered pitifully at his feet, then quickly melted back into the throng.

"It would have been an awful tragedy," Isobel said, turning to her brother, "if such precious things as these were lost in the coming holocaust, if they'd been caught in the unmaking."

I watched as Isaac removed an antique wooden box

from the pink backpack, the very same antique wooden box that Selwyn had taken to the Meatpacking District and sold to a fat oddities dealer who'd called himself Skunk Ape. Isaac passed the box to his sister, and he took a second object from the pack, a small gray silk pouch. I knew before he undid the drawstrings what was waiting inside.

Riddle me this, television audience: How the fuck does a vamp steal from a member of the Unseelie Court and live to tell the tale? I know it was a question had *me* on the edge of my fucking seat. Sure, to the living, we might seem all that, but as nasties go—heinousness being relative—we're really not so very far above ghouls, ourselves.

The wooden box wasn't locked, the way it'd been when Selwyn handed it over to Skunk Ape, and Isobel Snow opened the lid. She grinned like a kid on Christmas morning, and her teeth up close and in person were even worse than they'd been in the vision, worse than they'd been described in that anonymous document B had given me. Buckled, crooked, razor sharp. It seemed safe to assume dental hygiene and orthodontics weren't a big part of Hera Snow's approach to parenting. Anyway, Isobel set the box down on the flagstones at her feet and lifted the skull out of its velvet cradle. She stood, gazed into its empty sockets, then held it triumphantly above her head. All eyes turned towards her.

"Though his name has been lost," she said, and her voice swelled to fill the chamber, "behold the remains of he who, more than fifteen centuries ago, first received the Word. The Word that, on this night and before another dawn breaks, shall set us all free."

Like I said, *And the crowd went wild*.

Clearly, these two knew how to work a room.

As for me, I'd seen what was trapped in the cage behind them, and everything else had ceased to matter. My head swam with a sickening, intoxicating mix of hatred and sorrow, regret and bitterness. I hurt like I hadn't hurt since that night some five years before when Mercy Brown bedded me and murdered me on a filthy mattress. Like I never thought I'd hurt again. I was so small, so irrelevant, a spider pinned to a board, nailed down and twitching at the eye of a storm of plots and bullshit intrigues, agendas and subterfuge and contradiction. Pickman, B, the twins, Charlee, fuck them all equally and fuck their ambitions and greed. I cursed every soul and every soulless being that had ever been willing to maim and butcher and rape and destroy in the name of [Fill in the Fucking Blank]. I did not exclude myself.

My mind was swelling with blood and fire.

And I felt my Beast begin to stir. She wasn't going to need a megadose of *Aconitum* to wake up. Not tonight.

From the satin bag, Isaac produced the necklace that Aster, the Faerie bitch beekeeper of East 4th Street, had called the Tear of Dis. In the dim light, the diamonds twinkled dully, and the ruby leaked a glow of its own literally hellish creation. Isaac dropped the satin bag to the floor and turned to his sister, his bride, his partner in DIY End Times.

"My love," he said, "no throat but yours should ever wear this jewel." And then he unclasped the necklace and hung it around Isobel's neck. Still holding the skull in her left hand like some genderfuck Hamlet, she lovingly fondled the stone with the fingers of her right. Isaac leaned in close and bit her on the cheek, keeping her flesh clenched tightly between his teeth for a full minute or more. She didn't even wince.

"La Saignement de gorge," he said, when he'd finally released her. Isaac had bitten hard enough to break the skin, and a trickle of blood wound its way down Isobel's pale cheek. There was a scarlet smear on Isaac's lips. He licked it away and gently kissed her forehead.

I'd seen enough. I'd seen enough and back. I put my head down. I reached out and pulled the Madonna to me. It had come partly unwrapped, and I could see a corner of the dark volcanic stone, a hint of the graven image of Mother Hydra. I shut my eyes.

Behind my lids, I saw that burning field, a memory so vivid it might as well have been taking place in the here and now. The fire and the field, the white horse and its white riders, their armor white as snow.

"And Hell followed after," I said.

"My Lord, what would you have me do with this one?" Charlee asked, and then I felt his fingers twining themselves in my hair. He yanked my head back with enough force that my neck popped. I opened my eyes and stared up into his face. His features had hardened, and I wondered why I'd ever thought him pretty at all.

"In her way," Isaac replied, "the Twice-Damned has served us well. That she did so unwittingly is of no concern to me."

And Isobel said, "She has guarded the Mother and the Child, and she has traveled the long Night Road to bring them to us. Faithless, yes, faithless and treacherous and disbelieving. Infidel. But she has surely earned some meager reward for her tribulations. Some favor before death."

"If that's your wish, my Lady," said Charlee.

"Fuck you," I said, and I spat in his face. He smirked again and wiped my spittle away.

"We've come, at last, to the end of a tale," Isobel continued. "The end of one, which is also the beginning of another. There is a little space on the threshold for . . ." And Isobel trailed off and was silent for a moment. Charlee tightened his grip on my hair, and I glared up at him, unable to look away.

". . . an act of mercy," Isobel finished.

"Our poor cousin cannot speak," said Isaac.

"So she cannot whisper secrets," added his sister.

"Siobhan Quinn, we shall allow you—" began Isaac.

"—one final caress," finished Isobel.

I tried to pull free, and Charlee drove his knee into my back. He let my hair go then, and I crumpled to the ground, doubled over and tasting my own blood. Charlee had said he was older than me by at least a few decades, and he was a lot stronger than me. And, to tell the truth, I'd never been any good at the hand-to-hand melee shit. I'd always relied on guns and crossbows and enchanted lockets and pointy sticks and what the hell ever else got the job done.

"Cousin Selwyn is our smiling little lamb," Isobel said. "She told us much about you, Twice-Damned, before we took her tongue."

I'd seen what was in the cage.

Whatever else happened, I wouldn't be leaving Mount

Auburn with Selwyn. I was pretty damn sure I wouldn't be leaving at all. And I discovered that being fairly damn certain of my guaranteed doom, it cleared my head a little.

"Get up," Charlee growled, sounding hardly like himself at all. He grabbed my left shoulder and lifted me roughly to my feet.

"What's your percentage in all this?" I asked him. "Short con or long?"

He didn't reply. Instead, Charlee with two *e*'s took the Madonna from me, and shoved me, stumbling, towards the cage. The twins had stepped aside, moving as one, and there was Selwyn waiting behind the cold iron bars. It wasn't necessary for Charlee to push me again. I walked the rest of the way on my own.

In a dream of a fairy-tale forest and a burning autumn field, a girl with my name had said, "You saw. You saw us in a cage, an *awful* sort of cage. You saw that the twins had locked us up inside a cage."

Days and days ago, Selwyn had said, "In their eyes, of course, it makes me an abomination."

"We have shown mercy on her, also," said Isobel, and there was no hint of sarcasm in her voice. The madwoman absolutely believed what she was saying. "Twice-Damned, by the All Mother we have given her a *gift*, a gift that even my brother and I are denied."

Selwyn stared out at me, and her star-sapphire eyes had turned a rusty shade of amber, like blood in a glass of beer. There was nothing in those eyes but suffering.

"We are making her whole," said Isobel.

You saw that the twins had locked us up inside a cage.

The woman that had been Selwyn Throckmorton

was quickly being gnawed apart by whatever corrosive spell of germ-line genetic transmutation the twins had cast on her. She crouched in one filthy corner, her knees pulled up close to her chest. In places, her flesh bubbled and steamed as if someone had poured acid on it. Bones popped and shifted beneath her mottled skin as the double helices of her DNA were ripped apart and rebuilt. Tears streamed from her eyes, but they were the tears of a ghoul, sticky and yellow, pustulant. She opened her mouth, and only a strangled, choking sound escaped her ruined lips.

Do you know what's on the other side of the meadow, Quinn?

Whatever angle Selwyn had been playing, it had cost her everything. Like Mean Mister B, she'd crossed the twins, and like him, she'd been caught at it. He'd only lost a hand, his dignity, a few teeth. Lucky motherfucker, but then he always was. I think it's more likely than not that Selwyn had cast her lot with Richard Upton Pickman and his rebels, but, as it happens, I would never know for sure. Where the twins had sent her, she was never coming back from that place.

"I'm sorry," I said, and maybe I even meant it. I drew the Browning and put three bullets in her head. They did the trick.

And the ghouls, they finally shut up.

Isobel Snow was laughing, a quiet, uneasy titter.

Those scraps of my humanity the Bride of Quiet had somehow missed, those died in the space of three gunshots. *Bam, bam, bam.* That's all she wrote. Selwyn was gone, and with luck she wasn't hurting anymore. I like to tell myself she was dead already, before I pulled the trigger.

It was only the second time I'd ever killed out of kindness. It hasn't happened since.

I turned back to Isobel and Isaac, and I raised the pistol again, taking aim at the sister.

As the saying goes, you could have heard a pin drop.

I squeezed the trigger, and the 9mm roared again. The bullet went in through Isobel's left eye and took off most of the back of her head. She didn't go down immediately. There was this long, weird pause while she just stood there, swaying side to side, her remaining eye filled with hemorrhage and surprise. And then she bared her teeth, hissed, and I clearly heard the death rattle before she crumpled—very, very slowly, as though she were moving underwater. The ghoul skull tumbled from her hands and rolled away across the flagstones. And, what with the way their white hair was braided together, she dragged Isaac off his feet, as well, and he wound up on all fours beside her corpse. I took aim again.

Yeah, it did—right then—occur to me that there was no way in hell it could be *that* easy, avenging Selwyn, putting an end to what the twins had done and what they meant to do. What they'd set in motion. Putting an end to the twins themselves. Unless, of course, what was happening right that moment, Selwyn's and their undoing, me reprising my too-familiar role as executioner, was all they'd ever *really* set in motion, the inevitable and unintended consequences or their actions.

"Twice-Damned," said Charlee in a voice that boomed louder than the Browning. I didn't lower the pistol, but I did look his way.

Well, I looked towards the place where he'd *been*.

What stood there now, it wasn't human, and it wasn't a vampire. My first thought, *Where the fucking fuck did the fucking angel come from?*

Three fucks, when one just isn't fucking enough.

I knew what it was, even though I'd never laid eyes on a Djinn. To my knowledge, it had been an imp's age since anyone of earth had. B told me once that Djinn are like germs in a cheap whorehouse. You never see the bastards, but they're always there.

. . . in the midst of the four beasts, I heard a terrible, terrible voice saying to me, 'Come, child, and see.' And behold, in the midst of the whirlwind I looked . . .

"Fuck me," I whispered. There wasn't so much as a peep from the ghouls, but I could hear Isaac sobbing inconsolably over his dead sister.

Go head, I thought. *Go ahead and bawl your eyes out.*

The Djinn unfurled wings of fire, fire and smoke and incandescent gases, wings made of lightning and roiling, sulfurous clouds. The Basalt Madonna was clutched in the talons of its right hand. It took a step towards the Snows, a step towards me. I took a step backwards and bumped into Selwyn's cage.

"Which is what I get for underestimating boys who wear dresses," I said. "So, tell me, Smoky. What happens next?"

The Djinn flared its wide nostrils, exhaling steam, then stared down at the Madonna. The T-shirt had burned completely away, revealing the grotesque mother and child reunion and the pyrite whorl of the ammonite.

"All the time you held it," said the Djinn, and its voice was a hurricane. "All that time, you might have changed your fate, rewoven the skein of time, and yet you did not. Why is that, Siobhan Quinn, Twice-Damned?"

Its voice bruised the air, and I wanted to cover my aching ears.

"Did doing so not even occur to you?"

Oh, it had. Of course it fucking had. As soon as B told me what it was that hunk of rock did and why the Snows wanted it so badly, I began to wonder what would have to be undone, what single event in the shitty hit parade of my existence would have to be unbirthed, in order to set things right. Right for me, I mean. What would get me back to that moment before Selwyn and I climbed onto the subway? What would buy back the lost life of a homeless girl named Lily? How about the night I was attacked by Grumet and the Bride? Better yet, what would take me all the way back to the day before I ran away from home?

Don't think I didn't give it a long hard think.

But there was no guarantee anything would turn out any differently, was there? Or that it wouldn't be infinitely worse, because that's always an option. Better the hell you know. What I said to the Djinn was:

"I just couldn't stand the thought that I'd probably have to do all this same shit over again. Figured, best-case scenario, I'd still manage to fuck it up. Figured I probably wouldn't remember what I had unhappened, which meant I wouldn't know what to do differently.

"Once was enough."

The Djinn smiled, which is a sight I hope never to see again. Napalm dripped from its jaws and spattered across the floor at its feet.

"I admit," said the Djinn, "we had not considered that a fool could be so wise."

I glanced back to Isaac, who was still blubbering over the corpse of his sister. So much for the eldritch terror of the Snows. The dumbstruck ghouls were beginning to mutter among themselves as the shock wore off.

"You can destroy it?" I asked the Djinn.

"No," it said. "But we can consign it to the Greater Shadow, forever beyond the reach of Rās al-ghūl and man and any other who would seek after the *Qqi d'Evai Muba-dieb*. Past Sarkomand and Leng, there are bottomless vaults in the roots of mountains known only to the Sūrat al-Jinnī."

My head was spinning, and I tightened my grip on the trigger.

"Okay, well, that's wonderful. Fucking wonderful. So, asshole, why didn't you take it from me back in Manhattan and save us all this horror show? Why didn't you just find Selwyn before I even showed up and take it from *her*? Fuck, why didn't you just get proactive back in nineteen hundred and ninety whatever and stop Thing One and Thing Two here from having been *born*."

The Djinn laughed to itself, and the hollow place below Mount Auburn shuddered. Dirt and small stones rained down around me. I heard the retinue of ghouls yelp and curse.

"Because, Twice-Damned," said the Djinn, "it did not please me to do so. Now, do you mean to kill the half-breed King of Dogs, or shall I?"

I glared up at the sulfurous inferno of not-Charlee with two *e*'s.

"It did not fucking *please* you to fucking do so? You asshole. You son of a bitch."

"Twice-Damned," the Djinn said, "mind your place and know your limits. Events have unfurled as suited our design, and it is not remaining to you to question."

I'll never get used to the whole inscrutable plots of godlike beings thing. *It's none of your business, little baby monster, and you wouldn't understand, even if I deigned to tell you. Which I won't.* And I'm sure it makes for unsatisfying reading. But it is what it fucking is.

Anyway . . .

Isaac had dragged Isobel into his arms, and then he lifted his head and sneered at me, showing me his teeth, as she had done. Tears and snot and dirt streaked his face, and it was clear that all the fight and bluster had gone out of him. When his sister had died, she'd taken at least half of him with her.

"Why did you give me the *Aconitum*?" I asked the Djinn.

"Because," it replied, "you're going to have to find your own way out of this tomb. I cannot help."

"Because it wouldn't *please* you to do so," I whispered, and the Djinn didn't disagree.

With my free hand, I took the bottle from my pocket.

Isaac growled something in Ghūl. He was busy now trying to gather up all those globs of ruined gray matter and stuff them back into the hole in Isobel's head.

And I felt sick.

Not the sort of sick puking will ever make better.

"It's wrong," I said, "you two getting off this easy."

Then I pulled the trigger again.

And again.

I put ten rounds into him, emptying the clip, and then I let the gun slip from my fingers and clatter to the flagstones. I glanced back to where the Djinn who was not a vampire who was not a boy named Charlee with two *e*'s had stood, and there was only a sooty, scorched pattern on the floor of the chamber where it had been standing. The Djinn had taken its leave; enough fun and games for now, thank you one and all, and it had taken the Madonna with it.

Through the ringing in my ears, I could hear the frenzied yelping and yapping of the ghouls, and then I heard more gunshots. I sat down beside Selwyn's cage, her coffin, and I tried to make sense of the chaos unfolding around me. There were more ghouls pouring into the chamber. A lot more. But they were not those who'd sworn allegiance to Isaac and Isobel. These were ghouls who'd opposed the twins, Pickman's foot soldiers, his necropolis infantry. And not only ghouls, but dozens of night gaunts, their leathery wings battering the air, and gugs, too, and ghasts. They were all well armed, and they'd come to mop up. I considered doing nothing at all, sitting right where I was and letting the battle wash over me, crush me, rip me to fucking shreds, and then maybe the world would be done with me once and for all.

I seriously considered it.

Then I uncorked the bottle and took a long drink. My belly rolled, and the cramps began.

At the edge of a dream field, a girl with my name pushed her way through a wall of yellow-brown grass, and a great black wolf the black of Selwyn Throckmorton's hair followed her.

    And I followed it.

    Fade to black.

    Roll credits.

    The End.

AUTHOR'S NOTE

With this novel I conclude a trip that has been long and strange, indeed, and which has had a few highs and some truly astounding lows. It has been an experiment, and, admittedly, not one I can declare a success, but, as Mr. Vonnegut said, "And so it goes." My thanks to my agent, Merrilee Heifetz, who urged me to do this after reading Chapter One of *Blood Oranges*, which I'd actually written on a lark, as a joke, a protest against what "paranormal romance" has done to the once respectable genre of urban fantasy. I honestly never intended to write a whole Quinn book, much less three. Well, technically four, but I scrapped *Fay Grimmer* and wrote *Red Delicious* to replace it. My thanks to Amber Benson, who, one summer night in New Orleans, agreed to be the voice of Quinn. And my thanks to the many readers who stuck with this. At the very least, I hope you had fun. I will miss you, Aloysius, and I'll miss you too, Mean Mr. B. I'll even miss the damn seagulls.

On the 124th anniversary of Lovecraft's birth,
Caitlín R. Kiernan (Kathleen Tierney)
20 August 2014
Providence, Rhode Island